Candida Baker was born in London in 1955 into a theatrical and literary family. She visited Australia with a Royal Shakespeare Company production of *The Hollow Crown* in 1975, and emigrated to Sydney in 1977. Her first novel, *Women and Horses*, was published to critical acclaim in Australia in 1990, and a year later in America. *The Powerful Owl*, a collection of short stories, several of which had won prizes prior to publication, was published in 1994. Baker is also the creator of the *Yacker* series of interviews with Australian writers, and has written several children's books. Her short stories and essays have been published in numerous anthologies. As a journalist she has worked for *The Age*, *Time* magazine and the *Sydney Morning Herald*. She is currently editor of the *Weekend Australian Magazine*.

Jean Giono
The Horseman on the Roof 268

C. S. Lewis
The Horse and his Boy 274

Katharine S. Prichard
The Grey Horse 285

Rodney Hall
The Island in the Mind 304

Damon Runyon
Old Em's Kentucky Home 314

M. E. Patchett
Tam the Untamed 325

Jim Crace
Continent 345

Notes on the authors 366

Acknowledgments 374

Henry Lawson
The Buckjumper   182

Nicholas Evans
The Horse Whisperer   189

Candida Baker
The Cut   201

Elyne Mitchell
Silver Brumby, Silver Dingo   217

The Book of Job
Hast thou given the horse strength?   226

Peter Shaffer
Equus   228

R. Wilkes Hunter
The Breaking   239

Anna Sewell
Black Beauty   261

Lewis Carroll
The White Knight   265

THE PENGUIN BOOK OF THE

HORSE

EDITED BY CANDIDA BAKER

PENGUIN BOOKS

PENGUIN BOOKS

Published by the Penguin Group
Penguin Books Ltd, 27 Wrights Lane, London W8 5TZ, England
Penguin Putnam Inc., 375 Hudson Street, New York, New York 10014, USA
Penguin Books Australia Ltd, Ringwood, Victoria, Australia
Penguin Books Canada Ltd, 10 Alcorn Avenue, Toronto, Ontario, Canada M4V 3B2
Penguin Books (NZ) Ltd, Private Bag 102902, NSMC, Auckland, New Zealand

Penguin Books Ltd, Registered Offices: Harmondsworth, Middlesex, England

First published by Penguin Books Australia 1998
Published in Penguin Books 1999
1 3 5 7 9 10 8 6 4 2

Set in Monotype Centaur
Printed in England by Clays Ltd, St Ives plc

Contents

Introduction ix

Louis de Bernières
The War of Don Emmanuel's Nether Parts 1

Larry McMurtry
Comanche Moon 7

Tess Gallagher
The Lover of Horses 18

Monty Roberts
The Man Who Listens to Horses 42

Ernest Hemingway
War Cloud   60

Alistair MacLeod
In the Fall   76

Mary O'Hara
My Friend Flicka   104

Alan Le May
The Searchers   115

Robert Drewe
Our Sunshine   127

John Steinbeck
The Red Pony   129

Alice Hoffman
Here on Earth   137

D. H. Lawrence
The Rocking-Horse Winner   141

Alex Miller
The Tivington Nott   169

Introduction

I would love to know at what point mankind decided to stop hunting horses and to start riding them. I wonder who it was who made the connection that hunting *on* them, rather than *for* them, was a far more efficient use of energy. Whoever it was did man and horse a great service.

I am a rider. I have been most of my life. I have never ridden quite as well as I would like to, but horses have nevertheless become an integral part of my life, and perhaps even more importantly, my dreams. I dream of horses almost every night, and those horse dreams seem to tap me into a level of creative and collective memory far superior to my more mundane horseless dreams.

For me, the book which began the love affair – as I imagine it would have for many children – was *Black Beauty*. I was five years old and in hospital having my tonsils out, and I loved the book so much that I developed the ability to dream exactly what my father had read to me that evening. Over the years that enjoyable ability has lessened somewhat, but I still occasionally enjoy a good gallop on Flicka across the green grass of Wyoming. (One of the joys of editing this collection was the chance to explore landscapes I may never see in reality.)

What is it about horses? Why have we mythologised them so? Apollo and his horse-drawn chariot racing across the sky, perhaps most perfectly realised in their wondrous water setting in the gardens of Versailles; unicorns with their supposedly magical powers; Pegasus and his mighty wings: 'Hast thou given the horse strength?' roars the Book of Job. 'Hast thou clothed his neck with thunder? Canst thou make him afraid as a grasshopper? And the glory of his nostrils *is* terrible. He paweth in the valley, and rejoiceth in *his* strength.'

It is a somewhat curious irony that so many of the legends we have created around the horse are to do with flight, or freedom, or magic, when in actuality horsemen and women spend their lives breaking, taming, and in general, controlling the horse. But perhaps horse lovers sense this — that the horse always retains some little part for his, or her, self. Perhaps like cats, a horse can never be truly owned. As our human lives tame, restrict and contain us, a love of horses — riding them or simply watching them — keeps a tiny light alive for the ancient wildness within us all.

You don't have to be a horse rider to love horses. It would be hard to watch such majestic sights as the Grand National, the Kentucky Derby or the Melbourne Cup, and not be moved by the speed and grace of the racehorse. We have invented hundreds of sports involving the horse: steeple-chasing, racing, trotting, show-jumping, dressage, hunting, cross-country, rodeos, point-to-points, horse trekking, circuses, the dancing white Lipizzaner stallions, gymkhanas, the list goes on. Even more importantly we have used them to help us live our lives: for agriculture, transportation, commerce, industry, and not least, war.

What is even more remarkable is that the horse has

chosen to go along with us for the ride, so to speak. Even though he may be used as human food, or pet food, or glue, or at the least humiliated at the end of his life or even after death, the horse, it seems to me, has in the most noble way lowered his gracious head and allowed us to bridle him. Not only allowed us but has often, even mostly, appeared to actively enjoy the relationship between horse and rider. The old adage that you can lead a horse to water but you cannot make it drink stands true, and so too you cannot force a horse to jump or race, or dance, or perform a half-pass, and yet for humans they have done and will continue to do all these things.

In the past they have done much more. From the time when Genghis Khan chose horses as his means of transport as he swept into Asia, horses have accompanied men into battle. They have fought and died alongside them, and have, according to many reports, often purposely saved lives. Alexander had a horse called Bucephalus who was twenty-four the last time he was ridden into battle before a well-earned honorary retirement. Xenephon's riding principles are still adhered to today. If dog is man's best friend, then horse is man's best ally.

The horse, once harnessed, quickly became a military necessity which would allow those living in one spot to fight mounted invaders. Nomads lived on horseback – their whole lives revolved around horses – for fighting, hunting, stealing, and sport. Every modern use of the horse can be traced back to *Equus przevalskii Pojakoff*, the prehistoric wild horse of Mongolia, hunted to the brink of extinction, and now, thanks to several international breeding programmes, being reintroduced to the land of their ancestors. Even in these days of motorbikes, four-wheel drives and helicopters, the horse – Icelandic ponies for instance, or the stock horses in Australia and the Americas – remains an essential work tool in many isolated places.

Any horseperson will tell you that there are as many horse characteristics as there are human characteristics, which is perhaps why we have created a pantheon of Super Horses alongside our Batman and Superman: Fury, Black Beauty, Champion the Wonder Horse, even Mr Ed. And along with those icons there are also the wild ones which we hold dear to our hearts: the unbreakable brumby, the loco stallion, the skittish thoroughbred. (For the fullest description of horse nature possible, Monty Roberts must surely be the living expert. Reading his book, *The Man Who Listens to Horses*, it seemed to me as if horses themselves had decided to beam their message through this man, to explain why the horse, the ultimate flight creature, should always be treated with respect and gentleness by man, the ultimate fight creature.)

Before there was writing or riding our forebears painted pictures on cave walls of man hunting the horse; once humans rode, the pictures changed to show warriors displaying their horseback skills. I like to imagine that storytellers in those days told tales and wove magical myths for their tribes with stories of the fleetest of hoof, the quickest of spirit, the bravest of heart.

Then came the day when people began to record not just bloodlines, but the deeds of horses onto paper. As the horse was used less for work and war and more for sport, so the recording of its deeds increased. In these days of mass media, a great racehorse or showjumper will have its reputation kept alive forever just as surely as any fictional counterpart. In the last century or so, the horse has risen to lofty heights. It is often not just part of a story: it *is* the story.

Introduction

In this anthology I have collected tall tales and true. Stories, extracts, poems and prose which show horses in all their forms, from the most mythical to the truly prosaic. There are some obvious choices: Larry McMurtry, Nicholas Evans, Mary O'Hara and Anna Sewell; and I hope some not so obvious ones: D. H. Lawrence, Jim Crace and Jean Giono for instance.

Whether you are a rider or a reader, or both, I hope you enjoy reading this anthology as much as I have enjoyed editing it.

Candida Baker
Sydney, May 1998

'Why is Prince Hal an indoor character, and Tosca an outdoor girl? It is a question of their different veins of boldness. Hal, the excitable thoroughbred, has tremendous natural impulsion and an almost libertine boldness. He demands freedom and the right to assume complete control. But these he must not be allowed, and thus a valuable paradox is created; difficult to control, hemmed in by the limited spaces and the solid walls of the indoor ring, Hal acquires a sense of discipline — without losing his natural daring. His boldness soars. And so indoors — the bolder the horse, the better he jumps. Tosca, on the other hand, is ultra-careful, hates touching a fence, and on the indoor course often becomes over-anxious — thus losing her joie de vivre. In the open air, however, Tosca usually offers me total obedience, and so marshals herself that I can take her with deadly accuracy to all her fences.'

Jumping for Joy
Pat Smythe

Louis de Bernières

The War of Don Emmanuel's
Nether Parts

Don Emmanuel may have been the obvious and logical choice as emissary to Dona Constanza, but he was
a long way from being the best. This was because, ever
since someone had told him in an 'old-boy-just-a-
word-in-your-ear' manner that his Spanish was
unacceptably vulgar, especially in his choice of
adverbs, adjectives and common nouns, he had
adopted a style of speech when talking to influential
and respectable people which consisted partly of his
customarily outrageous bluntness, and partly of that
elaborate courtesy which one finds in medieval
romances. The not entirely unintended effect was that

of extreme sarcasm, and his reputation as an outstanding boor was thereby greatly enhanced, more especially as he never tried to abandon or modify his peasant's accent.

His customary mode of conveyance was an unfortunate bay horse with a white blaze on its forehead that had earned it the unromantic name of 'Careta'. The beast was unfortunate firstly in that, although Don Emmanuel was a fit and strong man, he had a very large belly as tight as a drum which contributed an unreasonable quantum of extra kilos to the horse's load. Secondly the horse was a pasero, which in this case does not mean a ferryman but a horse which has been carefully trained not to trot but to move at a steady, undulating lope. This was the one pace at which Don Emmanuel never rode it, so it had not only a sagging back, but also the depressed, irritated and frustrated air of a natural artist whom financial straits have reduced to taking a job as a bank clerk. The horse always breathed in hard when its master tightened its cinturon, and would stop in the middle of the river in order to exhale so that the girth would loosen and Don Emmanuel would fall off sideways. Don Emmanuel was very proud of his horse on account of this trick, and always quoted it as irrefutable proof that a horse can have a sense of humour. However, he took to waiting for the horse to breathe out before tightening the cinturon, and Careta became probably the only horse in the world to have discovered for itself some of the techniques of Hatha yoga.

Don Emmanuel rode his dispirited pasero through the only street of the pueblo, raising little plumes of dust that were caught up and whirled away by the dancing dust-devils, and wishing 'Buena' dia'!' in the customary nasal drawl to everyone he saw. He passed the three brothels with concrete floors, the little shop that sold machetes, alcohol, contraceptives, and the huge avocados that little boys stole from his own trees; he passed a small field of maize, Professor Luis' creaking little windmill that generated electricity, and turned left up the track to Dona Constanza's hacienda, all the while thinking of things he could say to irritate her.

Dona Constanza looked out of her window, where she had been reading a copy of *Vogue* that was already three years old, and witnessed his arrival with a fascinated mixture of dread and excitement. She watched him tie his horse to the lemon tree, his torso bare and his trousers hanging from halfway down his buttocks, and challenged herself to remain cool and dignified in the face of this impending trial of her patience.

Her maid, an unprepossessing and clumsy mulatta who affected oligarchic manners, ushered him into Dona Constanza's room and waited to be dismissed.

'Dona Constanza,' said Don Emmanuel, 'it is a sign of the exquisite times in which we live that a lady's maid may be as lovely as her mistress!'

The maid flushed with pleasure, and her mistress flinched visibly. 'Don Emmanuel, you are as charming as ever. Now, as I am very busy, as you see, perhaps you would tell me the purpose of your visit?'

Don Emmanuel made a show of scrutinising the degree of her industriousness and bowed, removing his straw sombrero with a flourish, 'Madam will forgive me for not perceiving her busyness. It is a sign of the highest breeding to be able to be busy whilst appearing idle to the uninformed observer.'

Her mouth tightened and her eyes flashed before she regained her composure. 'Senor is full of signs today. Now what is the purpose of your visit?'

'It has come to my ears, dear lady, that you intend to divert with a canal the very river which waters my land and that of the campesinos in order to replenish your piscina. I must say, as I know you appreciate frankness, that I and the local people will be fucked, buggered and immersed in guano of the finest Ecuadorean provenance before we permit such a thing to occur.'

'The permission,' she rallied, her temper rising almost immediately beyond control, 'is not yours or theirs to grant. I will do as I wish with the water on my land.'

'I appeal,' said Don Emmanuel, 'to your highly-developed social conscience and to your concern for my nether parts.'

'Your nether parts?' she repeated with astonishment.

'Indeed, Senora. In the dry season the Mula is the only water where I may rinse the dingleberries from my nether parts.'

'Dingleberries!' she exclaimed with mounting outrage.

'Dingleberries,' he said, assuming a professorial air, 'are the little balls of fluff that appear in one's underwear and sometimes entwine themselves in one's pubic hair. Frequently they are of a grey colour and woolly texture.'

Dona Constanza oscillated between amazement and fury before remarking icily, 'Indeed I should bear in mind your nether parts, as you call them, for I hear they often are found in the most unsavoury places.'

'Indeed,' said Don Emmanuel, 'it is often most unsavoury between one's legs, which is their usual location, as a lady of your wide experience will doubtless know, and this is why I appeal to you . . .'

But Dona Constanza was already leaving, and Don Emmanuel was already aware that he had allowed himself to fail in his mission out of perversity. He rode home with a heavy heart.

Larry McMurtry

Comanche Moon

Kicking Wolf was amused by the carelessness of Big Horse Scull, who put three men at a time to guard the rangers' horses and the two pack mules, but did not bother with guards for the Buffalo Horse. The men on guard were rotated at short intervals, too — yet Scull did not seem to think the Buffalo Horse needed watching.

'He does not think anyone would try to steal the Buffalo Horse,' Kicking Wolf told Three Birds, after they had watched the ranger and their horses for three nights.

'Scull is careless,' he added.

Three Birds, for once, had a thought he didn't want to keep inside himself.

'Big Horse is right,' Three Birds said. He pointed upward to the heavens, which were filled with bright stars.

'There are as many men as there are stars,' Three Birds said. 'They are not all here, but somewhere in the world there are that many men.'

'What are you taking about?' Kicking Wolf said.

Three Birds pointed to the North Star, a star much brighter than the little sprinkle of stars around it.

'Only one star shines to show where the north is,' Three Birds said. 'Only one star, of all the stars, shines for the north.'

Kicking Wolf was thinking it was pleasanter when Three Birds didn't try to speak his thoughts, but he tried to listen politely to Three Birds' harmless words about the stars.

'You are like the North Star,' Three Birds said. 'Only you of all the men in the world could steal the Buffalo Horse. That horse might be a witch – some say that it can fly. It might turn and eat you, when you go up to it. Yet you are such a thief that you are going to steal it anyway.

'Big Horse doesn't know that the North Star has come to take his horse,' he added. 'If he knew, he would be more careful.'

On the fourth night, after studying the situation well, Kicking Wolf decided it was time to approach the Buffalo Horse. The weather conditions were good: there was a three-quarter moon, and the brightness of the stars was dimmed just enough by scudding, fast-moving clouds. Kicking Wolf could see all he needed to see. He had carefully prepared himself by fasting, his bowels were empty, and he had rubbed sage all over his body. Scull even left a halter on the Buffalo Horse. Once Kicking Wolf has reassured the big horse with his touch and his stroking, all he would have to do would be to take the halter and quietly lead the Buffalo Horse away.

As he was easing along the ground on his belly, so that the lazy guards wouldn't see him, Kicking Wolf got a big shock: suddenly the Buffalo Horse raised its ear, turned its head, and looked right at him. Kicking Wolf was close enough then that he could see the horse's breath making little white clouds in the cold night.

When he realized that the Buffalo Horse knew he

was there, Kicking Wolf remembered Three Birds' warning that the horse might be a witch. For an instant, Kicking Wolf felt fear — big fear. In a second or two the big horse could be on him, trampling him or biting him before he could crawl away.

Immediately Kicking Wolf rose to a crouch, and got out of sight of the Buffalo Horse as fast as he could. He was very frightened, and he had not been frightened during the theft of a horse in many years. The Buffalo Horse had smelled him even though he had no smell and heard him even though he made no sound.

'I think he heard my breath,' he said, when he was safely back with Three Birds. 'A man cannot stop his breath.'

'The other horses didn't know you were there,' Three Birds told him. 'Only the Buffalo Horse noticed you.'

Though he was not ready to admit it, Kicking Wolf had begun to believe that Three Birds might be right. The Buffalo Horse might be a witch horse, a horse that could not be stolen.

'We could shoot it and see if it dies,' Three Birds suggested. 'If it dies it is not a witch horse.'

'Be quiet,' Kicking Wolf said. 'I don't want to shoot it. I want to steal it.'

'Why?' Three Birds asked. He could not quite fathom why Kicking Wolf had taken it into his head to steal the Buffalo Horse. Certainly it was a big stout horse whose theft would embarrass the Texans. But Three Birds took a practical view. If it was a witch horse, as he believed, then it could not be stolen, and if it wasn't a witch horse, then it was only another animal – an animal that would die some day, like all animals. He did not understand why Kicking Wolf wanted it so badly.

'It is the great horse of the Texans – it is the best horse in the world,' Kicking Wolf said, when he saw Three Birds looking at him quizzically.

Once he calmed down he decided he had been too hasty in his judgment. Probably the Buffalo Horse wasn't a witch horse at all – probably it just had an exceptionally keen nose. He decided to follow the rangers another day or two, so he could watch the horse a little more closely.

It was aggravating to him that Famous Shoes, the Kickapoo tracker, was with the Texans. Famous Shoes was bad luck, Kicking Wolf thought. He was a cranky man who was apt to turn up anywhere, usually just when you didn't want to see him. He enjoyed the protection of Buffalo Hump, though: otherwise some Comanche would have killed him long ago.

The old men said that Famous Shoes could talk to animals — they believed that there had been a time when all people had been able to talk freely with animals, to exchange bits of information that might be helpful, one to another. There were even a few people who supposed that Kicking Wolf himself could talk to horses — otherwise how could he persuade them to follow him quietly out of herds that were well guarded by the whites?

Kicking Wolf knew that was silly. He could not talk to horses, and he wasn't sure that anyone could talk to animals, anymore. But the old people insisted that some few humans still retained the power to talk with birds and beasts, and they thought Kicking Wolf might be such a person.

Kicking Wolf doubted it, but then some of the old ones were very wise; they might know more about the matter than he did. If the Kickapoo tracker could really talk to animals, then he might have spoken to the Buffalo Horse and told him Kicking Wolf meant to steal him. Whether he could talk to animals or not,

Famous Shoes was an exceptional tracker. He would certainly be aware that he and Three Birds were following the Texans. But he was a curious man. He might not have taken the trouble to mention this fact to the Texans — he might only have told the Buffalo Horse, feeling that was all that was necessary.

It was while watching the Buffalo Horse make water one evening that Kicking Wolf remembered old Queta, the grandfather of Heavy Leg, Buffalo Hump's oldest wife. Queta, too, had been a great horse thief; he was not very free with his secrets, but once, while drunk, he had mentioned to Kicking Wolf that the way to steal difficult horses was to approach them while they were pissing. When a horse made water it had to stretch out — it could not move quickly, once its flow started. Kicking Wolf had already noticed that the Buffalo Horse made water for an exceptionally long time. The big horse would stretch out, his legs spread and his belly close to the ground, and would pour out a hot yellow stream for several minutes. If Big Horse Scull was mounted when this happened he sometimes took a book out of his saddlebags and read it. On one occasion, while the Buffalo Horse was pissing, Scull did something very strange, something that went with the view that the Buffalo Horse was a witch horse. Scull slipped backward onto the big horse's rump, put his head on the saddle, and raised his legs. He stood on his head in the saddle while the Buffalo Horse pissed. Of course it was not unusual for men who were good riders to do feats of horsemanship — Comanche riders, particularly young riders, did them all the time. But neither Kicking Wolf nor Three Birds had ever seen a rider stand on his head while a horse was pissing.

'I thing Big Horse is crazy,' Three Birds said, when he saw that. Those were his last words on the subject and his only words on any subject for several days. Three Birds decided he had been talking too much; he went back to his old habit of keeping his thoughts inside himself.

Kicking Wolf decided he should wait until the Buffalo Horse was pissing before he approached him again. It would require patience, because horses did not always make water at night; they were more apt to wait and relieve themselves in the early morning.

When he mentioned his intention to Three Birds, Three Birds merely made a gesture indicating that he was not in the mood to speak.

Then, that very night, opportunity came. The men who were around the campfire were all singing; the Texans sang almost every night, even if it was cold. Kicking Wolf was not far from the Buffalo Horse when the big horse began to stretch out. As soon as the stream of piss was flowing from the horse's belly, Kicking Wolf moved, and this time the big horse did not look around. In a minute, Kicking Wolf was close to him and grasped the halter — the Buffalo Horse gave a little snort of surprise, but that was all. All the time the Buffalo Horse was pissing Kicking Wolf stroked him, as he had stroked the many horses he had stolen. When the yellow water ceased to flow Kicking Wolf pulled on the halter, and, to his relief, the big horse followed him. The great horse moved as quietly as he did, a fact that, for a moment, frightened Kicking Wolf. Maybe he was not the one playing the trick — maybe the Buffalo Horse *was* a witch horse, in which case the horse might be following so quietly only in order to get him off somewhere and eat him.

Soon, though, they were almost a mile from the ranger camp, and the Buffalo Horse had not eaten him or given him any trouble at all. It was following as meekly as a donkey — or more meekly; few donkeys were meek — then Kicking Wolf felt a great surge of pride. He had done what no other Comanche warrior could have done: he had stolen the Buffalo Horse, the greatest horse that he had ever taken, the greatest horse the Texans owned.

He walked another mile, and then mounted the Buffalo Horse and rode slowly to where he had left Three Birds. He did not want to gallop, not yet. None of the rangers were alert enough to pick up a horse's gallop at that distance, but Famous Shoes was there, and he might put his ear to the ground and hear the gallop.

Three Birds was in some kind of trance when Kicking Wolf rode up to him. Three Birds had their horses ready, but he himself was sitting on a blanket, praying. The man often prayed at inconvenient times. When he looked up from his prayer and saw Kicking Wolf coming on the Buffalo Horse all he said was, 'Ho!'

'I have stolen the Buffalo Horse,' Kicking Wolf said. 'You shouldn't be sitting on that dirty blanket praying. You should be making a good song about what I have done tonight. I went to the Buffalo Horse while he was making water, and I stole him. When Big Horse

Scull gets up in the morning he will be so angry he will want to make a great war on us.'

Three Birds thought that what Kicking Wolf said was probably true. Scull would make a great war, because his horse had been stolen. He immediately stopped praying and caught his horse.

'Let's go a long way now,' he said. 'All those Texans will be chasing us, when it gets light.'

'We will go a long way, but don't forget to make the song,' Kicking Wolf said.

Tess Gallagher

The Lover of Horses

They say my great-grandfather was a gypsy, but the most popular explanation for his behavior was that he was a drunk. How else could the women have kept up the scourge of his memory all these years, had they not had the usual malady of our family to blame? Probably he was both, a gypsy and a drunk.

Still, I have reason to believe the gypsy in him had more to do with the turn his life took than his drinking. I used to argue with my mother about this, even though most of the information I have about my great-grandfather came from my mother, who got it from her mother. A drunk, I kept telling her, would have had no initiative. He would simply have gone down with his failures and had nothing to show for it. But my great-grandfather had eleven children, surely a sign of industry, and he was a lover of horses. He had so many horses he was what people called 'horse poor'.

I did not learn, until I traveled to where my family originated at Collenamore in the west of Ireland, that my great-grandfather had most likely been a 'whisperer', a breed of men among the gypsies who were said to possess the power of talking sense into horses. These men had no fear of even the most malicious and dangerous horses. In fact, they would often take the wild animal into a closed stall in order to perform their skills.

Whether a certain intimacy was needed or whether the whisperers simply wanted to protect their secret conversations with horses is not known. One thing was certain — that such men gained power over horses by whispering. What they whispered no one knew. But the effectiveness of their methods was renowned, and anyone for counties around who had an unruly horse could send for a whisperer and be sure that the horse would take to heart whatever was said and reform his behavior from that day forth.

By all accounts, my great-grandfather was like a

huge stallion himself, and when he went into a field where a herd of horses was grazing, the horses would suddenly lift their heads and call to him. Then his bearded mouth would move, and though he was making sounds that could have been words, which no horse would have had reason to understand, the horses would want to hear; and one by one they would move toward him across the open space of the field. He could turn his back and walk down the road, and they would follow him. He was probably drunk my mother said, because he was swaying and mumbling all the while. Sometimes he would stop dead-still in the road and the horses would press up against him and raise and lower their heads as he moved his lips. But because these things were only seen from a distance, and because they have eroded in the telling, it is now impossible to know whether my great-grandfather said anything of importance to the horses. Or even if it was his whispering that had brought about their good behavior. Nor was it clear, when he left them in some barnyard as suddenly as he'd come to them, whether they had arrived at some new understanding of the difficult and complex relationship between men and horses.

Only the aberrations of my great-grandfather's relationship with horses have survived – as when he would bathe in the river with his favorite horse or when, as my grandmother told my mother, he insisted on conceiving his ninth child in the stall of a bay mare named Redwing. Not until I was grown and going through the family Bible did I discover that my grandmother had been this ninth child, and so must have known something about the matter.

These oddities in behavior lead me to believe that when my great-grandfather, at the age of fifty-two, abandoned his wife and family to join a circus that was passing through the area, it was not simply drunken bravado, nor even the understandable wish to escape family obligations. I believe the gypsy in him finally got the upper hand, and it led to such a remarkable happening that no one in the family has so far been willing to admit it: not the obvious transgression – that he had run away to join the circus – but that he was in all likelihood a man who had been stolen by a horse.

This is not an easy view to sustain in the society we live in. But I have not come to it frivolously, and have some basis for my belief. For although I have heard the story of my great-grandfather's defection time and again since childhood, the one image which prevails in all versions is that of a dappled gray stallion that had been trained to dance a variation of the mazurka. So impressive was this animal that he mesmerized crowds with his sliding step-and-hop to the side through the complicated figures of the dance, which he performed, not in the way of Lippizaners – with other horses and their riders – but riderless and with the men of the circus company as his partners.

It is known that my great-grandfather became one of these dancers. After that he was reputed, in my mother's words, to have gone 'completely to ruin'. The fact that he walked from the house with only the clothes on his back, leaving behind his own beloved horses (twenty-nine of them to be exact), further supports my idea that a powerful force must have held sway over him, something more profound than the miseries of drink or the harsh imaginings of his abandoned wife.

Not even the fact that seven years later he returned and knocked on his wife's door, asking to be taken back, could exonerate him from what he had done, even though his wife did take him in and looked after him until he died some years later. But the detail that no one takes note of in the account is that when my great-grandfather returned, he was carrying a saddle blanket and the black plumes from the headgear of one of the circus horses. This passes by even my mother as simply a sign of the ridiculousness of my great-grandfather's plight – for after all, he was homeless and heading for old age as a 'good for nothing drunk' and a 'fool for horses'.

No one has bothered to conjecture what these curious emblems – saddle blanket and plumes – must have meant to my great-grandfather. But he hung them over the foot of his bed – 'like a fool, my mother said. And sometimes when he got very drunk he would take up the blanket and, wrapping it like a shawl over his shoulders, he would grasp the plumes. Then he would dance the mazurka. He did not dance in the living room but took himself out into the field, where the horses stood at attention and watched as if suddenly experiencing the smell of the sea or a change of wind in the valley. 'Drunks don't care what they do,' my mother would say as she finished her story about my great-grandfather. 'Talking to a drunk is like talking to a stump.'

Ever since my great-grandfather's outbreaks of gypsy-necessity, members of my family have been stolen by things — by mad ambitions, by musical instruments, by otherwise harmless pursuits from mushroom hunting to childbearing or, as was my father's case, by the more easily recognized and popular obsession with card playing. To some extent, I still think it was failure of imagination in this respect that brought about his diminished prospects in the life of our family.

But even my mother had been powerless against the attraction of a man so convincingly driven. When she met him at a birthday dance held at the country house of one of her young friends, she asked him what he did for a living. My father pointed to a deck of cards in his shirt pocket and said, 'I play cards.' But love is such as it is, and although my mother was otherwise a deadly practical woman, it seemed she could fall in love with no man but my father.

So it is possible that the propensity to be stolen is somewhat contagious when ordinary people come into contact with people such as my father. Though my mother loved him at the time of the marriage, she soon began to behave as if she had been stolen from a more fruitful and upright life which she was always imagining might have been hers.

My father's card playing was accompanied, to no one's surprise, by bouts of drinking. The only thing that may have saved our family from a life of poverty was the fact that my father seldom gambled with money. Such were his charm and powers of persuasion that he was able to convince other players to accept his notes on everything from the fish he intended to catch next season to the sale of his daughter's hair.

I know about this last wager because I remember the day he came to me with a pair of scissors and said it was time to cut my hair. Two snips and it was done. I cannot forget the way he wept onto the backs of his hands and held the braids together like a broken noose from which a life had suddenly slipped. I was thirteen at the time and my hair had never been cut. It was his pride and joy that I had such hair. But for me it was only a burdensome difference between me and my classmates, so I was glad to be rid of it. What anyone else could have wanted with my long shiny braids is still a mystery to me.

∩ ∩ ∩

When my father was seventy-three he fell ill and the doctors gave him only a few weeks to live. My father was convinced that his illness had come on him because he'd hit a particularly bad losing streak at cards. He had lost heavily the previous month, and items of value, mostly belonging to my mother, had disappeared from the house. He developed the strange idea that if he could win at cards he could cheat the prediction of the doctors and live at least into his eighties.

By this time I had moved away from home and made a life for myself in an attempt to follow the reasonable dictates of my mother, who had counseled her children severely against all manner of rash ambition and foolhardiness. Her entreaties were leveled especially in my direction since I had shown a suspect enthusiasm for a certain pony at around the age of five. And it is true I felt I had lost a dear friend when my mother saw to it that the neighbours who owned this pony moved it to pasture elsewhere.

But there were other signs that I might wander off into unpredictable pursuits. The most telling of these was that I refused to speak aloud to anyone until the age of eleven. I whispered everything, as if my mind were a repository of secrets which could only be divulged in this intimate manner. If anyone asked me a question, I was always polite about answering, but I had to do it by putting my mouth near the head of my inquisitor and using only my breath and lips to make my reply.

My teachers put my whispering down to shyness and made special accommodations for me. When it came time for recitations I would accompany the teacher into the cloakroom and there whisper to her the memorized verses or the speech I was to have prepared. God knows, I might have continued on like this into the present if my mother hadn't plotted with some neighborhood boys to put burrs into my long hair. She knew by other signs that I had a terrible temper, and she was counting on that to deliver me into the world where people shouted and railed at one another and talked in an audible fashion about things both common and sacred.

When the boys shut me into a shed, according to plan, there was nothing for me to do but to cry out for help and to curse them in a torrent of words I had only heard used by adults. When my mother heard this she rejoiced, thinking that at last she had broken the treacherous hold of the past over me, of my great-grandfather's gypsy blood and the fear that against all her efforts I might be stolen away, as she had been, and as my father had, by some as yet unforeseen predilection. Had I not already experienced the consequences of such a life in our household, I doubt she would have been successful, but the advantages of an ordinary existence among people of a less volatile nature had begun to appeal to me.

It was strange, then, that after all the care my mother had taken for me in this regard, when my father's illness came on him, my mother brought her appeal to me. 'Can you do something?' she wrote, in her cramped, left-handed scrawl. 'He's been drinking and playing cards for three days and nights. I am at my wit's end. Come home at once.'

Somehow I knew this was a message addressed to the very part of me that most baffled and frightened my mother – the part that belonged exclusively to my father and his family's inexplicable manias.

When I arrived home my father was not there.

'He's at the tavern. In the back room,' my mother said. 'He hasn't eaten for days. And if he's slept, he hasn't done it here.'

I made up a strong broth, and as I poured the steaming liquid into a Thermos I heard myself utter syllables and other vestiges of language which I could not reproduce if I wanted to. 'What do you mean by that?' my mother demanded, as if a demon had leapt out of me. 'What did you say?' I didn't — I couldn't — answer her. But suddenly I felt that an unsuspected network of sympathies and distant connections had begun to reveal itself to me in my father's behalf.

There is a saying that when lovers have need of moonlight, it is there. So it seemed, as I made my way through the deserted town toward the tavern and card room, that all nature had been given notice of my father's predicament, and that the response I was waiting for would not be far off.

But when I arrived at the tavern and had talked my way past the barman and into the card room itself, I saw that my father had an enormous pile of blue chips at his elbow. Several players had fallen out to watch, heavy-lidded and smoking their cigarettes like weary gangsters. Others were slumped on folding chairs near the coffee urn with its empty 'Pay Here' styrofoam cup.

My father's cap was pushed to the back of his head so that his forehead shone in the dim light, and he grinned over his cigarette at me with the serious preoccupation of a child who has no intention of obeying anyone. And why should he, I thought as I sat down just behind him and loosened the stopper on the Thermos. The five or six players still at the table casually appraised my presence to see if it had tipped the scales of their luck in an even more unfavorable direction. Then they tossed their cards aside, drew fresh cards, or folded.

In the center of the table were more blue chips, and poking out from my father's coat pocket I recognized the promissory slips he must have redeemed, for he leaned to me and in a low voice, without taking his eyes from his cards, said, 'I'm having a hell of a good time. The time of my life.'

He was winning. His face seemed ravaged by the effort, but he was clearly playing on a level that had carried the game far beyond the realm of mere card playing and everyone seemed to know it. The dealer cocked an eyebrow as I poured broth into the plastic Thermos cup and handed it to my father, who slurped from it noisily, then set it down.

'Tell the old kettle she's got to put up with me a few more years,' he said, and lit up a fresh cigarette. His eyes as he looked at me, however, seemed over-brilliant, as if doubt, despite all his efforts, had gained a permanent seat at his table. I squeezed his shoulder and kissed him hurriedly on his forehead. The men kept their eyes down, and as I paused at the door, there was a shifting of chairs and a clearing of throats. Just outside the room I nearly collided with the barman, who was carrying in a fresh round of beer. His heavy jowls waggled as he recovered himself and looked hard at me over the icy bottles. Then he disappeared into the card room with his provisions.

I took the long way home, finding pleasure in the fact that at this hour all the stoplights had switched onto a flashing-yellow caution cycle. Even the teenagers who usually cruised the town had gone home or to more secluded spots. *Doubt*, I kept thinking as I drove with my father's face before me, that's the real thief. And I knew my mother had brought me home because of it, because she knew that once again a member of our family was about to be stolen.

Two more days and nights I ministered to my father at the card room. I would never stay long because I had the fear myself that I might spoil his luck. But many unspoken tendernesses passed between us in those brief appearances as he accepted the nourishment I offered, or when he looked up and handed me his beer bottle to take a swig from – a ritual we'd shared since my childhood.

My father continued to win – to the amazement of the local barflies who poked their faces in and out of the card room and gave the dwindling three or four stalwarts who remained at the table a commiserating shake of their heads. There had never been a winning streak like it in the history of the tavern, and indeed, we heard later that the man who owned the card room and tavern had to sell out and open a fruit stand on the edge of town as a result of my father's extraordinary good luck.

Twice during this period my mother urged the doctor to order my father home. She was sure my father would, at some fateful moment, risk the entire winnings in some mad rush toward oblivion. But his doctor spoke of a new 'gaming therapy' for the terminally ill, based on my father's surge of energies in the pursuit of his gambling. Little did he know that my father was, by that stage, oblivious to even his winning, he had gone so far into exhaustion.

Luckily for my father, the hour came when, for lack

of players, the game folded. Two old friends drove him home and helped him down from the pickup. They paused in the driveway, one on either side of him, letting him steady himself. When the card playing had ended there had been nothing for my father to do but to get drunk.

My mother and I watched from the window as the men steered my father toward the hydrangea bush at the side of the house, where he relieved himself with perfect precision on one mammoth blossom. Then they hoisted him up the stairs and into the entryway. My mother and I took over from there.

'Give 'em hell, boys,' my father shouted after the men, concluding some conversation he was having with himself.

'You betcha,' the driver called back, laughing. Then he climbed with his companion into the cab of his truck and roared away.

Tied around my father's waist was a cloth sack full of bills and coins which flapped and jingled against his knees as we bore his weight between us up the next flight of stairs and into the living room. There we deposited him on the couch, where he took up residence, refusing to sleep in his bed – for fear, my mother claimed, that death would know where to find him. But I preferred to think he enjoyed the rhythms of the household; from where he lay at the centre of the house, he could overhear all conversations that took place and add his opinions when he felt like it.

My mother was so stricken by the signs of his further decline that she did everything he asked, instead of arguing with him or simply refusing. Instead of taking his winnings straight to the bank so as not to miss a day's interest, she washed an old goldfish bowl and dumped all the money into it, most of it in twenty-dollar bills. Then she placed it on the coffee table near his head so he could run his hand through it at will, or let his visitors do the same.

'Money feels good on your elbow,' he would say to them. 'I played them under the table for that. Yes sir, take a feel of that!' Then he would lean back on his pillows and tell my mother to bring his guests a shot of whiskey. 'Make sure she fills my glass up,' he'd say to me so that my mother was certain to overhear. And my mother, who'd never allowed a bottle of whiskey to be brought into her house before now, would look at me as if the two of us were more than any woman should have to bear.

'If you'd only brought him home from that card room,' she said again and again. 'Maybe it wouldn't have come to this.'

This included the fact that my father had radically altered his diet. He lived only on greens. If it was green he would eat it. By my mother's reckoning, the reason for his change of diet was that if he stopped eating what he usually ate, death would think it wasn't him and go look for somebody else.

Another request my father made was asking my mother to sweep the doorway after anyone came in or went out.

'To make sure death wasn't on their heels; to make sure death didn't slip in as they left.' This was my mother's reasoning. But my father didn't give any reasons. Nor did he tell us finally why he wanted all the furniture moved out of the room except for the couch where he lay. And the money, they could take that away too.

But soon his strength began to ebb, and more and more family and friends crowded into the vacant room to pass the time with him, to laugh about stories remembered from his childhood or from his nights as a young man at the country dances when he and his older brother would work all day in the cotton fields, hop a freight train to town and dance all night. Then they would have to walk home, getting there just at daybreak in time to go straight to work again in the cotton fields.

'We were like bulls then,' my father would say in a burst of the old vigor, then close his eyes suddenly as if he hadn't said anything at all.

As long as he spoke to us, the inevitability of his condition seemed easier to bear. But when, at the last, he simply opened his mouth for food or stared silently toward the far wall, no one knew what to do with themselves.

My own part in that uncertain time came to me accidentally. I found myself in the yard sitting on a stone bench under a little cedar tree my father loved because he liked to sit there and stare at the ocean. The tree whispered, he said. He said it had a way of knowing what your troubles were. Suddenly a craving came over me. I wanted a cigarette, even though I don't smoke, hate smoking, in fact. I was sitting where my father had sat, and to smoke seemed a part of some rightness that had begun to work its way within me. I went into the house and bummed a pack of cigarettes from my brother. For the rest of the morning I sat under the cedar tree and smoked. My thoughts drifted with its shiftings and murmurings, and it struck me what a wonderful thing nature is because it knows the value of silence, the innuendos of silence and what they could mean for a word-bound creature such as I was.

I passed the rest of the day in a trance of silences, moving from place to place, revisiting the sites I knew my father loved – the 'dragon tree', a hemlock which stood at the far end of the orchard, so named for how the wind tossed its triangular head; the rose arbor where he and my mother had courted; the little marina where I sat in his fishing boat and dutifully smoked the hated cigarettes, flinging them one by one into the brackish water.

I was waiting to know what to do for him, he who would soon be a piece of useless matter of no more consequence than the cigarette butts that floated and washed against the side of his boat. I could feel some action accumulating in me through the steadiness of water raising and lowering the boat, through the sad petal-fall of roses in the arbor and the tossing of the dragon tree.

That night when I walked from the house I was full of purpose. I headed toward the little cedar tree. Without stopping to question the necessity of what I was doing, I began to break off the boughs I could reach and to pile them on the ground.

'What are you doing?' my brother's children wanted to know, crowding around me as if I might be inventing some new game for them.

'What does it look like?' I said.

'Pulling limbs off the tree,' the oldest said. Then they dashed away in a pack under the orchard trees, giggling and shrieking.

As I pulled the boughs from the trunk I felt a painful permission, as when two silences, tired of holding back, give over to each other some shared regret. I made my bed on the boughs and resolved to spend the night there in the yard, under the stars, with the hiss of the ocean in my ear, and the maimed cedar tree standing over me like a gift torn out of its wrappings.

My brothers, their wives and my sister had now begun their nightly vigil near my father, taking turns at staying awake. The windows were open for the breeze and I heard my mother trying to answer the question of why I was sleeping outside on the ground – 'like a damned fool' I knew they wanted to add.

'She doesn't want to be here when death comes for him,' my mother said, with an air of clairvoyance she had developed from a lifetime with my father. 'They're too much alike,' she said.

The ritual of night games played by the children went on and on long past their bedtimes. Inside the house, the kerosene lantern, saved from my father's childhood home, had been lit – another of his strange requests during the time before his silence. He liked the shadows it made and the sweet smell of the kerosene. I watched the darkness as the shapes of my brothers and sister passed near it, gigantic and misshapen where they bent or raised themselves or crossed the room.

Out on the water the wind had come up. In the orchard the children were spinning around in a circle, faster and faster until they were giddy and reeling with speed and darkness. Then they would stop, rest a moment, taking quick ecstatic breaths before plunging again into the opposite direction, swirling round and round in the circle until the excitement could rise no higher, their laughter and cries brimming over, then scattering as they flung one another by the arms or chased each other toward the house as if their lives depended on it.

I lay awake for a long while after their footsteps had died away and the car doors had slammed over the goodbyes of the children being taken home to bed and the last of the others had been bedded down in the house while the adults went on waiting.

It was important to be out there alone and close to the ground. The pungent smell of the cedar boughs was around me, rising up in the crisp night air toward the tree, whose turnings and swayings had altered, as they had to, in order to accompany the changes about to overtake my father and me. I thought of my great-grandfather bathing with his horse in the river, and of my father who had just passed through the longest period in his life without the clean feel of cards falling through his hands as he shuffled or dealt them. He was too weak now even to hold a cigarette; there was a burn mark on the hardwood floor where his last cigarette had fallen. His winnings were safely in the bank and the luck that was to have saved him had gone back to that place luck goes to when it is finished with us.

So this is what it comes to, I thought, and listened

to the wind as it mixed gradually with the memory of children's voices which still seemed to rise and fall in the orchard. There was a soft crooning of syllables that was satisfying to my ears, but ultimately useless and absurd. Then it came to me that I was the author of those unwieldy sounds, and that my lips had begun to work of themselves.

In a raw pulsing of language I could not account for, I lay awake through the long night and spoke to my father as one might speak to an ocean or the wind, letting him know by that threadbare accompaniment that the vastness he was about to enter had its rhythms in me also. And that he was not forsaken. And that I was letting him go. That so far I had denied the disreputable world of dancers and drunkards, gamblers and lovers of horses to which I most surely belonged. But from that night forward I vowed to be filled with the first unsavoury desire that would have me. To plunge myself into the heart of my life and be ruthlessly lost forever.

Monty Roberts

The Man Who Listens to Horses

So I was heading off to Nevada again, but this time without Larry and also three weeks ahead of my helpers and the trucks. I was 14 years old and had a driver's licence, but I was not qualified to drive a truck loaded with horses, so I used the services of the haulage company to transport myself, Brownie, Sergeant and Oriel up to the Campbell ranch.

I was going to be up there, just me and my horses, for three weeks. I'd have the time to move slowly and observe the mustangs without interfering with them in any way.

The Campbell ranch had prior information as to

where the family groups were likely to be. There'd be a group here and a group there — maybe 10 miles apart. I intended to bring each family group towards the trap in the barranca one by one, very slowly, observing them as I went.

Once again, I was glad to have Brownie as one of my saddle-horses for this all-important experience. I patted his neck as we rode out over the high desert ground. Oriel and Sergeant walked along behind, and in addition I had a dog, three pairs of binoculars, a hand-gun and a rifle. 'This time, Brownie, we'll see what'll happen, won't we?'

When we reached the first horizon I twisted around in my saddle and watched the outbuildings belonging to the Campbell ranch disappear from sight as we tucked down the opposite side of the slope. We were on our own.

It was great to be riding across this open ground again, with its rocky barrancas where cottonwood and aspen trees grew. I knew I must be extra vigilant for rattlesnakes and for the invisible crevices which were maybe six feet across, treacherous for horses.

As before, it was hot during the day and cold at night. Occasionally, rainstorms would lash down for an hour. Big, billowy, high-desert clouds would give rise to electrical storms.

I was living on a diet mostly of jerky – a cured meat – and pancake mix and salami, as well as oranges.

To find the first family group of horses, I was having to look closely for where they'd be getting their nutrition. They'd eat the sage and the chamis if they were desperate, but they preferred the grama, brome and rye grasses.

When I caught up with my first group, my aim was to integrate with the herd as closely as I could. Either they'd accept me as no threat – which meant I'd have to stay over a mile distant – or I'd have to get closer without their knowing I was there.

They caught my scent from a mile away and began to move off. They were little more than dots on the plateau, and already they were going away.

I left Oriel, my bay pack-horse, because he was proving rather clumsy and often stumbled over stones, the noise of which carried over vast distances – not that he cared. I was beginning to wonder about this Oriel character. His ears were always at half-mast, neither forwards nor backwards. Either he was a deep thinker or a little dumb, or maybe both.

Having lightly hobbled him and leaving Sergeant as well to keep him company, I continued on foot, leading Brownie.

The wild herd saw us pressing closer, and it was an achievement to get within a quarter of a mile of them. We used the barrancas as cover and stayed downwind, moving quietly.

Given the time to move slowly and think about what was happening, I was surprised by how hypersensitive the herd was to our presence. If Brownie just scuffed a rock, I could see their ears flick in our direction.

Now I was within a quarter of a mile of the herd, and I couldn't get any closer. I'd run out of cover and even though I was down-wind of them, they wouldn't allow us any more ground.

This was OK for a while. Brownie and I settled down by a cottonwood tree and I counted them up, trying to log their markings so that I could learn to distinguish one from another.

My binoculars became incredibly important. Nowadays I see young people strapping the virtual reality helmets on to their heads, entranced by the world they enter. This reminds me of the feeling I had when I looked through my binoculars at this herd of wild horses. Suddenly they were close enough to touch. I could observe their every movement in detail. I was there, among them.

I noticed in particular a dun mare with a dark stripe along her back and zebra stripes above her knees. Older than most of the others, with a heavier belly that hinted at many more pregnancies, she seemed to give a lot of commands in the group. It was she who ordered her group to move off. She started and the others followed, she stopped, and so did the others. It seemed she was the wisest, and they knew it.

What I was observing, in fact, was the dominant mare. No one had told me that wild horses were controlled by a dominant mare before, and I suspect a lot of people today still think that it's the stallion who runs the show. That isn't true. The breeding or dominant stallion, sometimes called the alpha male or lead male, will skirt the herd and defend it from marauders. His motivation is to prevent anyone or anything from stealing his harem.

But it was the dun mare who was in charge of the day-to-day running of this group. There was no mistaking it.

And then I saw an extraordinary sequence of

events. A light bay colt was behaving badly. He was about 20 months old, I guessed, with a vast amount of feathering around his fetlocks and down the backs of his legs and a mane running down well below his neck line. Right in the middle of the group, he took a run at a filly and gave her a kick. The filly squealed and hobbled off and this colt looked pleased with himself. He was only about 550 pounds in weight, but very aware of the fact that he was the owner of a pair of testicles.

As I watched, he committed another crime. A little foal approached him, snapping his mouth in a suckling action to indicate he was no threat but subservient, only a little foal. That didn't cut any ice with this colt; he launched himself at his younger cousin and took a bite out of his backside. He really was a terrorist – if he wasn't kicking, he was biting. Immediately after the attack, he pretended nothing had happened; he went neutral. It was as though he was trying to avoid having the blame pinned on him.

Each time he behaved badly, the dun mare – the matriarch – weaved a little closer to him. I became certain that she was watching to see if there was going to be any more of this behaviour. Even though she showed no sign of interest, she'd left her station and was getting closer to him all the time.

She witnessed about four such episodes before she made her move. Now she was within 20 yards, but this sugar-coloured colt couldn't help himself; he launched at a grown mare, grabbed the nap of her neck and bit down hard.

The dun mare didn't hesitate. In an instant she went from neutral to full-on anger; she pinned her ears back and ran at him, knocking him down. As he struggled to his feet, she whirled and knocked him down again.

While this chastisement was going on, the other members of the herd didn't turn a hair. It was as if they didn't know it was happening.

The dun mare ended by driving the colt out of the herd. She drove him out 300 yards and left him there, alone.

I thought, What in the hell am I seeing? I was amazed. The dun mare took up position on the edge of the herd to keep him in exile. She kept her eye on his eye, she faced up to him. She was freezing him out.

He was terrified to be left alone. For a flight animal, it's to be under a sentence of death; the predators will get you if you're separated from the group. He walked back and forth, his head close to the ground, executing this strange, uncomfortable gait several times. It looked like a sign of obedience, similar to a bow made by a human being.

Then the light bay colt made his way around to the other side of the herd and attempted to come back in that way, but the dun mare had followed his circle. Again she drove him out, running at him until he was about 300 yards away before returning to maintain her vigil on the edge of the herd. She kept her body square on to him, and she never once took her eye off his.

He stood there, and I noticed there was a lot of licking and chewing going on, although he hadn't eaten anything. I remembered the foal and how it had snapped its mouth, which is an obvious signal of humility as though it was saying, 'I'm not a threat to you.' Was this the more adult version? Was this colt saying the same thing to his matriarch?

By this time, some hours had passed and it was rapidly getting dark. I thought, Where's the moon? Am I going to see how this ends up?

I scooped up Brownie's reins and rode back to where Sergeant and Oriel were waiting. My intention was to take up a position for the night from where I could continue to observe what was happening with this confrontation between the dun mare and the adolescent colt.

When I got back, Oriel was standing with his nose in a bush. Then he lifted his head sharply, his whole body tense with surprise. A cloud of bees surrounded his head.

This was an emergency. Oriel took a few paces backwards and then tried a couple more sideways. He tried it with his head held low and then jerked it up again.

No luck.

Then he shook himself like a dog coming out of the water, but afterwards he was astonished to realise the bees were still there. This was a puzzle all right, and he'd nearly run out of tricks. There was only one thing for it: tossing his head up and down like a Texan 'nodding donkey'. His thinking obviously was, that if he did this for long enough the bees would get bored and leave.

Brownie, Sergeant and I kept our distance until the bees had gone. Oriel didn't seem unduly perturbed by the experience. It was one of life's many mysteries.

The sun sank surprisingly fast down the western slope of the sky, as though itself desiring rest from a hard day's work. I made camp and hurried to settle Brownie, Sergeant and Oriel with their feed.

Looking at the silhouettes of Brownie and Oriel as they stood nose to tail, no doubt conferring on the day's experiences, I wondered again about Brownie. Where used he to live? Who was his dominant mare? How did he relate to the family group?

The moonlight gave a different tint to the landscape and, since it was reflected from such a vast sky, it seemed to me that there was quite a lot of light available. I picked up my binoculars and found I could see clearly for quite a distance. In fact, unknown to me I was aided in my night-time observations by the fact that I was (and remain) totally colour-blind. This is a rare condition, quite separate from the more ordinary condition of confusing colours or being unable to separate them normally. When I was young, no one believed that I could only see in black and white, but I've subsequently learned that I see in a very different way from normally-sighted people. Professor Oliver Sacks, in his study of 'The Case of the Colour-blind Painter', describes how his subject had a car accident which caused him to lose all perception of colour: 'People's figures might be visible and recognizable half a mile off...his vision had become much sharper, "that of an eagle".' Particularly at night, it seems, the artist could see far better than a normal person, suddenly finding himself able to identify a number-plate from four blocks away. In fact, this artist was so distressed by his loss of colour that he took to being nocturnal.

Focusing and swinging the twin circles of the eyepiece here and there, I caught sight of my herd. I wanted to find out what was happening.

To my astonishment, the dun mare was now grooming the light bay colt. She was giving him little scrapes on his neck and hindquarters with her teeth, and generally fussing over him. She'd let him back in; and now she was keeping him close by and giving him a lot of attention. She worked away at the root of his tail, hips and withers.

So...after his purgatory, came heaven. As I watched, she groomed the hell out of him.

As it turned out, my periods of observation of the wild herds were particularly fruitful at night. Mustangs fear attacks from predators mostly at dawn and dusk; at night they could afford to relax and their social interaction was more marked. It became a habit to watch them by the light of the moon, and I slept usually from about 1.30 until 5.30 in the morning.

Puzzling over what I had just seen, I began to learn the language of 'Equus', as I now call it.

Of course, my comprehension of this silent language took more than these first few weeks alone out on the high desert of Nevada, but I was to continue rounding up mustangs for the Salinas Rodeo for the next two years.

It was certainly the single most important thing I saw — this matriarch disciplining the young, adolescent horses. There was a gang of adolescents she had to deal with, and it was educational to watch her do it because a lot happened. Their youthful energy drove them to do things, and their inexperience meant they made mistakes, much like the young of any species.

It was the dun mare's job to keep them in order — and over the three-week period, I watched every move.

Certainly, she went on and made a Christian out of that sugar-coloured colt. Often, like a child, he would reoffend immediately after being let back in, to test the disciplinary system and gain back the ground he'd lost. Maybe he'd start fighting with another colt or bothering the fillies.

The dun mare came right back and disciplined him again. She squared up to him and said, 'I don't like your actions. You're going away.'

He sinned a few more times, but she always drove him out and kept him out there before letting him back in and welcoming him into the group with extensive grooming. The third time he sinned, he practically owned up and walked out there by himself, grumbling about it but accepting his fate.

Then he came back in and stuck to the group like glue. He was a positive nuisance; he turned out so nice and co-operative, wandering about and asking everyone, 'D'you need any grooming?' when all they wanted was to be left alone to eat. For four whole days the dun mare had made the education of this awful brat her number one priority, and it had paid off.

As I watched the mare's training procedures with this and other adolescents, I began to cotton on to the language she used, and it was exciting to be able to recognise the exact sequence of signals that would pass between her and the adolescents. It really was a language – predictable, discernible and effective.

First and foremost, it was a silent language. It's worth dwelling on the silent aspect of her commands because it's easy to underrate a language which uses a different medium from our own.

As I was to learn much later, the most common form of communication on this planet takes place silently – in the dark of the deep sea, where animals use bioluminescence, intricate lighting systems, to attract mates, ward off predators, attract prey and otherwise convey all the signals necessary for their existence.

Body language is not confined to humans, nor to horses; it constitutes the most often used form of communication between animate objects on dry land, as well.

And here, moving as close as a quarter-mile from a herd of wild horses, I learned that the dun mare was constantly schooling the foals and yearlings without the need for sound. In their turn, they were reacting to the matriarch without the need for sound either. The stallion was operating his security system with a distinct need for silence, and meanwhile he was also investigating the potential for mating.

They were happy with one another, upset with one another, guiding one another and advising one another, and it was all done silently.

I was to realise that nothing was done by accident. Every small degree of a horse's movement occurs for a reason. Nothing is trivial. Nothing is to be dismissed.

Lying on my belly and watching these horses with my three different pairs of binoculars pressed for hours at a time to my eyes-sockets, straining to see all I could in the moonlight, I began to log their vocabulary.

I discovered that the key ingredient to the language 'Equus' is the positioning of the body and its direction of travel.

The attitude of the body relative to the long axis of the spine and the short axis – this is critical to their vocabulary. It *is* their vocabulary.

The dun mare squared up, eyes on eyes, with spine rigid and head pointed directly at the adolescent to drive him away, and he knew exactly what she meant. When he was malingering in his purgatory 200–300 yards away, he would know by her body position whether or not he was to be allowed back in.

If she was facing him, he wasn't. If she showed him part of her long axis, he could begin to consider himself invited back into the group. Before this act of forgiveness, she waited to see signs of penitence from him. These signals he gave – asking forgiveness –

would later be fundamental to the development of my technique.

If he walked back and forth in his isolated position with his nose close to the ground, then he was asking for a chance to re-negotiate his position with her. He was saying, 'I am obedient, and I'm willing to listen.'

If he showed her the long axis of his body, then he was offering the vulnerable areas to her and asking to be forgiven.

Their eye contact also spoke volumes. When she was holding him out there, she always kept an eye directly looking at his eye, sometimes for uncomfortably long periods of time. When her eye slid a short distance off his, he knew he might be allowed back in.

I came to realise that their reading of eye contact was extraordinarily subtle. Even when I was familiar to this herd, I could cause a horse to alter its direction and pace of movement by changing which part of its body I looked at – even from quite a distance away.

When the colt trotted out to suffer his exile, he'd be throwing his nose out in front of himself in a circular motion, which would mean, 'I didn't intend to do that, I'm sorry, it wasn't my idea, it just happened, it was the other guy's fault.'

Then the dun mare made a judgement as to whether she believed him or not. I could see her thinking about it. Sometimes she believed him, sometimes she didn't.

The licking and chewing action of the colt's mouth that I had observed was a signal from him that he was penitent. He was saying to her, 'Look, I'm a herbivore, I'm no threat to you, I'm eating over here.'

Observing these signals that passed with absolute regularity and predicability between the adolescent and the matriarch, it became clear to me that the pattern of behaviour set up within the group accounted for the 'yo-yo effect' as described to me by my Uncle Ray.

Press the young horse away, and his instinct is to return.

The dun mare advanced on him, then she retreated.

When I made this connection between the mare's disciplining of the adolescents and Uncle Ray's story, I can remember it was as if the synapses in my brain all clicked at the same time to tell me I'd found what I was looking for. A name sprang to my head – 'Advance and Retreat'.

After a time spent observing these signals, I could see how exact a language it was; there was nothing haphazard about it. These were precise messages, whole phrases and sentences which always meant the same thing, always had the same effect. They happened over and over again.

Perhaps I could use the same silent system of communication myself, as I'd observed employed by the dominant mare. If I understood how to do it, I could effectively cross over the boundary between man – the ultimate fight animal – and horse, the flight animal. Using their language, their system of communication, I could create a strong bond of trust. I would achieve cross-species communication.

'Advance and Retreat' also seemed to me to provide a psychological explanation as to why horses are 'into pressure' animals. If you place a finger against a horse's shoulder or flank and push, you'll find the weight of the animal swing against you, not away from you. To understand this phenomenon is to be half-way to achieving good results as a trainer of horses.

Over the years I would be able to add to my vocabulary in the language of 'Equus', but the more refined definitions – important as they'd become to my techniques – would all be contained within this overall, most important concept of 'Advance and Retreat'.

Ernest Hemingway

War Cloud

I guess looking at it, my old man was cut out for a fat guy, one of those regular little roly guys you see around, but he sure never got that way, except a little towards the last, and then it wasn't his fault, he was riding over the jumps only and he could afford to carry plenty of weight then. I remember the way he'd pull on a rubber shirt over a couple of jerseys and a big sweat shirt over that, and get me to run with him in the forenoon in the hot sun. He'd have, maybe, taken a trial trip with one of Razzo's skins early in the morning after just getting in from Torino at four o'clock in the morning and beating it out to the stables in a cab and then with the dew all over everything and the sun just starting to get going, I'd help him pull off his boots and he'd get into a pair of sneakers and all those sweaters and we'd start out.

'Come on, kid,' he'd say, stepping up and down on his toes in front of the jocks' dressing-room, 'let's get moving.'

Then we'd start off jogging around the infield once, maybe, with him ahead, running nice, and then turn out the gate and along one of those roads with all the trees along both sides of them that run out from San Siro. I'd go ahead of him when we hit the road and I could run pretty stout and I'd look around and he'd be jogging easy just behind me and after a little while I'd look around again and he'd begun to sweat. Sweating heavy and he'd just be dogging it along with his eyes on my back, but when he'd catch me looking at him he'd grin and say, 'Sweating plenty?' When my old man grinned, nobody could help but grin too. We'd keep right on running out towards the mountains and then my old man would yell, 'Hey, Joe!' and I'd look back and he'd be sitting under a tree with a towel he'd had around his waist wrapped around his neck.

I'd come back and sit down beside him and he'd pull a rope out of his pocket and start skipping rope out in the sun with the sweat pouring off his face and him skipping rope out in the white dust with the rope going cloppetty, cloppetty, clop, clop, clop, and the sun hotter, and him working harder up and down a patch of the road. Say, it was a treat to see my old man skip rope, too. He could whirr it fast or lop it slow and fancy. Say, you ought to have seen wops look at us sometimes, when they'd come by, going into town walking along with big white steers hauling the cart. They sure looked as though they thought the old man was nuts. He'd start the rope whirring till they'd stop dead still and watch him, then give the steers a cluck and a poke with the goad and get going again.

When I'd sit watching him working out in the hot sun I sure felt fond of him. He sure was fun and he done his work so hard and he'd finish up with a regular whirring that'd drive the sweat out on his face like water and then sling the rope at the tree and come over and sit down with me and lean back against the tree with the towel and a sweater wrapped around his neck.

'Sure is hell keeping it down, Joe,' he'd say and lean

back and shut his eyes and breathe long and deep, 'it ain't like when you're a kid.' Then he'd get up before he started to cool and we'd jog along back to the stables. That's the way it was keeping down to weight. He worried all the time. Most jocks can just about ride off all they want to. A jock loses about a kilo every time he rides, but my old man was sort of dried out and he couldn't keep down his kilos without all that running.

I remember once at San Siro, Regoli, a little wop, that was riding for Buzoni, came out across the paddock going to the bar for something cool; and flicking his boots with his whip, after he'd just weighed in and my old man had just weighed in too, and came out with the saddle under his arm looking red-faced and tired and too big for his silks and he stood there looking at young Regoli standing up to the outdoors bar, cool and kid-looking, and I says, 'What's the matter, Dad?' 'cause I thought maybe Regoli had bumped him or something and he just looked at Regoli and said, 'Oh, to hell with it,' and went on to the dressing-room.

Well, it would have been all right, maybe, if we'd stayed in Milan and ridden at Milan and Torino, 'cause if there ever were any easy courses, it's those two, 'Pianola, Joe', my old man said when he dismounted in the winning stall after what the wops thought was a hell of a steeplechase. I asked him once. 'This course rides itself. It's the pace you're going at, that makes riding the jumps dangerous, Joe. We ain't going any pace here, and they ain't really bad jumps either. But it's the pace always – not the jumps that makes the trouble.'

San Siro was the swellest course I'd ever seen, but the old man said it was a dog's life. Going back and forth between Mirafiore and San Siro and riding just about every day in the week with a train ride every other night.

I was nuts about the horses, too. There's something about it, when they come out and go up the track to the post. Sort of dancy and tight looking with the jock keeping a tight hold on them and maybe easing off a little and letting them run a little going up. Then once they were at the barrier it got me worse than anything. Especially at San Siro with that big green infield and the mountains way off and the fat wop starter with his big whip and the jocks fiddling them around and then the barrier snapping up and that bell going off and them all getting off in a bunch and then commencing to string out. You know the way a bunch of skins gets off. If you're up in the stand with a pair of glasses all you see is them plunging off and then the bell goes off and it seems like it rings for a thousand years and then they come sweeping round the turn. There wasn't ever anything like it for me.

But my old man said one day, in the dressing-room, when he was getting into his street clothes, 'None of these things are horses, Joe. They'd kill that bunch of skates for their hides and hoofs up at Paris.' That was the day he'd won the Premio Commercio with Lantorna, shooting her out of the field the last hundred metres like pulling a cork out of a bottle.

It was right after the Premio Commercio that we pulled out and left Italy. My old man and Holbrook and a fat wop in a straw hat that kept wiping his face with a handkerchief were having an argument at a table in the Galleria. They were all talking French and the two of them were after my old man about something. Finally he didn't say anything any more but just sat there and looked at Holbrook, and the two of them kept after him, first one talking and then the other, and the fat wop always butting in on Holbrook.

'You go out and buy me a *Sportsman*, will you, Joe?'

my old man said, and handed me a couple of soldi without looking away from Holbrook.

So I went out of the Galleria and walked over to in front of the Scala and bought a paper, and came back and stood a little way away because I didn't want to butt in and my old man was sitting back in his chair looking down at the coffee and fooling with a spoon and Holbrook and the big wop were standing and the big wop was wiping his face and shaking his head. And I came up and my old man acted just as though the two of them weren't standing there and said, 'Want an ice, Joe?' Holbrook looked down at my old man and said slow and careful, 'You son of a bitch,' and he and the fat wop went out through the tables.

My old man sat there and sort of smiled at me, but his face was white and he looked sick as hell and I was scared and felt sick inside because I knew something had happened and I didn't see how anybody could call my old man a son of a bitch, and get away with it. My old man opened up the *Sportsman* and studied the handicaps for a while and then he said, 'You got to take a lot of things in this world, Joe.' And three days later we left Milan for good on the Turin train for Paris, after an auction sale out in front of Turner's stables of everything we couldn't get into a trunk and a suitcase.

We got into Paris early in the morning in a long, dirty station the old man told me was the Gare de Lyon. Paris was an awful big town after Milan. Seems like in Milan everybody is going somewhere and all the trams run somewhere and there ain't any sort of mix-up, but Paris is all balled up and they never do straighten it out. I got to like it, though, part of it, anyway, and say, it's got the best racecourses in the world. Seems as though that were the thing that keeps it all going and about the only thing you can figure on is that every day the buses will be going out to whatever track they're running at, going right out through everything to the track. I never really got to know Paris well, because I just came in about once or twice a week with the old man from Maisons and he always sat at the Café de la Paix on the Opéra side with the rest of the gang from Maisons and I guess that's one of the busiest parts of the town. But, say, it is funny that a big town like Paris wouldn't have a Galleria, isn't it?

Well, we went out to live at Maisons-Lafitte, where just about everybody lives except the gang at Chantilly, with a Mrs Meyers that runs a boarding house. Maisons is about the swellest place to live I've ever seen in all my life. The town ain't so much, but there's a lake and a swell forest that we used to go off bumming in all day, a couple of us kids, and my old man made me a sling shot and we got a lot of things with it, but the best one was a magpie. Young Dick Atkinson shot a rabbit with it one day and we put it under a tree and were all sitting around and Dick had some cigarettes and all of a sudden the rabbit jumped up and beat into the brush and we chased it, but we couldn't find it. Gee, we had fun at Maisons. Mrs Meyers used to give me lunch in the morning and I'd be gone all day. I learned to talk French quick. It's an easy language.

As soon as we got to Maisons, my old man wrote to Milan for his licence and he was pretty worried till it came. He used to sit around the Café de Paris in Maisons with the gang; there were lots of guys he'd known when he rode up at Paris, before the war, lived at Maisons, and there's a lot of time to sit around because the work around a racing stable, for the jocks, that is, is all cleaned up by nine o'clock in the morning. They take the first batch of skins out to gallop

them at 5.30 in the morning and they work the second lot at 8 o'clock. That means getting up early all
right and going to bed early, too. If a jock's riding for
somebody too, he can't go boozing around because the
trainer always has an eye on him if he's a kid and if he
ain't a kid he's always got an eye on himself. So mostly
if a jock ain't working he sits around the Café de Paris
with the gang and they can all sit around about two or
three hours in front of some drink like a vermouth
and seltz and they talk and tell stories and shoot pool
and it's sort of like a club or the Galleria in Milan.
Only it ain't really like the Galleria because there
everybody is going by all the time and there's everybody around the tables.

Well, my old man got his licence all right. They
sent it through to him without a word and he rode a
couple of times. Amiens, up country and that sort of
thing, but he didn't seem to get any engagements.
Everybody liked him and whenever I'd come in to the
café in the forenoon I'd find somebody drinking with
him because my old man wasn't tight like most of
these jockeys that have got the first dollar they made
riding at the World's Fair in St Louis in nineteen
ought four. That's what my old man would say when

he'd kid George Burns. But it seemed like everybody steered clear of giving my old man any mounts.

We went out to wherever they were running every day with the car from Maisons and that was the most fun of all. I was glad when the horses came back from Deauville and the summer. Even though it meant no more bumming in the woods, 'cause then we'd ride to Enghein or Tremblay or St Cloud and watch them from the trainers' and jockeys' stand. I sure learned about racing from going out with that gang and the fun of it was going every day.

I remember once out at St Cloud. It was a big two-hundred-thousand-franc race with seven entries and War Cloud a big favourite. I went around to the paddock to see the horses with my old man and you never saw such horses. This War Cloud is a great big yellow horse that looks like just nothing but run. I never saw such a horse. He was being led around the paddock with his head down and when he went by me I felt all hollow inside he was so beautiful. There never was such a wonderful, lean, running-built horse. And he went around the paddock putting his feet just so and quiet and careful and moving easy like he knew just what he had to do and not jerking and standing up on

his legs and getting wild-eyed like you see these selling platers with a shot of dope in them. The crowd
was so thick I couldn't see him again except just his
legs going by and some yellow and my old man started
out through the crowd and I followed him over to the
jocks' dressing-room back in the trees and there was a
big crowd around there, too, but the man at the door
in a derby nodded to my old man and we got in and
everybody was sitting around and getting dressed and
pulling shirts over their heads and pulling boots on
and it all smelled hot and sweaty and linimenty and
outside was the crowd looking in.

The old man went over and sat down beside George
Gardner that was getting into his pants and said,
'What's the dope, George?' just in an ordinary tone of
voice 'cause there ain't any use him feeling around
because George either can tell him or he can't tell him.

'He won't win,' George says very low, leaning over
and buttoning the bottoms of his pants.

'Who will?' my old man says, leaning over close so
nobody can hear.

'Foxless,' George says, 'and if he does, save me a
couple of tickets.'

My old man says something in a regular voice to

George and George says, 'Don't ever bet on anything, I tell you,' kidding like, and we beat it out and through the crowd that was looking in over to the 100 franc mutuel machine. But I knew something big was up because George is War Cloud's jockey. On the way he gets one of the yellow odds-sheets with the starting prices on and War Cloud is only paying 5 for 10, Cefisidote is next at 3 to 1 and fifth down the list this Foxless is 8 to 1. My old man bets five thousand on Foxless to win and puts on a thousand to place and we went around back of the grandstand to go up the stairs and get a place to watch the race.

We were jammed in tight and first a man in a long coat with a grey tall hat and a whip folded up in his hand came out and then one after another the horses, with the jocks up and a stable-boy holding the bridle on each side and walking along, followed the old guy. That big yellow horse War Cloud came first. He didn't look so big when you first looked at him until you saw the length of his legs and the whole way he's built and the way he moves. Gosh, I never saw such a horse. George Gardner was riding him and they moved along slow, back of the old guy in the grey tall hat that walked along like he was the ringmaster in a circus. Back of

War Cloud, moving along smooth and yellow in the sun, was a good-looking black with a nice head with Tommy Archibald riding him; and after the black was a string of five more horses all moving along slow in a procession past the grandstand and the pesage. My old man said the black was Foxless and I took a good look at him and he was a nice-looking horse, all right, but nothing like War Cloud.

Everybody cheered War Cloud when he went by and he sure was one swell-looking horse. The procession of them went around on the other side past the pelouse and then back up to the near end of the course and the circus master had the stable-boys turn them loose one after another so they could gallop by the stands on their way up to the post and let everybody have a good look at them. They weren't at the post hardly any time at all when the gong started and you could see them way off across the infield all in a bunch starting on the first swing like a lot of little toy horses. I was watching them through the glasses and War Cloud was running well back, with one of the bays making the pace. They swept down and around and come pounding past and War Cloud was way back when they passed us and this Foxless horse in front and going smooth. Gee, it's awful when they go by you and then you have to watch them go farther away and get smaller and smaller and then all bunched up on the turns and then come around towards you into the stretch and you feel like swearing and god-damning worse and worse. Finally they made the last turn and came into the straightaway with the Foxless horse way out in front. Everybody was looking funny and saying 'War Cloud' in a sort of sick way and them pounding nearer down the stretch, and then some-thing come out of the pack right into my glasses like a horse-headed yellow streak and everybody began to yell 'War Cloud' as though they were crazy. War Cloud came on faster than I'd ever seen anything in my life and pulled up on Foxless that was going fast as any black horse could go with the jock flogging hell out of him with the gad and they were right dead neck and neck for a second but War Cloud seemed about twice as fast with those great jumps and that head out – but it was while they were neck and neck that they passed the winning post and when the numbers went up in the slots the first one was 2 and that meant Foxless had won.

I felt all trembly and funny inside, and then we were

all jammed in with the people going downstairs to stand in front of the board where they'd post what Foxless paid. Honest, watching the race I'd forgotten how much my old man had bet on Foxless. I'd wanted War Cloud to win so damned bad. But now it was all over it was swell to know we had a winner.

'Wasn't it a swell race, Dad?' I said to him.

He looked at me sort of funny with his derby on the back of his head. 'George Gardner's a swell jockey, all right,' he said. 'It sure took a great jockey to keep that War Cloud horse from winning.'

Of course I knew it was funny all the time. But my old man saying that right out like that sure took the kick out of it for me and I didn't get the real kick back again ever, even when they posted the numbers up on the board and the bell rang to pay off and we saw that Foxless paid 67.50 for 10. All round people were saying, 'Poor War Cloud! Poor War Cloud!' And I thought, I wish I were a jockey and could have rode him instead of that son of a bitch. And that was funny, thinking of George Gardner as a son of a bitch because I'd always liked him and besides he'd given us the winner, but I guess that's what he is, all right.

Alistair MacLeod

In the Fall

'We'll just have to sell him,' I remember my mother saying with finality. 'It will be a long winter and I will be alone here with only these children to help me. Besides he eats too much and we will not have enough feed for the cattle as it is.'

It is the second Saturday of November and already the sun seems to have vanished for the year. Each day dawns duller and more glowering and the waves of the gray Atlantic are sullen and almost yellow at their peaks as they pound relentlessly against the round smooth boulders that lie scattered as if by a careless giant at the base of the ever-resisting cliffs. At night,

when we lie in our beds, we can hear the waves rolling
in and smashing, rolling in and smashing, so relentless
and regular that it is possible to count rhythmically
between the thunder of each: one, two, three, four;
one, two, three, four.

It is hard to realize that this is the same ocean that
is the crystal blue of summer when only the thin oil
slicks left by the fishing boats or the startling whiteness of the riding sea gulls mar its azure sameness.
Now it is roiled and angry, and almost anguished,
hurling up the brown dirty balls of scudding foam,
the sticks of pulpwood from some lonely freighter,
the caps of unknown men, buoys from mangled fishing nets and the inevitable bottles that contain no
messages. And always also the shreds of blackened
and stringy seaweed that it has ripped and torn from
its own lower regions, as if this is the season for self-
mutilation – the pulling out of the secret, private,
unseen hair.

We are in the kitchen of our house and my mother
is speaking as she energetically pokes at the wood and
coal within her stove. The smoke escapes, billows
upward and flattens itself out against the ceiling.
Whenever she speaks she does something with her

hands. It is as if the private voice within her can only be liberated by some kind of physical action. She is tall and dark with high cheekbones and brown eyes. Her hair which is very long and very black is pulled back severely and coiled in a bun at the base of her neck where it is kept in place by combs of coral.

My father is standing with his back toward us and is looking out the window to where the ocean pounds against the cliffs. His hands are clasped behind his back. He must be squeezing them together very tightly because they are almost white – especially the left. My father's left hand is larger than his right and his left arm is about three inches longer than normal. That is because he holds his stevedore's hook in his left hand when he works upon the waterfront in Halifax. His complexion is lighter than my mother's and his eyes are gray which is also the predominant colour of his thinning hair.

We have always lived on the small farm between the ocean and the coal-mining town. My father has always worked on his land in the summer and at one time he would spend his winters working within the caverns of the coal mine. Later when he could bear the under-ground no longer he had spent the time from

November to April as an independent coal-hauler or
working in his wood lot where he cut timbers for the
mine roof's support. But it must have been a long
time ago for I can scarcely remember a time when the
mine worked steadily or a winter when he has been
with us and I am almost fourteen. Now each winter he
goes to Halifax but he is often a long time in going.
He will stand as he does now, before the window, for
perhaps a week or more and then he will be gone and
we will see him only at Christmas and on the odd
weekend; for he will be over two hundred miles away
and the winter storms will make travelling difficult
and uncertain. Once, two years ago, he came home for
a weekend and the blizzard came so savagely and with
such intensity that he could not return until Thursday.
My mother told him he was a fool to make such a
journey and that he had lost a week's wages for nothing — a week's wages that she and six children could
certainly use. After that he did not come home again
until it was almost spring.

'It wouldn't hurt to keep him another winter,' he
says now, still looking out the window. 'We've kept
him through all of them before. He doesn't eat much
now since his teeth have gone bad.'

'He was of some use before,' says my mother shortly and rattling the lids of her stove. 'When you were home you used him in the woods or to haul coal — not that it ever got us much. These last years he's been worthless. It would be cheaper to rent a horse for the summer or perhaps even hire a tractor. We don't need a horse anymore, not even a young one, let alone one that will probably die in March after we've fed him all that time.' She replaces the stove lids — all in their proper places.

They are talking about our old horse Scott who has been with us all of my life. My father had been his driver for two winters in the underground and they had become fond of one another and in the time of the second spring, when he left the mine forever, the man had purchased the horse from the Company so that they might both come out together to see the sun and walk upon the grass. And that the horse might be saved from the blindness that would inevitably come if he remained within the deeps, the darkness that would make him like itself.

At one time he had even looked like coal, when his coat was black and shiny strong, relieved by only a single white star in the center of his forehead; but that too was a long time ago and now he is very gray about the eyes and his legs are stiff when he first begins to walk.

'Oh, he won't die in March,' says my father. 'He'll be okay. You said the same thing last fall and he came through okay. Once he was on the grass again he was like a two-year-old.'

For the past three or four years Scott has had heaves. I guess heaves come to horses from living too near the ocean and its dampness, like asthma comes to people, making them cough and sweat and struggle for breath. Or perhaps from eating dry and dusty hay for too many winters in the prison of a narrow stall. Perhaps from old age too. Perhaps from all of them. I don't know. Someone told my little brother David who is ten that dampening the hay would help, and last winter from early January when Scott began to cough really bad, David would take a dipper of water and sprinkle it on the hay after we'd put it in the manger. Then David would say the coughing was much better and I would say so too.

'He's not a two-year-old,' says my mother shortly and begins to put on her coat before going out to feed her chickens. 'He's old and useless and we're not running a rest home for retired horses. I am alone here with six children and I have plenty to do.'

Long ago when my father was a coal-hauler and before he was married he would sometimes become drunk, perhaps because of his loneliness, and during a short February day and a long February night he had drunk and talked and slept inside the bootlegger's oblivious to the frozen world without until in the next morning's dehydrated despair he had staggered to the door and seen both horse and sleigh where he had left them and where there was no reason for them to be. The coal was glowing black on the sleigh beneath the fine powdered snow that seems to come even when it is coldest, seeming more to form like dew than fall like rain, and the horse was standing like a gray ghostly form in the early morning's darkness. His own black coat was covered with the hoarfrost that had formed of yesterday's sweat, and tiny icicles hung from his nose.

My father could not believe that the horse had waited for him throughout the night of bitter cold, untied and unnecessary, shifting his feet on the squeaking snow, and flickering his muscles beneath the frozen harness. Before that night he had never been waited for by any living thing and he had buried his face in the hoarfrost mane and stood there quietly for a long, long time, his face in the heavy black hair and the ice beading on his cheeks.

He has told us this story many times even though it bores my mother. When he tells it David sits on his lap and says that he would have waited too, no matter how long and no matter how cold. My mother says she hopes David would have more sense.

'Well, I have called MacRae and he is to come for him today,' my mother says as she puts on her coat and prepares to feed her chickens. 'I wanted to get it over with while you were still here. The next thing I know you'll be gone and we'll be stuck with him for another winter. Grab the pail, James,' she says to me. 'Come and help me feed the chickens. At least there's some point in feeding them.'

'Just a minute,' he says. 'Just a goddamn minute.' He turns quickly from the window and I see his hands turn into fists and his knuckles white and cold. My mother points to the younger children and shakes her head. He is temporarily stymied because she has so often told him he must not swear before them and while he hesitates we take our pails and escape.

As we go to where the chickens are kept, the ocean waves are even higher, and the wind has risen so that we have to use our bodies to shield the pails that we carry. If we do not their contents will be scooped out and scattered wildly to the skies. It is beginning to rain and the drops are so driven by the fierceness of the wind that they ping against the galvanized sides of the pails and sting and then burn upon our cheeks.

Inside the chicken house it is warm and acrid as the chickens press around us. They are really not chickens any more but full-grown capons which my mother has been raising all summer and will soon sell on the Christmas market. Each spring she gets day-old chicks and we feed them ground-up hardboiled eggs and chick-starter. Later we put them into outside pens and then in the fall into this house where they are fattened. They are Light Sussex which is the breed my mother favors because they are hardy and good weight-producers. They are very, very white now with red combs and black and gold glittering eyes and with a ring of startling black at the base of their white, shining necks. It is as if a white fluid had been poured over their heads and cascaded down their necks to where it suddenly and magically changed to black after exposure to the air. The opposite in color but the same in luster. Like piano keys.

My mother moves about them with ease and they are accustomed to her and jostle about her as she fills their troughs with mash and the warm water we have brought. Sometimes I like them and sometimes I do not. The worst part seems to be that it doesn't really matter. Before Christmas they will all be killed and dressed and then in the spring there will be another group and they will always look and act and end in the same way. It is hard to really like what you are planning to kill and almost as hard to feel dislike, and when there are many instead of one they begin to seem almost as the blueberries and strawberries we pick in summer. Just a whole lot of them to be alive in their way for a little while and then to be picked and eaten, except it seems the berries would be there anyway but the capons we are responsible for and encourage them to eat a great deal, and try our best to make them warm and healthy and strong so that we may kill them in the end. My father is always uncomfortable around them and avoids them as much as possible. My friend Henry Van Dyken says that my father feels that way because he is Scottish, and that

Scotsmen are never any good at raising poultry or flowers because they think such tasks are for women and that they make a man ashamed. Henry's father is very good at raising both.

As we move about the closeness of the chicken house the door bangs open and David is almost blown in upon us by the force of the wind and the rain. 'There's a man with a big truck that's got an old bull on it,' he says. 'He just went in the house.'

When we enter the kitchen MacRae is standing beside the table, just inside the door. My father is still at the window, although now with his back to it. It does not seem that they have said anything.

MacRae, the drover, is in his fifties. He is short and heavyset with a red face and a cigar in the corner of his mouth. His eyes are small and bloodshot. He wears Wellington boots with his trousers tucked inside them, a broad western-style belt, and a brown suede jacket over a flannel shirt which is open at the neck exposing his reddish chest-hair. He carries a heavy stock whip in his hand and taps it against the side of his boot. Because of his short walk in the wind-driven rain his clothes are wet and now in the warmth of the kitchen they give off a steamy, strong odor that mingles uncomfortably with that of his cigar. An odor that comes of his jostling and shoving the countless frightened animals that have been carried on the back of his truck, an odor of manure and sweat and fear.

'I hear you've got an old knacker,' he says now around the corner of his cigar. 'Might get rid of him for mink-feed if I'm lucky. The price is twenty dollars.'

My father says nothing, but his eyes which seem the gray of the ocean behind him remind me of a time when the log which Scott was hauling seemed to ricochet wildly off some half-submerged obstacle, catching the man's legs beneath it until it smashed into a protruding stump, almost uprooting it and knocking Scott back upon his haunches. And his eyes then in their grayness had reflected fear and pain and almost a mute wonder at finding himself so painfully trapped by what seemed all too familiar.

And it seemed now that we had, all of us, conspired against him, his wife and six children and the cigar-smoking MacRae, and that we had almost brought him to bay with his back against the ocean-scarred window so pounded by the driving rain and with all of us ringed before him. But still he says nothing although I think his mind is racing down all the possible avenues of argument, and rejecting all because he knows the devastating truth that awaits him at the end of each: 'There is no need of postponing it; the truck is here and there will never be a better opportunity; you will soon be gone; he will never be any younger; the price will never be any higher; he may die this winter and we will get nothing at all; we are not running a rest home for retired horses; I am alone here with six children and I have more than enough to do; the money for his feed could be spent on your children; don't your children mean more to you than a horse; it is unfair to go and leave us here with him to care for.'

Then with a nod he moves from the window and starts toward the door. 'You're not...' begins David, but he is immediately silenced by his mother. 'Be quiet,' she says. 'Go and finish feeding the chickens,' and then, as if she cannot help it, 'At least there is some point in feeding them.' Almost before my father stops, I know she is sorry about the last part. That she fears that she has reached for too much and perhaps even now has lost all she had before. It is like when you attempt to climb one of the almost vertical sea-washed cliffs, edging upward slowly and groping with blue-tipped fingers from one tiny crevice to the next and then seeing the tantalizing twig which you cannot resist seizing, although even as you do, you know it can be grounded in nothing for there is no vegetation there nor soil to support it and the twig is but a reject tossed up there by the sea, and even then you are tensing yourself for the painful, bruising slide that must inevitably follow. But this time for my mother, it does not. He only stops and looks at her for a moment before forcing open the door and going out into the wind. David does not move.

'I think he's going to the barn,' says my mother then with surprising softness in her voice, and telling me with her eyes that I should go with him. By the time MacRae and I are outside he is already halfway to the barn; he had no hat nor coat and is walking sideways and leaning and knifing himself into the wind which blows his trousers taut against the outlines of his legs.

As MacRae and I pass the truck I cannot help but look at the bull. He is huge and old and is an Ayrshire. He is mostly white except for the almost cherry-red markings of his massive shoulders and on his neck and jowls. His heavy head is forced down almost to the truck's floor by a reinforced chain halter and by a rope that has been doubled through his nose ring and fastened to an iron bar bolted to the floor. He has tried to turn his back into the lashing wind and rain and his bulk is pressed against the truck's slatted side at an unnatural angle to his grotesquely fastened head. The floor of the truck is greasy and slippery with a mixture of the rain and his own excrement, and each time he attempts to move, his feet slide and threaten to slip from under him. He is trembling with the strain, and the muscles in his shoulders give involuntary little twitches and his eyes roll upward in their sockets. The rain mingles with his sweat and courses down his flanks in rivulets of gray.

'How'd you like to have a pecker on you like that fella,' shouts MacRae into the wind. 'Bet he's had his share and driven it into them little heifers a good many times. Boy you get hung like that, you'll have all them horny little girls squealen for you to take 'em behind the bushes. No time like it with them little girls, just when the juice starts runnen in 'em and they're finding out what it's for.' He runs his tongue over his lips appreciatively and thwacks his whip against the sodden wetness of his boot.

Inside the barn it is still and sheltered from the

storm. Scott is in the first stall and then there is a vacant one and then those of the cattle. My father has gone up beside Scott and is stroking his nose but saying nothing. Scott rubs his head up and down against my father's chest. Although he is old he is still strong and the force of his neck as he rubs almost lifts my father off his feet and pushes him against the wall.

'Well, no time like the present,' say MacRae, as he unzips his fly and begins to urinate in the alleyway behind the stalls.

The barn is warm and close and silent, and the odor from the animals and from the hay is almost sweet. Only the sound of MacRae's urine and the faint steam that rises from it disturb the silence and the scene. 'Ah sweet relief,' he says rezipping his trousers and giving his knees a little bend for adjustment as he turns towards us. 'Now let's see what we've got here.'

He puts his back against Scott's haunches and almost heaves him across the stall before walking up beside him to where my father stands. The inspection does not take long; I suppose because not much is expected of future mink-feed. 'You've got a good halter on him there,' says MacRae. 'I'll throw in a dollar for it, you won't be needing it anyway.' My father looks at him for what seems a very long time and then almost imperceptibly nods his head. 'Okay,' says MacRae, 'twenty-one dollars, a deal's a deal.' My father takes the money, still without saying anything, opens the barn door and without looking backward walks through the rain toward his house. And I follow him because I do not know what else to do.

Within the house it is almost soundless. My mother goes to the stove and begins rinsing her teapot and moving her kettle about. Outside we hear MacRae starting the engine of his truck and we know he is going to back it against the little hill beside the barn. It will be easier to lead his purchase from there. Then it is silent again, except for the hissing of the kettle which is now too hot and which someone should move to the back of the stove; but nobody does.

And then all of us are drawn with a strange fascination to the window, and, yes, the truck is backed against the little hill as we knew and MacRae is going into the barn with his whip still in his hand. In a moment he reappears leading Scott behind him.

As he steps out of the barn the horse almost stumbles but regains his balance quickly. Then the two ascend the little hill, both of them turning their faces from the driving rain. Scott stands quietly while MacRae lets down the tailgate of his truck. When the tailgate is lowered it forms a little ramp from the hill to the truck and MacRae climbs it with the halter-shank in his hand, tugging it impatiently. Scott places one foot on the ramp and we can almost hear, or perhaps I just imagine it, the hollow thump of his hoof upon the wet planking; but then he hesitates, withdraws his foot and stops. MacRae tugs at the rope but it has no effect. He tugs again. He comes halfway down the little ramp, reaches out his hand, grasps the halter itself and pulls; we can see his lips moving and he is either coaxing or cursing or both; he is facing directly into the rain now and it is streaming down his face. Scott does not move. MacRae comes down from the truck and leads Scott in a wide circle through the wet grass. He goes faster and faster, building up speed and soon both man and horse are almost running. Through the grayness of the blurring, slanting rain they look almost like a black-and-white movie that is badly out of focus. Suddenly without changing speed MacRae hurries up the ramp of the truck and the almost trotting horse follows him, until his hoof strikes the tailboard. Then he stops suddenly. As the rope jerks taut, MacRae who is now in the truck and has been carried forward by his own momentum is snapped backward; he bounces off the side of the bull, loses his footing on the slimy planking and falls into the wet filth of the truck box's floor. Almost before we can wonder if he is hurt, he is back upon his feet; his face is livid and his clothes are smeared with manure and running brown rivulets; he brings the whip, which he has somehow never relinquished even in his fall, down savagely between the eyes of Scott, who is still standing rigidly at the tailgate. Scott shakes his head as if dazed and backs off into the wet grass trailing the rope behind him.

It has all happened so rapidly that we in the window do not really know what to do, and are strangely embarrassed by finding ourselves where we are. It is almost as if we have caught ourselves and each other doing something that is shameful. Then David breaks the spell. 'He is not going to go,' he says, and then almost shouts, 'He is just not going to go – ever. Good for him. Now that he's hit him, it's for sure. He'll never go and he'll have to stay.' He rushes toward my father and throws his arms around his legs.

And then the door is jerked open and MacRae is

standing there angrily with his whip still in his hand. His clothes are still soggy from his fall and the water trails from them in brown drops upon my mother's floor. His face is almost purple as he says, 'Unless I get that fucken horse on the truck in the next five minutes the deal's off and you'll be a goddamn long time tryen to get anybody else to pay that kinda money for the useless old cocksucker.'

It is as if all of the worst things one imagines happening suddenly have. But it is not at all as you expected. And I think I begin to understand for the first time how difficult and perhaps how fearful it is to be an adult and I am suddenly and selfishly afraid not only for myself now but for what it seems I am to be. For I had somehow always thought that if one talked like that before women or small children or perhaps even certain men that the earth would open up or lightning would strike or that at least many people would scream and clap their hands over their ears in horror or that the offender if not turned to stone would certainly be beaten by a noble, clean-limbed hero. But it does not happen that way at all. All that happens is the deepening of the thunder-cloud grayness in my father's eyes and the heightening of the color in my mother's cheeks. And I realize also with a sort of shock that in spite of Scott's refusal to go on the truck nothing has really changed. I mean not really; and that all of the facts remain awfully and simply the same: that Scott is old and that we are poor and that my father must soon go away and that he must leave us either with Scott or without him. And that it is somehow like my mother's shielding her children from 'swearing' for so many years, only to find one day that it too is there in its awful reality in spite of everything that she had wished and wanted. And even as I am thinking this my father goes by MacRae who is still standing in the ever-widening puddles of brown, seeming like some huge growth that is nourished by the foul-smelling waters that he himself has brought.

David who had released my father's legs with the entrance of MacRae makes a sort of flying tackle for them now but I intercept him and find myself saying as if from a great distance my mother's phrases in something that sounds almost like her voice, 'Let's go and finish feeding the chickens.' I tighten my grip on his arm and we almost have to squeeze past MacRae whose bulk is blocking the doorway and who has not yet made a motion to leave.

Out of doors my father is striding directly into the

slashing rain to where Scott is standing in something like puzzlement with his back to the rain and his halter-shank dangling before him. When he sees my father approach he cocks his ears and nickers in recognition. My father who looks surprisingly slight with his wet clothes plastered to his body takes the rope in his hand and moves off with the huge horse following him eagerly. Their movement seems almost that of the small tug docking the huge ocean freighter, except that they are so individually and collectively alive. As they approach the truck's ramp, it is my father who hesitates and seems to flinch, and it is his foot which seems to recoil as it touches the planking; but on the part of Scott there is no hesitation at all; his hooves echo firmly and confidently on the strong wet wood and his head is almost pressed into the small of my father's back, he is so eager to get to wherever they are going.

He follows him as I have remembered them all of my life and imagined them even before. Following wildly through the darkened caverns of the mine in its dryness as his shoes flashed sparks from the tracks and the stone; and in its wetness with both of them up to their knees in water, feeling rather than seeing the landing of their splashing feet and with the coal cars thundering behind them with such momentum that were the horse to stumble the very cars he had set in motion would roll over him, leaving him mangled and grisly to be hauled above ground only as carrion for the wheeling gulls. And on the surface, following, in the summer's heat with the jolting hay wagon and the sweat churned to froth between his legs and beneath his collar, fluttering white on the blackness of his glistening coat. And in the winter, following, over the semi-frozen swamps as the snapping, whistling logs snaked behind him, grunting as he broke through the shimmering crystal ice which slashed his fetlocks and caused a scarlet trail of bloodied perforations on the whiteness of the snow. And in the winter, too, with the ton of coal upon the sleigh, following, even over the snowless stretches, driven bare by the wind, leaning low with his underside parallel and almost touching the ground, grunting, and swinging with violent jolts to the right and then to the left, moving the sleigh forward only by moving it sideways, which he had learned was the only way it would move at all.

Even as my father is knotting the rope, MacRae is hurrying past us and slamming shut the tailgate and dropping down the iron bolts that will hold it in its place. My father climbs over the side of the box and down as MacRae steps onto the running board and up into the cab. The motor roars and the truck lurches forward. It leaves two broad wet tracks in the grass like the trails of two slimy, giant slugs and the smell of its exhaust hangs heavy on the air. As it makes the turn at the bottom of the lane Scott tries to turn his head and look back but the rope has been tied very short and he is unable to do so. The sheets of rain come down like so many slanted, beaded curtains making it impossible to see what we know is there, and then there is only the receding sound of the motor, the wet trails on the grass and the exhaust fumes in the air.

It is only then that I realize that David is no longer with me, but even as the question comes to the surface so also does its answer and I run toward the squawking of the chicken house.

Within the building it is difficult to see and difficult to breathe and difficult to believe that so small a boy could wreak such havoc in so short a time. The air is thick with myriad dust particles from the disturbed floor, and bits of straw and tiny white scarlet-flecked feathers eddy and dip and swirl. The frightened capons, many of them already bloodied and mangled, attempt short and ungainly flights, often colliding with each other in mid-air. Their overfed bodies are too heavy for their weak and unused wings and they are barely able to get off the floor and flounder for a few feet before thumping down to dusty crippled landings. They are screaming with terror and their screams seem as unnatural as their flights, as if they had been terribly miscast in the most unsuitable of roles. Many of them are already lifeless and crumpled and dustied and bloodied on the floor, like sad, gray, wadded newspapers that had been used to wipe up blood. The sheen of their feathers forever gone.

In the midst of it all David moves like a small blood-spattered dervish swinging his axe in all directions and almost unknowingly, as if he were blindfolded. Dust has settled on the dampness of his face and the tears make tiny trails through its grayness, like lonely little rivers that have really nothing to water. A single tiny feather is plastered to his forehead and he is coughing and sobbing, both at the same time.

When my father appears beside me in the doorway he seems to notice for the first time that he is not alone. With a final exhausted heave he throws the axe at my father, 'Cocksucker,' he says in some kind of small, sad parody of MacRae, and bolts past us through the door almost colliding with my mother who now comes from out of the rain. He has had very little strength with which to throw the axe and it clatters uselessly off the wall and comes to rest against my father's boot, wet and bloodied with feathers and bits of flesh still clinging to its blade.

I am tremendously sorry for the capons, now so ruined and so useless, and for my mother and for all the time and work she has put into them for all of us. But I do not know what to do and I know not what to say.

As we leave the melancholy little building the wind cuts in from the ocean with renewed fury. It threatens to lift you off your feet and blow you to the skies and your crotch is numb and cold as your clothes are flattened hard against the front of your body, even as they tug and snap at your back in insistent, billowing balloons. Unless you turn or lower your head it is impossible to breathe for the air is blown back almost immediately into your lungs and your throat convulses and heaves. The rain is now a stinging sleet which is rapidly becoming the winter's first snow. It is impossible to see into it, and the ocean off which it rushes is lost in the swirling whiteness although it thunders and roars in its invisible nearness like the heavy bass blending with the shrieking tenor of the wind. You hear so much that you can hardly hear at all. And you are almost immobile and breathless and blind and deaf. Almost but not quite. For by turning and leaning your body and your head, you can move and breathe and see and hear a little at a time. You do not gain much but you can hang on to what little you have and your toes curl almost instinctively within your shoes as if they are trying to grasp the earth.

I stop and turn my face from the wind and look back the way I have come. My parents are there, blown together behind me. They are not moving, either, only trying to hold their place. They have turned sideways to the wind and are facing and leaning into each other with their shoulders touching, like the end-timbers of a gabled roof. My father puts his arms around my mother's waist and she does not remove them as I have always seen her do. Instead she reaches up and removes the combs of coral from the heaviness of her hair. I have never seen her hair in all its length before and it stretches out now almost parallel to the earth, its shining blackness whipped by the wind and glistening like the snow that settles and melts upon it. It surrounds and engulfs my father's head and he buries his face within its heavy darkness, and draws my mother closer toward him. I think they will stand there for a long, long time, leaning into each other and into the wind-whipped snow and with the ice freezing to their cheeks. It seems that perhaps they should be left alone so I turn and take one step and then another and move forward a little at a time. I think I will try to find David, that perhaps he may understand.

Mary O'Hara

My Friend Flicka

When Ken went to bed that night, he kissed his
mother, and then threw his arms around her and held
her fiercely for a moment.

Smiling, she put her hand on his head. 'Well,
Kennie –' her violet eyes were soft and understanding.

He went upstairs, smiling back at her over his
shoulder, having a secret with her. He knew that she
knew.

He lit the candle in his room and stood staring at
the flickering light. This was like a last day. The last
day before school is out, or before Christmas, or
before his mother came back after a visit in the East.

Tomorrow was the day when, really, his life would begin. He would get his colt.

He had been thinking about the filly all day. He could still see her streaking past him, the wild terrified eyes turned to him in appeal – the hair blown back from her face like a girl's – and the long, slim legs moving so fast they were a blur, like the spokes of a wheel.

He couldn't quite remember the colour of her. Orange – pink – tangerine colour – tail and mane white, like the hair of an Albino boy at school. *Albino* – of course, her grand-sire *was* the Albino – the famous Albino stud. He felt a little uneasiness at this; Albino blood wasn't safe blood for a filly to have. But perhaps she hadn't much of it. Perhaps the cream tail and mane came from Banner, her sire. Banner had a cream tail and mane too when he was a colt; lots of sorrel colts had. He hoped she would be docile and good – not like Rocket. Which would she take after? Rocket? Or Banner? He hadn't had time to get a good look into her eyes. Rocket's eyes had that wild, wicked, white ring around them –

Ken began to undress. Walking around his room, his eyes caught sight of the pictures on the wall – they didn't interest him.

The speed of her! *She had run away from Banner.* He kept thinking about that. It hardly seemed possible. His father always said Rocket was the fastest horse on the ranch, and now Rocket's filly had run away from Banner.

He had gone up to look at her again that afternoon; hadn't been able to keep away. He had ridden up on Baldy and found the yearlings all grazing together on the far side of Saddle Back. And when they saw him and Baldy, they all took off across the mountain.

Ken had galloped along the crest above them watching the filly. Footing made no difference to her. She floated across the ravines, always two lengths ahead of the others. Her pinkish cream mane and tail whipped in the wind. Her long delicate legs had only to aim, it seemed, at a particular spot, for her to reach it and sail on. She seemed to Ken a fairy horse. She was simply nothing like any of the others.

Riding down the mountain again Ken had traced back all his recollections of her. The summer before, when he and Howard had seen the spring colts, he hadn't especially noticed her. He remembered that he had seen her even before that, soon after she was born. He had been out with Gus, one day, in the meadow, during the spring holiday. They were clearing some driftwood out of the irrigation ditch, and they had seen Rocket standing in a gully on the hillside, quiet for once, and eyeing them cautiously.

'Ay bet she got a colt,' said Gus: and they walked carefully up the draw. Rocket gave a wild snort, thrust her feet out, shook her head wickedly, then fled away. And as they reached the spot, they saw standing there the wavering, pinkish colt, barely able to keep its feet. It gave a little squeak and started after its mother on crooked, wobbling legs.

'Yee whiz! Look at de little *flicka!*' said Gus.

'What does *flicka* mean, Gus?'

'Swedish for little gurl, Ken –'

He had seen the filly again late in the fall. She was half pink, half yellow – with streaked untidy looking hair. She was awkward and ungainly, with legs too long, haunches a little too high.

And then he had gone away to school and hadn't seen her again until now – *she ran away from Banner* – Her eyes – they had looked like balls of fire this morning. What colour were they? Banner's were brown with flecks of gold, or gold with flecks of brown – Her speed and her delicate curving lines made him think of a greyhound he had seen running once, but really she was more like just a little girl than anything – the way her face looked, the way her blonde hair blew – a little girl –

Ken blew out the light and got into bed, and before the smile had faded from his face, he was asleep –

'I'll take that sorrel filly of Rocket's; the one with the cream tail and mane.'

Ken made his announcement at the breakfast table.

After he spoke there was a moment's astonished silence. Nell groped for recollection, and said, 'A sorrel filly? I can't seem to remember that one at all – what's her name?'

But Rob remembered. The smile faded from his face as he looked at Ken. *'Rocket's filly,* Ken?'

'Yes, sir.' Ken's face changed too. There was no mistaking his father's displeasure.

'I was hoping you'd make a wise choice. You know what I think of Rocket – that whole line of horses –'

Ken looked down; the colour ebbed from his cheeks. 'She's fast, Dad, and Rocket's fast –'

'It's the worst line of horses I've got. There's never

one amongst them with real sense. The mares are hellions and the stallions outlaws: they're untamable.'

'I'll tame her.'

Rob guffawed. 'Not I nor anyone, has ever been able to really tame any one of them.'

Kennie's chest heaved.

'Better change your mind, Ken. You want a horse that'll be a real friend to you, don't you?'

'Yes –' Kennie's voice was unsteady.

'Well, you'll never make a friend of that filly. Last fall after all the colts had been weaned and separated from their dams, she and Rocket got back together – no fence'll hold 'em – she's all out and scarred up already from tearing through barbed wire after that bitch of a mother of hers.'

Kennie looked stubbornly at his plate.

'Change your mind?' asked Howard briskly.

'No.'

'I don't remember seeing her this year,' said Nell.

'No,' said Rob. 'When I drove you up a couple of months ago to look them over and name them and write down their descriptions, there was a bunch missing, don't you remember?'.

'Oh, yes – then she's never been named –'

'I've named her,' said Ken. 'Her name is Flicka.'

'Flicka,' said Nell cheerfully. 'That's a pretty name.'

But McLaughlin made no comment, and there was a painful silence.

Ken felt he ought to look at his father, but he was afraid to. Everything was changed again, they weren't friends any more. He forced himself to look up, met his father's angry eyes for a moment, then quickly looked down again.

'Well,' McLaughlin barked. 'It's your funeral – or hers. Remember one thing. I'm not going to be out of pocket on account of this – every time you turn around you cost me money –'

Ken looked up, wonderingly, and shook his head.

'Time's money, remember,' said his father. 'I had planned to give you a reasonable amount of help in breaking and taming your colt. Just enough. But there's no such thing as enough with those horses.'

Gus appeared at the door and said, 'What's today, Boss?'

McLaughlin shouted, 'We're going out on the range to bring in the yearlings. Saddle Taggert, Lady and Shorty.'

Gus disappeared, and McLaughlin pushed his chair

back. 'First thing to do is get her in. Do you know where the yearlings are?'

'They were on the far side of the Saddle Back late yesterday afternoon – the west end, down by Dale's ranch.'

'Well, you're the Boss on this round-up – you can ride Shorty.'

McLaughlin and Gus and Ken went out to bring the yearlings in. Howard stood at the County gate to open and close it.

They found the yearlings easily. When they saw that they were being pursued, they took to their heels. Ken was entranced to watch Flicka – the speed of her, the power, the wildness – she led the band.

He sat motionless, just watching and holding Shorty in when his father thundered past on Taggert and shouted, 'Well, what's the matter? Why didn't you turn 'em?'

Ken woke up and galloped after them.

Shorty brought in the whole band. The corral gates were closed, and an hour was spent shunting the ponies in and out and through the chutes until Flicka was left alone in the small round branding corral. Gus mounted Shorty and drove the others away, through the gate, and up the Saddle Back.

But Flicka did not intend to be left. She hurled herself against the poles which walled the corral. She tried to jump them. They were seven feet high. She caught her front feet over the top rung, clung, scrambled, while Kennie held his breath for fear the slender legs would be caught between the bars and snapped. Her hold broke, she fell over backwards, rolled, screamed, tore around the corral.

One of the bars broke. She hurled herself again. Another went. She saw the opening, and as neatly as a dog crawls through a fence, inserted her head and forefeet, scrambled through and fled away, bleeding in a dozen places.

As Gus was coming back, just about to close the gate to the County Road, the sorrel whipped through it, sailed across the road and ditch with her inimitable floating leap, and went up the side of the Saddle Back like a jack rabbit.

From way up the mountain, Gus heard excited whinnies, as she joined the band he had just driven up, and the last he saw of them they were strung out along the crest running like deer.

'Yee whiz!' said Gus, and stood motionless and staring until the ponies had disappeared over the ridge.

Then he closed the gate, remounted Shorty, and rode back to the corrals.

Walking down from the corrals, Rob McLaughlin gave Kennie one more chance to change his mind. 'Better pick a horse that you have some hope of riding one day. I'd have got rid of this whole line of stock if they weren't so damned fast that I've had the fool idea that someday there might turn out one gentle one in the lot, and I'd have a race horse. But there's never been one so far, and it's not going to be Flicka.'

'It's not going to be Flicka,' chanted Howard.

'Maybe she *might* be gentled,' said Ken; and although his lips trembled, there was fanatical determination in his eye.

'Ken,' said McLaughlin, 'it's up to you. If you say you want her, we'll get her. But she wouldn't be the first of that line to die rather than give in. They're beautiful and they're fast, but let me tell you this, young man, they're *loco!*'

Ken flinched under his father's direct glance.

'If I go after her again, I'll not give up *whatever comes*, understand what I mean by that?'

'Yes.'

'What do you say?'

'I want her.'

'That's settled then,' and suddenly Rob seemed calm and indifferent. 'We'll bring her in again tomorrow or next day – I've got other work for this afternoon.'

Alan Le May

The Searchers

Mart woke up in the blackness before the winter dawn. He pulled on his pants, and started up the fire in the wood range before he finished dressing. As he took down his ragged laundry from behind the stove, he was of a mind to leave Amos's stuff hanging there, but he couldn't quite bring himself to it. He made a bundle of Amos's things, and tossed it into their room. By the time he had wolfed a chunk of bread and some leavings of cold meat, Tobe and Abner were up.

'I got to fetch that stuff Amos wants,' he said, 'from over – over at his house. You want to show me what team?'

'Better wait while we hot up some breakfast, hadn't you?'

'I et already.'

They didn't question it. 'Take them little fat bays, there, in the nigh corral – the one with the shelter shed.'

'I want you to take notice of what a pretty match they be,' said Tobe with shining pride. 'We call 'em Sis and Bud. And pull? They'll outlug teams twice their heft.'

'Sis is about the only filly we ever did bust around here,' Abner said. 'But they balanced so nice, we just couldn't pass her by. Oh, she might cow-kick a little –'

'A little? She hung Ab on the top bar so clean he just lay there flappin'.'

'Feller doesn't mind a bust in the pants from Sis, once he knows her.'

'I won't leave nothing happen to 'em,' Mart promised.

He took the team shelled corn, and brushed them down while they fed. He limbered the frosty straps of the harness with his gloved hands, and managed to be hooked and out of there before Amos was up.

Even from a distance the Edwards place looked strangely barren. Hard to think why, at first, until you remembered that the house now stood alone, without its barn, sheds, and haystacks. The snow hid the black char and the ash of the burned stuff, as if it never had been. Up on the hill, where Martha, and Henry, and the boys were, the snow had covered even the crosses he had carved.

Up close, as Mart neared the back gallery, the effect of desolation was even worse. You wouldn't think much could happen to a sturdy house like that in just a few months, but it already looked as if it had been unlived in for a hundred years. Snow was drifted on the porch, and slanted deep against the door itself, unbroken by any tracks. In the dust-glazed windows Laurie's wreaths were ghostly against empty black.

When he had forced the door free of the iced sill, he found a still cold inside, more chilling in its way than the searing wind of the prairie. A thin high music that went on for ever in the empty house was the keening of the wind in the chimneys. Almost everything he remembered was repaired and in place, but a grey film of dust lay evenly, in spite of Laurie's Christmas dusting. Her cake plate was crumbless, centring a pattern of innumerable pocket-mouse tracks in the dust upon the table.

He remembered something about that home-made table. Underneath it, an inch or so below the top, a random structural member made a little hidden shelf. Once when he and Laurie had been five or six, the Mathisons had come over for a taffy pull. He showed Laurie the secret shelf under the table, and they stored away some little square-cut pieces of taffy there. Afterward, one piece of taffy seemed to be stuck down; he wore out his fingers for months trying to break it loose. Years later he found out that the stubbornly stuck taffy was really the ironhead of a lag screw that you couldn't see where it was, but only feel with your fingers.

He found some winter clothes he sure could use, including some heavy socks Martha and Lucy had knitted for him. Nothing that had belonged to Martha and the girls was in the closets. He supposed some shut trunks standing around held whatever of their stuff the Comanches had left. He went to a little chest that had been Debbie's, with some idea of taking something of hers with him, as if for company; but he stopped himself before he opened the chest. I got these hands she used to hang on to, he told himself. I don't need nothing more. Except to find her.

He was in no hurry to get back. He wanted to miss supper at the Mathisons' for fear he would lash out at Amos in front of the others; so, taking his time about everything he did, he managed to fool away most of the day.

A red glow from the embers in the stove was the only light in the Mathison house as he put away the good little team, but a lamp went up in the kitchen before he went in. Laurie was waiting up, and she was put out with him.

'Who gave you the right to lag out till all hours, scaring the range stock?'

'Amos and me always night on the prairie,' he reminded her. 'It's where we live.'

'Not when I'm waiting up for you.' She was wrapped twice around in a trade-blanket robe cinched up with a leather belt. Only the little high collar of her flannel nightgown showed, and a bit of blue-veined instep between her moccasins and the hem. Actually she had on more clothes than he had ever seen her wear in her life; there was no reason for the rig to seem as intimate as it somehow did.

He mumbled, 'Didn't go to make work,' and went to throw his rag-pickings in the grandmother room.

Amos was not in his bunk; his saddle and every-thing he had was gone.

'Amos rode on,' Laurie said unnecessarily.

'Didn't he leave no word for me?'

'Any word,' she corrected him. She shook down the grate and dropped fresh wood in the firebox. 'He just said, tell you he had to get on.' She pushed him gently backward against a bench, so that he sat down. 'I mended your stuff,' she said. 'Such as could be saved.'

He thought of the saddle-worn holes in the thighs of his other drawers. 'Goddle mighty,' he whispered.

'Don't know what your purpose is,' she said, 'getting so red in the face. I have brothers, haven't I?'

'I know, but –'

'I'm a woman, Martie.' He had supposed that was the very point. 'We wash and mend your dirty old stuff for you all our lives. When you're little, we even wash you. How a man can make out to get bashful in front of a woman, I'll never know.'

He couldn't make any sense out of it. 'You talk like a feller might just as leave run around stark nekkid.'

'Wouldn't bother me. I wouldn't try it in front of Pa, was I you, so long as you're staying on.' She went to the stove to fix his supper.

'I'm not staying, Laurie. I got to catch up with Amos.'

She turned to see if he meant it. 'Pa was counting on you. He's running your cattle now, you know, along with his own —'

'Amos's cattle.'

'He let both winter riders go, thinking you and Amos would be back. Of course, riders aren't too hard to come by. Charlie MacCorry put in for a job.'

'MacCorry's a good fast hand,' was all he said.

'I don't know what you think you can do about finding Debbie that Amos can't do.' She turned to face him solemnly, her eyes very dark in the uneven light. 'He'll find her now, Mart. Please believe me. I know.'

He waited, but she went back to the skillet without explanation. So now he took a chance and told her the truth. 'That's what scares me, Laurie.'

'If you're thinking of the property,' she said, 'the land, the cattle —'

'It isn't that,' he told her. 'No, no. It isn't that.'

'I know Debbie's the heir. And Amos has never had anything in his life. But if you think he'd let harm come to one hair of that child's head on account of all that, then I know you're a fool.'

He shook his head. 'It's his black fits,' he said; and wondered how he could make a mortal danger sound so idiotic.

'What?'

'Laurie, I swear to you, I've seen all the fires of hell come up in his eyes, when he so much as thinks about getting a Comanche in his rifle sights. You haven't seen him like I've seen him. I've known him to take his knife . . .' He let that drop. He didn't want to tell Laurie some of the things he had seen Amos do. 'Lord knows I hate Comanches. I hate 'em like I never knew a man could hate nothin'. But you slam into a bunch of 'em, and kill some – you know what happens to any little white captives they got hold of, then? They get their brains knocked out. It's happened over and over again.'

He felt she didn't take any stock in what he was saying. He tried again, speaking earnestly to her back. 'Amos is a man can go crazy wild. It might come on him when it was the worst thing could be. What I counted on, I hoped I'd be there to stop him, if such thing come.'

She said faintly, 'You'd have to kill him.'

He let that go without answer. 'Let's have it now.

Where's he gone, where you're so sure he'll find her?'

She became perfectly still for a moment. When she moved again, one hand stirred the skillet, while the other brought a torn-open letter out of the breast of her robe, and held it out to him. He recognised the letter that had been left with Aaron Mathison for Amos. His eyes were on her face, questioning, as he took it.

'We hoped you'd want to stay on,' she said. All the liveliness was gone from her voice. 'But I guess I knew. Seems to be only one thing in the world you care about any more. So I stole it for you.'

He spread out the single sheet of ruled tablet paper the torn envelope contained. It carried a brief scrawl in soft pencil, well smeared.

Laurie said, 'Do you believe in second sight? No, of course you don't. There's something I dread about this, Martie.'

The message was from a trader Mart knew about, over on the Salt Fork of the Brazos. He called himself Jerem (for Jeremiah) Futterman — an improbable name at best, and not his own. He wasn't supposed to trade with Indians there any more, but he did, covering up by claiming that his real place of business was far to the west in the Arroyo Blanco, outside of Texas. The note said:

I bougt a small size dress off a
Injun. If this here is a peece of
yr chiles dress bring reward, I know
where they gone.

Pinned to the bottom of the sheet with a horseshoe nail was a two-inch square of calico. The dirt that greyed it was worn evenly into the cloth, as if it had been unwashed for a long time. The little flowers on it didn't stand out much now, but they were there. Laurie was leaning over his shoulder as he held the sample to the light. A strand of her hair was tickling his neck, and her breath was on his cheek, but he didn't even know.

'Is it hers?'

He nodded.

'Poor little dirty dress . . .'

He couldn't look at her. 'I've got to get hold of a horse. I just got to get me a horse.'

'Is that all that's stopping you!'

'It isn't stopping me. I'll catch up to him. I got to.'

'You've got horses, Martie.'

'I — what?'

'You've got Brad's horses. Pa said so. He means it, Martie. Amos told us what happened at the Warrior. A lot of things you left out.'

Mart couldn't speak for a minute, and when he could he didn't know what to say. The skillet started to smoke, and Laurie went to set it to the back of the range.

'Most of Brad's ponies are turned out. But the Fort Worth stud is up. He's coming twelve, but he'll out-game anything there is. And the good light gelding — the fast one, with the blaze.'

'Why, that's Sweet-face,' he said. He remembered Laurie naming that colt herself, when she was thirteen years old. 'Laurie, that's your own good horse.'

'Let's not get choosey, Bub. Those two are the ones Amos wanted to trade for and take. But Pa held them back for you.'

'I'll turn Sweet-face loose to come home,' he promised, 'this side Fiddler's Crick. I ought to cross soon after daylight.'

'Soon after — by starting when?'

'Now,' he told her.

He was already in the saddle when she ran out through the snow, and lifted her face to be kissed. She ran back into the house abruptly and the door closed behind her. He jabbed the Fort Worth stud, hard, with one spur. Very promptly he was bucked back to his senses, and all but thrown. The stallion conveyed a hard, unyielding shock like no horse Mart had ever ridden, as if he were made all of rocks and iron bands. Ten seconds of squealing contention cleared Mart's head, though he thought his teeth might be loosened a little; and he was on his way.

Robert Drewe

Our Sunshine

This is how she introduces herself: 'Good afternoon, would you come and hold my horse's thing?'

The lady loves the chase, and is famous in the district for hunting on this dark bay stallion. She rides Lord Byron so hard over such long distances that sometimes he doesn't have time to piss. When she makes her request it's a Monday afternoon – I'm employed shaping foundation stones – and Lord Byron's been holding on since Saturday's hunt.

This time his bladder's paralysed from the strain. Looks to me like colic, only worse. Two stablehands are struggling to hold him. He's groaning and slick with sweat, sighing, kicking at his swollen belly, peering with a longing, uneasy expression at his flanks.

This lady pushes her brown hair from her eyes, rolls up her sleeve, oils her arm and plunges up into Lord Byron's sheath. He's well retracted from pain and nerves. She frowns. 'Got it,' she says, and, grunting, hauls it all out and drops it across my hands.

'Hold on,' she tells me.

And then the boys and I all need to hold on very hard. Lord Byron trembles and skitters and lurches us back and forth across the paddock because she's got this veterinarian's metal catheter, Jesus, it must be five feet long, pointed at the business end, and she oils it too, and grabs him, pushes it inside and forwards and threads it ever upwards.

A terrible shiver overcomes Lord Byron. Suddenly we're up to our shins, nearly floating in the downpour, and shivering almost as much as him.

'There,' says Mrs C. 'Watch your boots.'

John Steinbeck

The Red Pony

When the triangle sounded in the morning, Jody dressed more quickly even than usual. In the kitchen, while he washed his face and combed back his hair, his mother addressed him irritably. 'Don't you go out until you get a good breakfast in you.'

He went to the dining-room and sat at the long white table. He took a steaming hotcake from the platter, arranged two fried eggs on it, covered them with another hotcake and squashed the whole thing with his fork.

His father and Billy Buck came in. Jody knew from the sound on the floor that both of them were wearing flat-heeled shoes, but he peered under the table to make sure. His father turned off the oil lamp, for the day had arrived, and he looked stern and disciplinary, but Billy Buck didn't look at Jody at all. He avoided the shy questioning eyes of the boy and soaked a whole piece of toast in his coffee.

Carl Tiflin said crossly, 'You come with us after breakfast!'

Jody had trouble with his food then, for he felt a kind of doom in the air. After Billy had tilted his saucer and drained the coffee which had slopped into it, and had wiped his hands on his jeans, the two men stood up from the table and went out into the morning light together, and Jody respectfully followed a little behind them. He tried to keep his mind from running ahead, tried to keep it absolutely motionless.

His mother called, 'Carl! Don't you let it keep him from school.'

They marched past the cypress, where a singletree hung from a limb to butcher the pigs on, and past the black iron kettle, so it was not a pig killing. The sun shone over the hill and threw long, dark shadows of the trees and buildings. They crossed a stubble-field to shortcut to the barn. Jody's father unhooked the door and they went in. They had been walking toward the sun on the way down. The barn was black as night in contrast and warm from the hay and from the beasts. Jody's father moved over towards the one box stall. 'Come here!' he ordered. Jody could begin to see things now. He looked into the box stall and then stepped back quickly.

A red pony colt was looking at him out of the stall. Its tense ears were forward and a light of disobedience was in its eyes. Its coat was rough and thick as an airedale's fur and its mane was long and tangled. Jody's throat collapsed in on itself and cut his breath short.

'He needs a good currying,' his father said, 'and if I ever hear of you not feeding him or leaving his stall dirty, I'll sell him off in a minute.'

Jody couldn't bear to look at the pony's eyes any more. He gazed down at his hands for a moment, and he asked very shyly, 'Mine?' No one answered him. He put his hand out towards the pony. Its grey nose came close, sniffing loudly, and then the lips drew back and the strong teeth closed on Jody's fingers. The pony shook its head up and down and seemed to laugh with amusement. Jody regarded his bruised fingers. 'Well,' he said with pride – 'well, I guess he can bite all right.'

The two men laughed, somewhat in relief. Carl Tiflin went out of the barn and walked up a side-hill to be by himself, for he was embarrassed, but Billy Buck stayed. It was easier to talk to Billy Buck. Jody asked again – 'Mine?'

Billy became professional in tone. 'Sure! That is, if you look out for him and break him right. I'll show you how. He's just a colt. You can't ride him for some time.'

Jody put out his bruised hand again, and this time the red pony let his nose be rubbed. 'I ought to have a carrot,' Jody said. 'Where'd we get him, Billy?'

'Bought him at a sheriff's auction,' Billy explained. 'A show went broke in Salinas and had debts. The sheriff was selling off their stuff.'

The pony stretched out his nose and shook the forelock from his wild eyes. Jody stroked the nose a little. He said softly, 'There isn't a – saddle?'

Billy Buck laughed. 'I'd forgot. Come along.'

In the harness-room he lifted down a little saddle of red morocco leather. 'It's just a show saddle,' Billy Buck said disparagingly, 'It isn't practical for the brush, but it was cheap at the sale.'

Jody couldn't trust himself to look at the saddle

either, and he couldn't speak at all. He brushed the shining red leather with his finger-tips, and after a long time he said, 'It'll look pretty on him though.' He thought of the grandest and prettiest thing he knew. 'If he hasn't a name already, I think I'll call him Gabilan Mountains,' he said.

Billy Buck knew how he felt. 'It's a pretty long name. Why don't you just call him Gabilan? That means hawk. That would be a fine name for him.' Billy felt glad. 'If you will collect tail hair, I might be able to make a hair rope for you sometime. You could use it for a hackamore.'

Jody wanted to go back to the box stall. 'Could I lead him to school, do you think – to show the kids?'

But Billy shook his head. 'He's not even halter-broke yet. We had a time getting him here. Had to almost drag him. You better be starting for school though.'

'I'll bring the kids to see him here this afternoon,' Jody said.

Six boys came over the hill half an hour early that afternoon, running hard, their heads down, their fore-arms working, their breath whistling. They swept by the house and cut across the stubble-field to the barn.

And then they stood self-consciously before the pony, and then they looked at Jody with eyes in which there was a new admiration and a new respect. Before today Jody had been a boy, dressed in overalls and a blue shirt – quieter than most, even suspected of being a little cowardly. And now he was different. Out of a thousand centuries they drew the ancient admiration of the footman for the horseman. They knew instinctively that a man on a horse is spiritually as well as physically bigger than a man on foot. They knew that Jody had been miraculously lifted out of equality with them, and had been placed over them. Gabilan put his head out of the stall and sniffed them.

'Why'n't you ride him?' the boys cried. 'Why'n't you braid his tail with ribbons like in the fair?' 'When you going to ride him?'

Jody's courage was up. He too felt the superiority of the horseman. 'He's not old enough. Nobody can ride him for a long time. I'm going to train him on the long halter. Billy Buck is going to show me how.'

'Well, can't we even lead him around a little?'

'He isn't even halter broke,' Jody said. He wanted to be completely alone when he took the pony out for the first time. 'Come and see the saddle.'

They were speechless at the red morocco saddle, completely shocked out of comment. 'It isn't much use in the brush,' Jody explained. 'It'll look pretty on him though. Maybe I'll ride bareback when I go into the brush.'

'How you going to rope a cow without a saddle horn?'

'Maybe I'll get another saddle for every day. My father might want me to help him with the stock.' He let them feel the red saddle, and showed them the brass chain throat-latch on the bridle and the big brass buttons at each temple where the headstall and brow band crossed. The whole thing was too wonderful. They had to go away after a little while, and each boy, in his mind, searched among his possessions for a bribe worthy of offering in return for a ride on the red pony when the time should come.

Jody was glad when they had gone. He took brush and currycomb from the wall, took down the barrier of the box stall and stepped cautiously in. The pony's eyes glittered, and he edged around into kicking position. But Jody touched him on the shoulder and rubbed his high arched neck as he had always seen Billy Buck do, and he crooned, 'So-o-o, boy,' in a deep voice. The pony gradually relaxed his tenseness. Jody curried and brushed until a pile of dead hair lay in the stall and until the pony's coat had taken on a deep red shine. Each time he finished he thought it might have been done better. He braided the mane into a dozen little pigtails, and he braided the forelock, and then he undid them and brushed the hair out straight again.

Jody did not hear his mother enter the barn. She was angry when she came, but when she looked in at the pony and at Jody working over him, she felt a curious pride rise up in her. 'Have you forgot the wood-box?' she asked gently. 'It's not far off from dark and there's not a stick of wood in the house, and the chickens aren't fed.'

Jody quickly put up his tools, 'I forgot, ma'am.'

'Well, after this do your chores first. Then you won't forget. I expect you'll forget lots of things now if I don't keep an eye on you.'

'Can I have carrots from the garden for him, ma'am?'

She had to think about that, 'Oh — I guess so, if you only take the big tough ones.'

'Carrots keep the coat good,' he said, and again she felt the curious rush of pride.

Alice Hoffman

Here on Earth

Hollis has begun to have his dream about the horse again, that awful dream that always wakes him in the middle of the night and leaves him out of breath and sweaty and ready to run. He supposes that you cannot really murder a horse; that is something humans do to each other. You kill a horse, just as you would a cow or a sheep, but somehow it's not the same. It's uglier. It gives you nightmares, year in and year out and maybe even for the rest of your life.

If you are going to do it, Hollis knows, do it speedily and in the dark. Plan it out carefully, and be aware of what hours the grooms and the trainers keep. Make certain to get half your money up front, and be sure it's a great deal of money. After all, the owner of a dead racehorse stands to collect quite a bit from his insurance company. That's why he's paying you. All you have to realize is a single indelible fact: Just because you walk away after you've been paid doesn't mean you won't be dreaming about it afterwards, when you're no longer as hungry or as young.

Here's the thing about killing a horse – its screams are far worse than any sound a man can produce. Wear earplugs, work fast; be sure you're done and over the fence before they realize their pain. It's a lot of money for someone with no education and no training and no heart at all. It's a small fortune, if you can stand the way they scream when you shatter their cannon bones and knees with a hammer or a wrench. When you start to have bad dreams, go back and ask for more money from the owners. Don't call it blackmail; it's simply an extra payment for a job well done. After all, the horse wasn't running well, and that's what such horses are meant to do. Invest your money wisely, in land and condominiums and the market, and do it before you get hurt, because there will always be a horse who will fight for its life.

That is the one he always dreams about, the last one in Miami, a job so botched the owner never collected, even though the horse had been a Preakness winner and was insured for two million. Horses have hotter blood than humans, that's what Hollis believes, and he was covered with blood by the time he was finished. He had to stand in the shower for hours, and even then the cold water was a pale remedy. That horse, a white thoroughbred, had refused to go down. Hollis had blood under his fingernails and all over his boots; two weeks later, after he'd headed back to Massachusetts, he was brushing his teeth in the bathroom of his rented rooms above the Lyon Cafe when he found horse's blood in the rim of his ear. A single red thread which couldn't tie him to any crime, and could be easily scrubbed away with a damp washcloth, and yet that mark seems to have been a curse. He still does not like to look at himself in the mirror, for fear he'll see blood, and to this day he despises the color red.

That horse continues to follow Hollis while he sleeps. He runs in pastures that are as red as blood; he races through guilt and grief. Kill something, and it's yours forever. At night, you will be at your victim's mercy, but that's only temporary. Dreams, after all, are worthless things — Hollis knows that. They can't reach you on the street where you walk; they can only torment a man with a conscience, any fool who allows it.

D. H. Lawrence

The Rocking-Horse Winner

There was a woman who was beautiful, who started with all the advantages, yet she had no luck. She married for love, and the love turned to dust. She had bonny children, yet she felt they had been thrust upon her, and she could not love them. They looked at her coldly, as if they were finding fault with her. And hurriedly she felt she must cover up some fault in herself. Yet what it was that she must cover up she never knew. Nevertheless, when her children were present, she always felt the centre of her heart go hard. This troubled her, and in her manner she was all the more gentle and anxious for her children, as if she loved them very much. Only she herself knew that at the centre of her heart was a hard little place that could not feel love, no, not for anybody. Everybody else said of her: 'She is such a good mother. She adores her children.' Only she herself, and her children themselves, knew it was not so. They read it in each other's eyes.

There were a boy and two little girls. They lived in a pleasant house, with a garden, and they had discreet servants, and felt themselves superior to anyone in the neighbourhood.

Although they lived in style, they felt always an anxiety in the house. There was never enough money. The mother had a small income and the father had a small income, but not nearly enough for the social position which they had to keep up. The father went into town to some office. But though he had good prospects, these prospects never materialized. There was always the grinding sense of the shortage of money, though the style was always kept up.

At last the mother said: 'I will see if I can't make something.' But she did not know where to begin. She racked her brains, and tried this thing and the other, but could not find anything successful. The failure made deep lines come into her face. Her children were growing up, they would have to go to school. There must be more money, there must be more money. The father, who was always very handsome and expensive in his tastes, seemed as if he never *would* be able to do anything worth doing. And the mother, who had a great belief in herself, did not succeed any better, and her tastes were just as expensive.

And so the house came to be haunted by the unspoken phrase: *There must be more money! There must be more money!* The children could hear it all the time, though nobody said it aloud. They heard it at Christmas when the expensive and splendid toys filled the nursery. Behind the shining modern rocking-horse, behind the smart doll's house, a voice would start whispering: 'There *must* be more money! There *must* be more money!' and the children would stop playing, to listen for a moment. They would look into each other's eyes, to see if they had all heard. And each one saw in the eyes of the other two that they too had heard. 'There *must* be more money! There *must* be more money!'

It came whispering from the springs of the still-swaying rocking-horse, and even the horse, bending his wooden champing head, heard it. The big doll, sitting so pink and smirking in her new pram, could hear it quite plainly, and seemed to be smirking all the more self-consciously because of it. The foolish puppy, too, that took the place of the teddy-bear, he was looking so extraordinarily foolish for no other reason but that he heard the secret whisper all over the house: 'There *must* be more money!'

Yet nobody ever said it aloud. The whisper was everywhere, and therefore no one spoke it. Just as no one ever says: 'We are breathing!' in spite of the fact that breath is coming and going all the time.

'Mother,' said the boy Paul one day, 'why don't we keep a car of our own? Why do we always use uncle's, or else a taxi?'

'Because we're the poor members of the family,' said the mother.

'But why *are* we, mother?'

'Well—I suppose,' she said slowly and bitterly, 'it's because your father had no luck.'

The boy was silent for some time.

'Is luck money, mother?' he asked, rather timidly.

'No, Paul. Not quite. It's what causes you to have money.'

'Oh!' said Paul vaguely. 'I thought when Uncle Oscar said *filthy lucker*, it meant money.'

'*Filthy lucre* does mean money,' said the mother. 'But it's lucre not luck.'

'Oh!' said the boy. 'Then what is luck, mother?'

'It's what causes you to have money. If you're lucky you have money. That's why it's better to be born lucky than rich. If you're rich, you may lose your money. But if you're lucky, you will always get more money.'

'Oh! Will you? And is father not lucky?'

'Very unlucky, I should say,' she said bitterly.

The boy watched her with unsure eyes.

'Why?' he asked.

'I don't know. Nobody every knows why one person is lucky and another unlucky.'

'Don't they? Nobody at all? Does *nobody* know?'

'Perhaps God. But He never tells.'

'He ought to, then. And aren't you lucky either, mother?'

'I can't be, if I married an unlucky husband.'

'But by yourself, aren't you?'

'I used to think I was, before I married. Now I think I am very unlucky indeed.'

'Why?'

'Well — never mind! Perhaps I'm not really,' she said.

The child looked at her to see if she meant it. But

he saw, by the lines of her mouth, that she was only trying to hide something from him.

'Well, anyhow,' he said stoutly, 'I'm a lucky person.'

'Why?' said his mother, with a sudden laugh.

He stared at her. He didn't even know why he had said it.

'God told me,' he asserted, brazening it out.

'I hope He did, dear!' she said, again with a laugh, but rather bitter.

'He did, mother!'

'Excellent!' said the mother, using one of her husband's exclamations.

The boy saw she did not believe him; or rather, that she paid no attention to his assertion. This angered him somewhere, and made him want to compel her attention.

He went off by himself, vaguely, in a childish way, seeking for the clue to 'luck'. Absorbed, taking no heed of other people, he went about with a sort of stealth, seeking inwardly for luck. He wanted luck, he wanted it. When the two girls were playing dolls in the nursery, he would sit on his big rocking-horse, charging madly into space, with a frenzy that made the little girls peer at him uneasily. Wildly the horse careered, the waving dark hair of the boy tossed, his eyes had a strange glare in them. The little girls dared not speak to him.

When he had ridden to the end of his mad little journey, he climbed down and stood in front of his rocking-horse, staring fixedly into its lowered face. Its red mouth was slightly open, its big eye was wide and glassy-bright.

'Now!' he would silently command the snorting steed. 'Now, take me to where there is luck! Now take me!'

And he would slash the horse on the neck with the little whip he had asked Uncle Oscar for. He *knew* the horse could take him to where there was luck, if only he forced it. So he would mount again and start on his furious ride, hoping at last to get there. He knew he could get there.

'You'll break your horse, Paul!' said the nurse.

'He's always riding like that! I wish he'd leave off!' said his elder sister Joan.

But he only glared down on them in silence. Nurse gave him up. She could make nothing of him. Anyhow, he was growing beyond her.

One day his mother and his Uncle Oscar came in when he was on one of his furious rides. He did not speak to them.

'Hallo, you young jockey! Riding a winner?' said his uncle.

'Aren't you growing too big for a rocking-horse? You're not a very little boy any longer, you know,' said his mother.

But Paul only gave a blue glare from his big, rather close set eyes. He would speak to nobody when he was in full tilt. His mother watched him with an anxious expression on her face.

At last he suddenly stopped forcing his horse into the mechanical gallop and slid down.

'Well, I got there!' he announced fiercely, his blue eyes still flaring, and his sturdy long legs straddling apart.

'Where did you get to?' asked his mother.

'Where I wanted to go,' he flared back at her.

'That's right, son!' said Uncle Oscar, 'Don't you stop till you get there. What's the horse's name?'

'He doesn't have a name,' said the boy.

'Gets on without all right?' asked the uncle.

'Well he has different names. He was called Sansovino last week.'

'Sansovino, eh? Won the Ascot. How did you know this name?'

'He always talks about horse-races with Bassett,' said Joan.

The uncle was delighted to find that his small nephew was posted with all the racing news. Bassett, the young gardener, who had been wounded in the left foot in the war and had got his present job through Oscar Cresswell, whose batman he had been, was a perfect blade of the 'turf'. He lived in the racing events, and the small boy lived with him.

Oscar Cresswell got it all from Bassett.

'Master Paul comes and asks me, so I can't do more than tell him, sir,' said Bassett, his face terribly serious, as if he were speaking of religious matters.

'And does he ever put anything on a horse he fancies?'

'Well – I don't want to give him away – he's a young sport, a fine sport, sir. Would you mind asking him himself? He sort of takes a pleasure in it, and perhaps he'd feel I was giving him away, sir, if you don't mind.'

Bassett was serious as a church.

The uncle went back to his nephew and took him off for a ride in the car.

'Say, Paul, old man, do you ever put anything on a horse?' the uncle asked.

The boy watched the handsome man closely.

'Why, do you think I oughtn't to?' he parried.

'Not a bit of it! I thought perhaps you might give me a tip for the Lincoln.'

The car sped on into the country, going down to Uncle Oscar's place in Hampshire.

'Honour bright?' said the nephew.

'Honour bright, son!' said the uncle.

'Well then, Daffodil.'

'Daffodil! I doubt it, sonny. What about Mirza?'

'I only know the winner,' said the boy. 'That's Daffodil.'

'Daffodil eh?'

There was a pause. Daffodil was an obscure horse comparatively.

'Uncle!'

'Yes, son?'

'You won't let it go any further, will you? I promised Bassett.'

'Bassett be damned, old man! What's he got to do with it?'

'We're partners. We've been partners from the first. Uncle, he lent me my first five shillings, which I lost. I promised him, honour bright, it was only between

me and him; only you gave me that ten-shilling note I
started winning with, so I thought you were lucky.
You won't let it go any further, will you?'

The boy gazed at his uncle from those big, hot,
blue eyes, set rather close together. The uncle stirred
and laughed easily.

'Right you are, son! I'll keep your tip private.
Daffodil, eh? How much are you putting on him?'

'All except twenty pounds,' said the boy. 'I keep that
in reserve.'

The uncle thought it a good joke.

'You keep twenty pounds in reserve, do you, you
young romancer? What are you betting then?'

'I'm betting three hundred,' said the boy gravely. 'But
it's between you and me, Uncle Oscar! Honour bright?'

The uncle burst into a roar of laughter.

'It's between you and me all right, you young Nat
Gould,' he said, laughing. 'But where's your three
hundred?'

'Bassett keeps it for me. We're partners.

'You are, are you! And what is Bassett putting on
Daffodil?'

'He won't go quite as high as I do, I expect. Perhaps
he'll go a hundred and fifty.'

'What, pennies?' laughed the uncle.

'Pounds,' said the child, with a surprised look at his uncle. 'Bassett keeps a bigger reserve than I do.'

Between wonder and amusement Uncle Oscar was silent. He pursued the matter no further, but he determined to take his nephew with him to the Lincoln races.

'Now, son,' he said, 'I'm putting twenty on Mirza, and I'll put five on for you on any horse you fancy. What's your pick?'

'Daffodil, uncle.'

'No, not the fiver on Daffodil!'

'I should if it was my own fiver,' said the child.

'Good! Good! Right you are! A fiver for me and a fiver for you on Daffodil.'

The child had never been to a race-meeting before, and his eyes were blue fire. He pursed his mouth tight and watched. A Frenchman just in front had put his money on Lancelot. Wild with excitement, he flayed his arms up and down, yelling '*Lancelot! Lancelot!*' in his French accent.

Daffodil came in first, Lancelot second, Mirza third. The child, flushed and with eyes blazing, was curiously serene. His uncle brought him four five-pound notes, four to one.

'What am I to do with these?' he cried, waving them before the boy's eyes.

'I suppose we'll talk to Bassett,' said the boy. 'I expect I have fifteen hundred now; and twenty in reserve; and this twenty.'

His uncle studied him for some moments.

'Look here, son!' he said. 'You're not serious about Bassett and that fifteen hundred, are you?'

'Yes, I am. But it's between you and me, uncle. Honour bright?'

'Honour bright all right, son! But I must talk to Bassett.'

'If you'd like to be a partner, uncle, with Bassett and me, we could all be partners. Only, you'd have to promise, honour bright, uncle, not to let it go beyond us three. Bassett and I are lucky, and you must be lucky, because it was your ten shillings I started winning with...'

Uncle Oscar took both Bassett and Paul into Richmond Park for an afternoon, and there they talked.

'It's like this, you see, sir,' Bassett said. 'Master Paul would get me talking about racing events, spinning yarns, you know, sir. And he was always keen on knowing if I'd made or if I'd lost. It's about a year since, now, that I put five shillings on Blush of Dawn for him: and we lost. Then the luck changed with that ten shillings he had from you: that we put on Singhalese. And since that time, it's been pretty steady, all things considering. What do you say, Master Paul?'

'We're all right when we're sure,' said Paul. 'It's when we're not quite sure that we go down.'

'Oh, but we're careful then,' said Bassett.

'But when are you *sure*?' smiled Uncle Oscar.

'It's Master Paul, sir,' said Bassett in a secret, religious voice. 'It's as if he had it from heaven. Like Daffodil, now, for the Lincoln. That was as sure as eggs.'

'Did you put anything on Daffodil?' asked Oscar Cresswell.

'Yes, sir, I made my bit.'

'And my nephew?'

Bassett was obstinately silent, looking at Paul.

'I made twelve hundred, didn't I, Bassett? I told uncle I was putting three hundred on Daffodil.'

'That's right,' said Bassett nodding.

'But where's the money?' asked the uncle.

'I keep it safe locked up, sir. Master Paul he can have it any minute he likes to ask for it.'

'What, fifteen hundred pounds?'

'And twenty! And *forty*, that is, with the twenty he made on the course.'

'It's amazing!' said the uncle.

'If Master Paul offers you to be partners, sir, I would, if I were you: if you'll excuse me,' said Bassett.

Oscar Cresswell thought about it.

'I'll see the money,' he said.

They drove home again, and sure enough, Bassett came round to the garden-house with fifteen hundred pounds in notes. The twenty pounds reserve was left with Joe Glee, in the Turf Commission deposit.

'You see it's all right, uncle, when I'm *sure*! Then we go strong, for all we're worth. Don't we, Bassett?'

'We do that, Master Paul.'

'And when are you sure?' said the uncle, laughing.

'Oh, well, sometimes I'm *absolutely* sure, like about Daffodil,' said the boy; 'and sometimes I have an idea; and sometimes I haven't even an idea, have I, Bassett? Then we're careful, because we mostly go down.'

'You do, do you! And when you're sure, like about Daffodil, what makes you sure, sonny?'

'Oh, well, I don't know,' said the boy uneasily. 'I'm sure, you know, uncle; that's all.'

'It's as if he had it from heaven, sir,' Bassett reiterated.

'I should say so!' said the uncle.

But he became a partner. And when the Leger was coming on Paul was 'sure' about Lively Spark, which was a quite inconsiderable horse, Bassett went for five hundred, and Oscar Cresswell two hundred. Lively Spark came in first, and the betting had been ten to one against him. Paul had made ten thousand.

'You see, he said, 'I was absolutely sure of him.'

Even Oscar Cresswell had cleared two thousand.

'Look here, son,' he said, 'this sort of thing makes me nervous.'

'It needn't, uncle! Perhaps I shan't be sure again for a long time.'

'But what are you going to do with your money?' asked the uncle.

'Of course,' said the boy, 'I started it for mother. She said she had no luck, because father is unlucky, so I thought if I was lucky, it might stop whispering.'

'What might stop whispering?'

'Our house. I *hate* our house for whispering.'

'What does it whisper?'

'Why – why' – the boy fidgeted – 'why, I don't

know. But it's always short of money, you know, uncle.'

'I know it, son, I know it.'

'You know people send mother writs, don't you, uncle?'

'I'm afraid I do,' said the uncle.

'And then the house whispers, like people laughing at you behind your back. It's awful, that is! I thought if I was lucky –'

'You might stop it,' added the uncle.

The boy watched him with big blue eyes, that had an uncanny cold fire in them, and he said never a word.

'Well, then!' said the uncle. 'What are we doing?'

'I shouldn't like mother to know I was lucky,' said the boy.

'Why not, son?'

'She'd stop me.'

'I don't think she would.'

'Oh!' – and the boy writhed in an odd way – 'I *don't* want her to know, uncle.'

'All right, son! We'll manage it without her knowing.'

They managed it very easily. Paul, at the other's suggestion, handed over five thousand pounds to his uncle, who deposited it with the family lawyer, who was then to inform Paul's mother that a relative had put five thousand pounds into his hands, which sum was to paid out a thousand pounds at a time, on the mother's birthday, for the next five years.

'So she'll have a birthday present of a thousand pounds for five successive years,' said Uncle Oscar. 'I hope it won't make it all the harder for her later.'

Paul's mother had her birthday in November. The house had been 'whispering' worse than ever lately, and, even in spite of his luck, Paul could not bear up against it. He was very anxious to see the effect of the birthday letter, telling his mother about the thousand pounds.

When there were no visitors, Paul now took his meals with his parents, as he was beyond the nursery control. His mother went into town nearly every day. She had discovered that she had an odd knack of sketching furs and dress materials so she worked secretly in the studio of a friend who was the chief 'artist' for the leading drapers. She drew the figures of ladies in furs and ladies in silk and sequins for the newspaper advertisements. This young woman artist earned several thousand pounds a year, but Paul's mother only made several hundreds, and she was again dissatisfied. She so wanted to be first in something, and she did not succeed, even in making sketches for drapery advertisements.

She was down to breakfast on the morning of her birthday. Paul watched her face as she read her letters. He knew the lawyer's letter. As his mother read it, her face hardened and became more expressionless. Then a cold determined look came on her mouth. She hid the letter under the pile of others, and said not a word about it.

'Didn't you have anything nice in the post for your birthday, mother?' said Paul.

'Quite moderately nice,' she said, her voice cold and absent.

She went away to town without saying more.

But in the afternoon Uncle Oscar appeared. He said Paul's mother had had a long interview with the lawyer, asking if the whole five thousand could not be advanced at once, as she was in debt.

'What do you think, uncle?' said the boy.

'I leave it to you, son.'

'Oh, let her have it, then! We can get some more with the other,' said the boy.

'A bird in the hand is worth two in the bush, laddie!' said Uncle Oscar.

'But I'm sure to *know* for the Grand National; or the Lincoln-shire; or else the Derby. I'm sure to know for *one* of them,' said Paul.

So Uncle Oscar signed the agreement, and Paul's mother touched the whole five thousand. Then something very curious happened. The voices in the house suddenly went mad, like a chorus of frogs on a spring evening. There were certain new furnishings, and Paul had a tutor. He was *really* going to Eton, his father's school, in the following autumn. There were flowers in the winter, and a blossoming of the luxury Paul's mother had been used to. And yet the voices in the house behind the sprays of mimosa and almond-blossom, and from under the piles of iridescent cushions, simply trilled and screamed in a sort of ecstasy: 'There *must* be more money! Oh-h-h; there *must* be more money! Oh, now, now-w! Now-w-w – there *must* be more money! – More than ever! More than ever!'

It frightened Paul terribly. He studied away at his Latin and Greek with his tutor. But his intense hours were spent with Bassett. The Grand National had gone by; he had not 'known', and had lost a hundred pounds. Summer was at hand. He was in agony for the Lincoln. But even for the Lincoln he didn't 'know', and he lost fifty pounds. He became wild-eyed and strange, as if something were going to explode in him.

'Let it alone, son! Don't you bother about it!' urged Uncle Oscar. But it was as if the boy couldn't really hear what his uncle was saying.

'I've got to know for the Derby. I've got to know for the Derby!' the child reiterated, his big blue eyes blazing with a sort of madness.

His mother noticed how overwrought he was.

'You'd better go to the seaside. Wouldn't you like to go now to the seaside, instead of waiting? I think you'd better,' she said, looking down at him anxiously, her heart curiously heavy because of him.

But the child lifted his uncanny blue eyes.

'I couldn't possibly go before the Derby, mother!' he said. 'I couldn't possibly!'

'Why not?' she said, her voice becoming heavy when she was opposed. 'Why not? You can still go from the seaside to see the Derby with your Uncle Oscar, if that's what you wish. No need for you to wait here. Besides, I think you care too much about these races. It's a bad sign. My family has been a gambling family, and you won't know till you grow up how much damage it has done. But it has done damage. I shall have to send Bassett away, and ask Uncle Oscar not to talk racing to you, unless you promise to be reasonable about it: go away to the seaside and forget it. You're all nerves!'

'I'll do what you like, mother, so long as you don't send me away till after the Derby,' the boy said.

'Send you away from where? Just from this house?'

'Yes,' he said, gazing at her.

'Why, you curious child, what makes you care about this house so much suddenly? I never knew you loved it.'

He gazed at her without speaking. He had a secret within a secret, something he had not divulged, even to Bassett or to his Uncle Oscar.

But his mother, after standing undecided and a little bit sullen for some moments, said:

'Very well, then! Don't go to the seaside till after the Derby, if you don't wish it. But promise me you won't think so much about horse-racing, and *events*, as you call them!'

'Oh, no,' said the boy casually. 'I won't think much about them, mother. You needn't worry. I wouldn't worry, mother, if I were you.'

'If you were me and I were you,' said his mother, 'I wonder what we *should* do!'

'But you know you needn't worry mother, don't you?' the boy repeated.

'I should be awfully glad to know it,' she said wearily.

'Oh, well, you *can*, you know. I mean, you *ought* to know you needn't worry,' he insisted.

'Ought I? Then I'll see about it,' she said.

Paul's secret of secrets was his wooden horse, that which had no name. Since he was emancipated from a nurse and a nursery-governess, he had had his rocking-horse removed to his own bedroom at the top of the house.

'Surely you're too big for a rocking-horse!' his mother had remonstrated.

'Well, you see, mother, till I can have a *real* horse, I like to have *some* sort of animal about,' had been his quaint answer.

'Do you feel he keeps you company?' she laughed.

'Oh yes! He's very good, he always keeps me company, when I'm there,' said Paul.

So the horse, rather shabby, stood in an arrested prance in the boy's bedroom.

The Derby was drawing near, and the boy grew more

and more tense. He hardly heard what was spoken to him, he was very frail, and his eyes were really uncanny. His mother had sudden strange seizures of uneasiness about him. Sometimes, for half an hour, she would feel a sudden anxiety about him that was almost anguish. She wanted to rush to him at once, and know that he was safe.

Two nights before the Derby, she was at a big party in town, when one of her rushes of anxiety about her boy, her first-born, gripped her heart till she could hardly speak. She fought with the feeling, might and main, for she believed in common sense. But it was too strong. She had to leave the dance and go downstairs to telephone to the country. The children's nursery-governess was terribly surprised and startled at being rung up in the night.

'Are the children all right, Miss Wilmot?'

'Oh yes, they are quite all right.'

'Master Paul? Is he all right?'

'He went to bed as right as a trivet. Shall I run up and look at him?'

'No,' said Paul's mother reluctantly. 'No! Don't trouble. It's all right. Don't sit up. We shall be home fairly soon.' She did not want her son's privacy intruded upon.

'Very good,' said the governess.

It was about one o'clock when Paul's mother and father drove up to their house. All was still. Paul's mother went to her room and slipped off her white fur cloak. She had told her maid not to wait up for her. She heard her husband downstairs, mixing a whisky and soda.

And then, because of the strange anxiety at her heart, she stole upstairs to her son's bedroom. Noiselessly she went along the upper corridor. Was there a faint noise? What was it?

She stood, with arrested muscles, outside his door listening. There was a strange, heavy, and yet not loud noise. Her heart stood still. It was a soundless noise, yet rushing and powerful. Something huge, in violent hushed motion. What was it? What in God's name was it? She ought to know. She felt that she knew the noise. She knew what it was.

Yet she could not place it. She couldn't say what it was. And on and on it went, like a madness.

Softly, frozen with anxiety and fear, she turned the door handle.

The room was dark. Yet in the space near the window, she heard and saw something plunging to and fro. She gazed in fear and amazement.

Then suddenly she switched on the light, and saw her son, in his green pyjamas, madly surging on the rocking-horse. The blaze of light suddenly lit him up, as he urged the wooden horse, and lit her up, as she stood, blonde, in her dress of pale green and crystal, in the doorway.

'Paul!' she cried. 'Whatever are you doing?'

'It's Malabar!' he screamed in a powerful, strange voice. 'It's Malabar!'

His eyes blazed at her for one strange and senseless second, as he ceased urging his wooden horse. Then he fell with a crash to the ground, and she, all her tormented motherhood flooding upon her, rushed to gather him up.

But he was unconscious, and unconscious he remained, with some brain-fever. He talked and tossed, and his mother sat stonily by his side.

'Malabar! It's Malabar! Bassett, Bassett, I *know*! It's Malabar!'

So the child cried, trying to get up and urge the rocking-horse that gave him inspiration.

'What does he mean by Malabar?' asked the heart-frozen mother.

'I don't know,' said the father stonily.

'What does he mean by Malabar?' she asked her brother Oscar.

'It's one of the horses running for the Derby,' was the answer.

And, in spite of himself, Oscar Cresswell spoke to Bassett, and himself put a thousand on Malabar: at fourteen to one.

The third day of the illness was critical: they were waiting for a change. The boy, with his rather long, curly hair, was tossing ceaselessly on the pillow. He neither slept nor regained consciousness, and his eyes were like blue stones. His mother sat, feeling her heart had gone, turned actually into a stone.

In the evening, Oscar Cresswell did not come, but Bassett sent a message, saying could he come up for one moment, just one moment? Paul's mother was very angry at the intrusion, but on second thoughts she agreed. The boy was the same. Perhaps Bassett might bring him to consciousness.

The gardener, a shortish fellow with a little brown moustache and sharp little brown eyes, tiptoed into the room, touched his imaginary cap to Paul's mother, and stole to the bedside, staring with glittering, small-ish eyes at the tossing dying child.

'Master Paul!' he whispered. 'Master Paul! Malabar came in first all right, a clean win. I did as you told me. You've made over seventy thousand pounds, you have; you've got over eighty thousand. Malabar came in all right, Master Paul.'

'Malabar! Malabar! Did I say Malabar, mother? Did I say Malabar? Do you think I'm lucky, mother? I knew Malabar, didn't I? Over eighty pounds! I knew, didn't I know I knew? Malabar came in all right. If I ride my horse till I'm sure, then I tell you, Bassett, you can go as high as you like. Did you go for all you were worth, Bassett?'

'I went a thousand on it, Master Paul.'

'I never told you, mother, that if I can ride my horse, and *get there*, then I'm absolutely sure, – oh, absolutely! Mother, did I ever tell you? I *am* lucky!'

'No you never did,' said his mother.

But the boy died in the night.

And even as he lay dead, his mother heard her brother's voice saying to her: 'My God, Hester, you're eighty-odd thousand to the good, and a poor devil of a son to the bad. But, poor devil, poor devil, he's best gone out of a life where he rides his rocking-horse to find a winner.'

Alex Miller

The Tivington Nott

The horse is no trouble to me. As the weeks go by I
realize it's a decision he's made. I'm no Irishman to
work magic with horses. Nor a gypsy. It's him. He has
decided I'm okay. And pretty soon the Tiger starts
showing more than an idle interest. The ease with
which I get along with Kabara intrigues him. But he
keeps his distance. Leaving it all to me. Not making
his interest too plain; watching to see how things work
out. Making no move to get to know Kabara. Nothing
like that. Staying a stranger to the horse.

And that's his mistake.

I'm watching the Tiger too. Keeping abreast of his

little schemes as they're running through his head. I have to. And I don't think he understands that this horse is not really the good-natured nag he appears to be, but is a potential stroke of lightning. Looking back it is easy to see how Tiger makes this mistake. He sees me crawling all over Kabara without any caution and jogging along the Wiveliscombe road with a loose rein and no saddle.

But *I* never forget the energy of this entire, and his potential for something like heroic action. You can't touch him without knowing it, no matter what you might imagine from a distance.

It's in his blood.

A feeling that he's preparing for something.

A big day when it's all going to come together for him. When all the lineage, and all the breeding and all the care and all the years and the generations of refining are going to be called finally into action. He has a performance in him, and being close to him I feel it. But it's held in reserve and would have to be *called* out of him at the big moment. His rider would have to be his equal in potential or the limit would not be reached. That's the way he makes me feel. He's ordered, disciplined, quietly under control. A matter of stillness and finesse. Waiting. For the day. This is the only way it makes sense. My 'good' reflexes are a joke in comparison with his. Kabara can react and restore his balance again in the instant before I have had time to register what is going on. So I don't kid myself. I'm just taking care of him. He's out of my class. Out of Alsop's too. Out of most people's. Needing someone as special as himself to call out that performance. So I don't try anything fancy with him. I let him know what's going on, but I let *him* lead.

I say nothing to anyone about all this. And between haymaking and everything else, whenever we get the odd chance, which turns out to be mostly around late evening, me and Kabara are left alone to get on with things for a while. The Tiger keeps his eye on us and slips the odd question about the horse, but I don't say too much and I can see he's seriously starting to entertain the idea of hunting on him one day himself. Maybe it's no more than an outlandish fantasy at this stage rather than an actual idea. But the germ of it's there sure enough.

This horse is not an Exmoor hunter. Without superior horsemanship he's the wrong horse for this place. The first time I take him out on the Chains he panics when his feet start sinking into the bog. The local ponies skip their way over such places. Kabara thinks the earth is opening under him. And when I show it to him again, dismounting and leading him forward, giving him a good look, he makes it clear we aren't going that way. Ever.

It was about then that I decided to let him take over. Thundering along on the sound heather of the table-lands suited him just fine. But getting among the bogs and drainage ditches and old broken bits and pieces of sheep fencing, the worst of which was downed wire hidden among the bracken, was not something that interested him at all.

And it wasn't courage he lacked.

He had too much sense. Too much instinct for himself and for his own preservation. I could point him down the steepest combe and it wouldn't worry him. He'd pick his way without fear. Alert to every danger.

The one day, when there was a brief lull before the beginning of the harvest, I took him out early. Had him ready and saddled up in the yard before daylight so we could get away straight after milking, taking my breakfast with me and heading for the remote streams at the headwaters of the Barle. Taking Kabara to visit

the lonely spot where I had discovered the soiling pit
of the Tivington nott.

By midday we were there. Out on the tops. Then
down through the steep larch woods rising up on
either side of us and at the bottom a black and peaty
wallow. The air rich with the stench of wet earth and
rotting vegetation.

Private here. Unvisited. The depth of the wood,
where the great stag-without-horns rolls and soils,
cooling his body in the black mud, away from any eyes
but those of the wilderness.

As we step forward, entering the dim glade, there's
a whiff of mint hanging in the still air. He has moved
out silently ahead of us, crushing the wild herb that
grows on the edge of the stream as he stepped away. I
can see his slot there, the brown mud circulating
slowly where the hollow he has left has filled with
water. And a tiny whirlpool where his dew claws have
shifted a pebble.

Kabara's senses are stretched to the limit here.
Picking up the smell of the male deer close by. A
tremor running through his withers, transferring his
readiness to me. There is a balance now in the horse,
as if his hooves are not quite touching the ground, an

alertness that tempts me to action. To leap miraculously into the dark forest after the deer.

I am still.

Watching.

But we are not going to see the nott. He is in the shadows, watching *us* I dare say. I examine each dark patch of shade with care, letting my gaze rest for a moment on every uncertain shape amongst the gloomy conifers. But I can't tell where he might be. A knowing survivor. Somewhere between sixteen and twenty years old, Morris has told me. Surviving now by infinite skill and care. Old for a red stag. He's eluded the hunt on numerous occasions. Tricked them. And created a legend for himself. Many consider him dead. And none of them know he has moved to these woods or they'd come after him again. It is their practice always to take a nott stag whenever one presents himself, for they fear that notts will breed and diminish the elegance of the species.

I'm not about to tell them where he is.

Tell them nothing. *They're* the locals. And he's a long way from Tivington now. They chased him once too often and he shifted his ground right out of the district, crossing the Beacon and the Quarme and the Exe and setting himself up way over here.

I discovered him by chance and swore Morris to secrecy. Being from Wiltshire makes the secret easier for Morris to keep. A local couldn't hang onto such a hot piece of information for long. To harbour a stag for the hunt is the ambition of every yokel in this neck of the woods. And keeping the whereabouts of the Tivington nott a secret would burn a hole in their brains. Simple as that. You couldn't trust them with the information.

The Tiger would give money to know it.

They'll find him anyway. One day. Of their own accord. And when they do he'll be on the run again. Sooner or later, when the Arctic weather is tightening his belly, he'll sneak into someone's turnip field. And then some half-witted labourer, arriving to shift the hurdles, will see his great slot there, superimposed on the sheep tracks of the day before and frozen into the mud in the morning. The footprint of the devil staring him in the face.

The yokel will drop everything and run to tell his master. Crazy to see those big hounds having a go. Howling and wailing and crying on the trail. Lighting everybody up with his news that there's a warrantable stag harbouring in the area.

Except you don't need a warrant to hunt a nott. It's open season on them all year round.

Solitary. Always on guard. Never at ease with the herd.

It was late one October afternoon a year ago that I found him. I'm following this stream to its source. Just for the pleasures of exploration and of being on my own. It's Bampton Fair day and the Tiger's been forced by one of his own traditions to give us most of the day off. He'd squirm out of it if he could, but Morris doesn't ask on these occasions. The local custom is good enough for him. He makes sure the Tiger knows what his plans are in good time, and he and his wife go visiting her parents, over to Monksilver for the day.

Too bad for the Tiger.

I get out as fast as I can too. As soon as the milking's done I'm gone. It's either that or get trapped by Tiger into doing some five-minute job that ends up taking all day.

I get away.

Right out of the place. Gone. Saying nothing. On my own. Heading off by a roundabout route till I'm way out on the moor. Keeping always to cover.

Making the most of my opportunity for penetrating the wilderness.

Soon I've got my head down and I'm moving along quietly. Up the twisting track of the steep combe. Going deeper into the woods. Following the stream-bed and checking the small things. On the lookout for the unusual. Letting nothing pass. Turning the stones in the water. Sniffing at the weeds and herbs and seeking among the dense variety to get to a knowledge of it. It absorbs me. I never know what I am going to come across next. Human beings have been moving through this landscape for thousands of years. Leaving this and that behind. Not much, but something, every now and then, a thing out of place among the leaves and water-worn pebbles because of shape or texture. No more than a stone itself maybe. Odd thing out. Giving you the sense it has been brought. And the flow of the stream is always uncovering new layers.

Crawling, when I have to, through the tough under-growth, and wading when there's no other way. Squirming and pushing and scrabbling my way right into the silent coverts that no one visits. To see what's there. And I sit without moving under the ripe canopy of thorn and bramble. Staring. Hardly breathing.

Feeling it all close and intense around me. Waiting for me to move on so that it can return to action. And rising in me the feeling that I want to break my fear against its wary inhabitants. Surprise them. Hunt them.

And such feelings keep me there for a while in rapt attention.

Then I go on. Moving away from it. Returning to the enjoyment of the day. And I don't notice that I'm entering the mouth of a hidden glade under the dark canopy of the larches, and the stream-bank on either side a bed of needles. Soft and deep. Undisturbed.

Until the nott barks a sudden warning. I stop dead in my tracks. My heart thumping. I don't know what it is and can see nothing at first.

Then, stationary in the dark jumble of shadows, I see him. The wide-set, slanting eyes of a satyr. Wild and aggressive. Staring directly into mine. Neither of us moving. His thick neck-hair shaggy and standing out, knotted and sopping, with black mud cascading from his flanks. Something mad and savage rising from the wallow to confront me.

Staring at him it takes me seconds to work out that I am looking at a red stag and not at something from rumour and fear.

Alone in the woods with an escaped maniac.

Running won't get me far. One swift stride and he'd be on me. It's October and the rut is in full swing. And although I've heard often enough that stags will not attack humans, even during the rut, I feel sure this sudden confrontation will prove the exception to that.

Dripping with muck, caught unexpectedly in his most private moment, the breath steaming from his wide nostrils, surrounded by the rich peaty stench of his soiling pit and the acid aroma of his heated body. This animal does not look afraid of me.

Despite his lack of antlers there is no mistaking him for a hind. His stink is of maleness and there is in his gaze that obsessed look of arousal that is not something to be argued with. The general belief is that notts do not achieve breeding rights over their antlered brothers during the rut, but with the belief is a superstitious fear of the exception. I have never seen a nott before this day, but this one is unmistakable. He is something different. An aberration even among such outcasts as his own kind. I can see that. Who knows what he might do? He looks to me to be capable of anything. A sudden extreme.

I'm not hanging around to find out.

I ease my weight onto my toes and very slowly, taking extreme care to make no sudden movement, I
make ready to start backing off. The instant I tense up
he barks again. I freeze. It is a sharp, urgent warning.
A mad shout in the forest. And a wave of fear goes
through me. As if in slow-motion I see him gathering
himself. Then he leaps away to one side and is gone.

I take hold of a branch, steadying myself,
listening...

The woods are silent again and still. Only his smell
remains. As if I have imagined him but for that and
for the fact that my heart is racing. I stand there for
some minutes. Uncertain whether to go at once or
stay. Cautiously, then, I approach his soiling pit. An
intruder now in this glade. I look down at the watery
slurry of the pit where he was cooling himself a
moment ago. It is in a depression to one side of the
stream and hidden by a stand of bracken that has
asserted itself despite the larches. It is a soak. A source
that perhaps becomes a running spring in wet years.
Though these sources seem to stay the same whether
the years are wet or dry. All around me is the intimate
evidence of the old stag's activities... He was here
before the bear and the boar and was hunted by the

wolf since the beginning of his line. And he is here still. The wild red deer has survived them all.

Preserved for pleasure.

Standing here in the intense quiet I get the feeling I am being watched. I look around. Stare into the deepening shadows of the wood. Nothing moves. There's not the sound of a bird or the least rustle of a branch. No breeze. The late afternoon air of the high combe is growing cold. I hold my breath, straining my hearing, staring hard at the grey lichened trunks of the larches around me – thousand-year-old granite pillars.

Nothing.

Only there, faintly, in the extreme distance and barely penetrating this deep wooded cleft in the hills, the sound of a clocktower bell from a village somewhere. That's all.

I head for home.

Striking down the stream at a good pace. And then from behind me there comes the sudden roaring challenge of the old stag assured and firm in his rut. The whole darkening combe around me filling and echoing with his deep bellowing, low, archaic and malicious towards men and hounds and horses, tailing off into a bolking and rattling in his throat.

Henry Lawson

The Buckjumper

There were about a dozen bush natives, from any-where, most of them lanky and easygoing, hanging about the little slab-and-bark hotel on the edge of the scrub at Capertee Camp (a teamster's camp) when Cobb & Co's mail-coach and six came dashing down the sidling from round Crown Ridge, in all its glory, to the end of the twelve-mile stage. Some dusty, wiry, ill-used hacks were hanging to the fence and to saplings about the place. The fresh coach-horses stood ready in a stockyard close to the shanty. As the coach climbed the nearer bank of the creek at the foot of the ridge, six of the bushmen detached themselves from veranda-posts, from their heels, from the clay floor of the veranda and the rough slab wall against which they'd been resting, and joined a group of four or five who stood round one. He stood with his back to the corner post of the stockyard, his feet well braced out in front of him, and contemplated the toes of his tight new 'lastic-side boots and whistled softly. He was a clean-limbed, handsome fellow, with riding-cords, leggings, and a blue sash; he was Graeco-Roman-nosed, blue-eyed, and his glossy, curly black hair bunched up in front of the brim of a new cabbage-tree hat, set well back on his head.

'Do it for a quid, Jack?' asked one.

'Damned if I will, Jim!' said the young man at the post. 'I'll do it for a fiver – not a blanky sprat less.'

Jim took off his hat and shoved it round, and bobs were chucked into it. The result was about thirty shillings.

Jack glanced contemptuously into the crown of the hat.

'Not me!' he said, showing some emotion for the first time. 'D'yer think I'm going to risk me blanky neck for your blanky amusement for thirty blanky bob? I'll ride the blanky horse for a fiver, and I'll feel the blankly quids in my pocket before I get on.'

Meanwhile the coach had dashed up to the door of the shanty. There were about twenty passengers aboard – inside, on the box-seat, on the tailboard, and hanging on to the roof – most of them Sydney men going up to the Mudgee races. They got down and went inside with the driver for a drink, while the stablemen changed horses. The bushmen raised their voices a little and argued.

One of the passengers was a big, stout, hearty man – a good-hearted, sporting man and a racehorse owner, according to his brands. He had a round red face and a white cork hat. 'What's those chaps got on outside?' he asked the publican.

'Oh, it's a bet they've got on about riding a horse,' replied the publican. 'The flash-looking chap with the sash is Flash Jack, the horse-breaker; and they reckon they've got the champion outlaw in the district out there – that chestnut horse in the yard.'

The sporting man was interested at once, and went out and joined the bushmen.

'Well, chaps! What have you got on here?' he asked cheerily.

'Oh,' said Jim carelessly, 'it's only a bit of a bet about ridin' that blanky chestnut in the corner of the yard there.' He indicated an ungroomed chestnut horse, fenced off by a couple of long sapling poles in a corner of the stockyard. 'Flash Jack there – he reckons he's the champion horse-breaker round here – Flash Jack reckons he can take it out of that horse first try.'

'What's up with the horse?' inquired the big, red-faced man. 'It looks quiet enough. Why, I'd ride it myself.'

'Would yer?' said Jim, who had hair that stood straight up, and an innocent, inquiring expression. 'Looks quiet, does he? *You* ought to know more about horses than to go by the looks of 'em. He's quiet enough just now, when there's no one near him; but you should have been here an hour ago. That horse has killed two men and put another chap's shoulder out – besides breaking a cove's leg. It took six of us all the morning to run him in and get the saddle on him; and now Flash Jack wants to back out of it.'

'Euraliar!' remarked Flash Jack cheerfully. 'I said I'd ride that blanky horse out of the yard for a fiver. I ain't goin' to risk my blanky neck for nothing and only to amuse you blokes.'

'He said he'd ride the horse inside the yard for a quid,' said Jim.

'And get smashed against the rails!' said Flash Jack. 'I would be a fool. I'd rather take my chance outside in the scrub – and it's rough country round here.'

'Well, how much do you want?' asked the man in the mushroom hat.

'A fiver, I said,' replied Jack indifferently. 'And the blanky stuff in my pocket before I get on the blanky horse.'

'Are you frightened of us running away without paying you?' inquired one of the passengers who had gathered round.

'I'm frightened of the horse bolting with me without me being paid,' said Flash Jack. 'I know that horse; he's got a mouth like iron. I might be at the bottom of a cliff on Crown Ridge road in twenty minutes with my head caved in, and then what chance for the quids?'

'You wouldn't want 'em then,' suggested a passenger. 'Or, say! – we'd leave the fiver with the publican to bury you.'

Flash Jack ignored that passenger. He eyed his boots and softly whistled a tune.

'All right!' said the man in the cork hat, putting his hand in his pocket. 'I'll start with a quid; stump up, you chaps.'

The five pounds were got together.

'I'll lay a quid to half a quid he don't stick on ten minutes!' shouted Jim to his mates as soon as he saw that the event was to come off. The passengers also betted amongst themselves. Flash Jack, after putting the money in his breeches-pocket, let down the rails and led the horse into the middle of the yard.

'Quiet as an old cow!' snorted a passenger in disgust. 'I believe it's a sell!'

'Wait a bit,' said Jim to the passenger, 'wait a bit and you'll see.'

They waited and saw.

Flash Jack leisurely mounted the horse, rode slowly out of the yard, and trotted briskly round the corner of the shanty and into the scrub, which swallowed him more completely than the sea might have done.

Most of the other bushmen mounted their horses and followed Flash Jack to a clearing in the scrub, at a safe distance from the shanty; then they dismounted and hung on to saplings, or leaned against their horses, while they laughed.

At the hotel there was just time for another drink. The driver climbed to his seat and shouted, 'All aboard!' in his usual tone. The passengers climbed to their places, thinking hard. A mile or so along the road the man with the cork hat remarked, with much truth:

'Those blanky bushmen have got too much time to think.' The bushmen returned to the shanty as soon as the coach was out of sight and proceeded to 'knock down' the fiver.

Nicholas Evans

The Horse Whisperer

Smoky came back into the ring with the things Tom had sent him to get. They'd had to do this a few months back at a clinic down in New Mexico, so Smoky pretty much knew the score. Quietly though, away from all those watching, Tom took him through the process again so there wouldn't be any mistakes and nobody would get hurt.

Smoky listened gravely, nodding now and again. When Tom saw he had it straight in his head the two of them went over toward Pilgrim. He'd moved away to the far side of the arena and you could tell by the way he worked his ears that he sensed something was about to happen and that it might not be fun. He let Tom come to him and rub his neck but didn't take his eyes off Smoky who stood a few yards off with all those ropes and things in his hand.

Tom unhitched the bridle and in its place slipped on the rope halter Smoky handed him. Then, one at a time, Smoky passed him the ends of two long ropes that were coiled over his arm. Tom fastened one under the halter and the other to the horn of the saddle.

He worked calmly, giving Pilgrim no cause for fear. The subterfuge made him feel bad, knowing what was to come and how the trust he'd built with the horse would now have to be broken before it could be restored. Maybe he'd got it wrong just now, he thought. Maybe what had happened between him and Annie had affected him in some way that Pilgrim sensed. Most likely all the horse had sensed was Grace's fear. But you could never be quite sure, even he, what else was going on in their minds. Maybe from somewhere deep inside him, Tom was telling the horse he didn't want it to work, for when it worked that was the end and Annie would be gone.

He asked Smoky for the hobble. It was made out of an old strip of sacking and rope. Smoothing his hand down Pilgrim's left foreleg, he lifted the hoof. The horse only shifted slightly. Tom soothed him all the time with his hand and his voice. Then, when the horse was still, he slipped the sling of sacking over the hoof and made sure it was snug. The other end was rope and with it he hoisted the weight of the raised hoof and made it fast to the horn of the saddle. Pilgrim was now a three-legged animal. An explosion waiting to happen.

It happened, as he knew it would, as soon as Tom moved away and took one of the lines, the halter one, from Smoky. Pilgrim tried to move and found himself crippled. He lurched and hopped on his right foreleg and the feeling scared him so badly that he jolted and hopped again and scared himself even worse.

If he couldn't walk, then maybe he could run, so now he tried and his eyes filled with panic at the feel of it. Tom and Smoky braced themselves and leaned back on their lines, forcing him around them in a circle maybe fifteen feet in radius. And round and round he went, like a crazed rocking horse with a broken leg.

Tom glanced at the faces that watched from the rail. He could see Grace had grown pale and that Annie was now holding her and he cussed himself for giving them the choice and not insisting they go inside and save themselves the pain of this sorry sight.

Annie had her hands on Grace's shoulders and the knuckles had gone white. Every muscle in their two bodies was clenched and jerked at each agonized hop that Pilgrim made.

'Why's he doing this?' Grace cried.

'I don't know.'

'It'll be okay, Grace,' Frank said. 'I saw him do this one time before.' Annie looked at him and tried to smile. His face belied the comfort of his words. Joe and the twins looked almost as worried as Grace.

Diane said quietly, 'Maybe you'd better take her inside.'

'No,' Grace said. 'I want to watch.'

By now Pilgrim was covered in sweat. But still he kept going. As he ran his hobbled foot jabbed the air like a wild, deformed flipper. His jolting gait sent up a burst of red sand at every step and it hung over the three of them like a fine red mist.

It seemed to Annie so wrong, so out of character, for Tom to be doing this. She had seen him be firm with horses before but never causing pain or suffering. Everything he'd done with Pilgrim had been designed to build up trust and confidence. And now he was hurting him. She just couldn't understand.

At last the horse stopped. And as soon as he did Tom nodded to Smoky and they let the two lines go slack. Then off he went again and they tightened the lines and kept the pressure on until he stopped. They gave him slack again. The horse stood there, his wet sides heaving. He was panting like some desperate asthmatic smoker and the sound was so rasping and terrible that Annie wanted to block her ears.

Now Tom was saying something to Smoky. Smoky nodded and handed him his line then went to get the coiled lasso he'd left lying on the sand. He swung a wide loop in the air and at the second attempt got it to fall over the horn of Pilgrim's saddle. He pulled it tight then took the other end to the far side of the arena and tied it in a quick-release to the bottom rail. He came back and took the other two lines from Tom.

Now Tom went to the rail and started putting pressure on the lasso line. Pilgrim felt it and braced himself. The pressure was downward and the horn of the saddle tilted.

'What's he doing?' Grace's voice was small and fearful.

Frank said, 'He's trying to get him to go down on his knees.'

Pilgrim fought long and hard and when at last he did kneel, it was only for a moment. He then seemed to summon some last surge of effort and stood again. Three times more he went down and got up again, like some reluctant convert. But the pressure Tom was putting on the saddle was too strong and relentless and finally the horse crashed down on his knees and stayed down.

Annie could feel the relief in Grace's shoulders. But it wasn't over. Tom kept the pressure on. He yelled to Smoky now to drop the other lines and come and help him. And together they hauled on the lasso line.

'Why don't they let him be!' Grace said. 'Haven't they hurt him enough?'

'He's got to lie down,' Frank said.

Pilgrim snorted like a wounded bull. There was foam spewing at his mouth. His flanks were filthy where the sand had stuck to his sweat. Again he fought for a long time. But again it was too much. And at last, slowly, he keeled over on his side and lay his head on the sand and was still.

It seemed to Annie a total, humiliating surrender. She could feel Grace's body start to shake with sobs. She felt tears well in her own eyes and was powerless to stop them. Grace turned and buried her face in Annie's chest.

'Grace!' It was Tom.

Annie looked up and saw he was standing with Smoky by Pilgrim's prone body. They looked like two hunters at the carcass of a kill.

'Grace?' he called again. 'Will you come here please?'

'No! I won't!'

He left Smoky and headed toward them. His face was grim, almost unrecognizable, as though he were possessed by some dark or vengeful force. She kept her arms around Grace to shelter her. Tom stopped in front of them.

'Grace? I'd like you to come with me.'

'No, I don't want to.'

'You've got to.'

'No, you'll only hurt him some more.'

'He's not hurt. He's okay.'

'Oh sure!'

Annie wanted to intervene, to protect her. But so daunting was Tom's intensity that instead she let him take her daughter from her hands. He gripped the child by her shoulders and made her look at him.

'You've go to do this Grace. Trust me.'

'Do what?'

'Come with me and I'll show you.'

Reluctantly, she let him lead her across the arena. Driven by the same protective urge, Annie climbed unbidden over the rail and followed. She stopped a few yards short, but near enough in case she was needed. Smoky tried a smile but saw right away it was inappropriate. Tom looked at her.

'It'll be okay Annie.' She barely nodded.

'Okay Grace,' Tom said. 'I want you to stroke him. I want you to start with his hindquarters and rub him and move his legs and feel him all over.'

'What's the point? He's good as dead.'

'Just do as I say.'

Grace walked hesitantly to the horse's rear. Pilgrim didn't lift his head from the sand but Annie could see his one eye try to follow her.

'Okay. Now stroke him. Go on. Start with his leg there. Go on. Waggle it around. That's it.'

Grace cried out, 'His body feels all dead and limp! What have you done to him?'

Annie had a sudden vision of Grace in her coma in the hospital.

'He'll be okay. Now put your hand on his hip and rub him. Do it Grace. Good.'

Pilgrim didn't move. Gradually Grace worked her way along him, smearing the dust on his heaving, sweaty sides, working his limbs to Tom's instruction. At last she rubbed his neck and the wet, silky side of his head.

'Okay. Now I want you to stand on him.'

'What!' Grace looked at him as if he were mad.

'I want you to stand on him.'

'No way.'

'Grace . . .'

Annie took a step forward. 'Tom . . .'

'Be quiet Annie.' He didn't even look at her. And now he almost shouted, 'Do as I say, Grace. Stand on him. Now!'

It was impossible to disobey. Grace started to cry. He took her hand and led her into the curve of Pilgrim's belly.

'Now step up. Go on, step up on him.'

And she did. And with the tears streaming on her face, she stood frail, like a maimed soul, on the beaten flank of the creature she loved most in all the world and sobbed at her own brutality.

Tom turned and saw Annie was crying too but he

paid no attention and turned back to Grace and told her she could now get down.

'Why are you doing this?' Annie begged. 'It's so cruel and humiliating.'

'No, you're wrong.' He was helping Grace to get down and didn't look at Annie.

'What?' Annie said scornfully.

'You're wrong. It's not cruel. He had the choice.'

'What are you talking about?'

He turned and looked at her at last. Grace was still crying beside him, but he paid her no heed. Even in her tears, the poor girl seemed as unable as Annie to believe Tom could be like this, so hard and pitiless.

'He had the choice to go on fighting life or to accept it.'

'He had no choice.'

'He did. It was hard as hell, but he could have gone on. Gone on making himself more and more unhappy. But what he chose to do instead was to go to the brink and look beyond. And he saw what was there and he chose to accept it.'

He turned to Grace and put his hands on her shoulders. 'What just happened to him, laying down like that, was the worst thing he could imagine. And you know what? He found out it was okay. Even you standing on him was okay. He saw you meant him no harm. The darkest hour comes before the dawn. That was Pilgrim's darkest hour and he survived it. Do you understand?'

Grace was wiping her tears and trying to make sense of it. 'I don't know,' she said. 'I think so.'

Tom turned and looked at Annie and she saw something soft and imploring in his eyes now, something at last that she knew and could latch on to.

'Annie? Do you understand? It's real, real important you understand this. Sometimes what seems like surrender isn't surrender at all. It's about what's going on in our hearts. About seeing clearly the way life is and accepting it and being true to it, whatever the pain, because the pain of not being true to it is far, far greater. Annie, I know you understand this.'

She nodded and wiped her eyes and tried to smile. She knew there was some other message here, one that was only for her. It was not about Pilgrim but about them and what was happening between them. But although she pretended to, she didn't understand it and could only hope that the time would come when she might.

∩ ∩ ∩

Grace watched them undo Pilgrim's hobble and the ropes tied to his halter and saddle. He lay there a moment, looking up at them with one eye, not moving his head. Then, a little uncertainly, he staggered to his feet. He shrugged and whinnied and blew and then took a few steps to see he was all in one piece.

Tom told Grace to lead him to the tank at the side of the arena and she stood beside him while he took a good long drink. When he'd finished he lifted his head and yawned and everyone laughed.

'There go the butterflies!' Joe called.

Then Tom put the bridle back on and told Grace to put her foot in the stirrup. Pilgrim stood still as a house. Tom took her weight on his shoulder and she swung her leg and sat in the saddle.

She felt no fear. She walked him first one way around the arena then the other. Then she took him up to a lope and it was fine and collected and smooth as silk.

It was a while before she realized everyone was cheering, just like they had the day she rode Gonzo.

But this was Pilgrim. Her Pilgrim. He'd come through. And she could feel him beneath her, like he always used to be, giving and trusting and true.

Candida Baker

The Cut

It did not immediately occur to Helena that when her husband, her almost ex-husband she should say, called her a ballbreaker, during the last and final row before he flung out of the house forever, that there was some basis in fact for what she felt was the unfairest thing anybody had ever said to her.

It wasn't until a few months later when she was spring cleaning the house – dabbling in a futile fashion around the edges of her old life, trying to bleach Spencer into oblivion – that she found a note. 'Hi,' it said, 'how are you? Kath and I have settled into country life very easily, and I have to say that being a country vet is much more pleasurable than treating rich men's racehorses. Come and visit sometime, love Tom.'

This note from a lover she hadn't seen for almost twenty years caused Helena such a surge of distress that she put it in the back pocket of her jeans and forgot it in a flurry of cleaning fluid.

It wasn't until much later, when she had settled all the horses and made herself dinner, that she pulled the note out again and studied it. It seemed particularly poignant in her current circumstances. Firstly, it reminded her that she could easily have married Tom, and not Spencer – in which case she could still be living a life of gumbooted bliss – and it also reminded her that someone close to her had called her a ball-breaker before.

She'd met Tom when she was working at the city showground for one of the livery stables where he was the resident vet, so he knew from the start about the problems she was having with one of the horses she looked after – King, a chestnut Arab stallion who was so vicious that she had to enter his box armed with a pitchfork.

The thing about her relationship with Tom was that she liked fucking him. It didn't occur to her at any point that he had fallen in love with her. She thought they were simply having a good time.

'So,' said Tom, as she stood in the stable, the horse quivering up against the wall, red drops plopping onto the straw below. 'That's that then.' And he passed them to her delicately: two marbled round soft pieces of flesh. 'What a ballbreaker you are my dear, and I mean that most literally.'

She stood there, the balls in her hands, cradling them gently, not wanting to press into their flesh, not wanting to feel the warmth still contained in them – their almost life. 'I'm sorry.'

'Oh,' he said, 'That's okay. I'll get over you. I just wish I hadn't agreed to castrate this poor bugger for nothing. I could at least have charged like a wounded bull, if you'll excuse the metaphor.'

And he did get over her. He had his contented country life shoving his hands inside animals of all kinds, and she, always happy to move on, forgot him, or almost. The livery stable owner, who had given her King on the quiet because the owner had never paid his bills, had been the one to suggest castration. 'Cut his balls off,' he said, 'and send him to the bush, he'll be a different horse. Just don't tell me about it.'

∩ ∩ ∩

When Helena was fourteen, she had an Anglo-Arab colt, Lawrence. (The name was her father's idea of a joke.) For some reason when Lawrence, or Larry, as he became known, was castrated she and her mother were there. It had been snowing for days, the snow was thick and heavy in the field. Helena was excited, it was an adventure — at least to begin with. Except of course, she had never seen anything like it, had not in her wildest nightmares thought that such things happened — the twitch on the nose, the forcing of the white-eyed trembling, sweating horse against the wall, the curved knife, and the blood on the snow, the purest red against the purest white.

∩ ∩ ∩

In just a few days King had recovered enough from his ordeal to be trucked out late one night to a property in the country where he became so quiet that he could be ridden with only a halter, and the kids could play underneath his stomach without him moving a muscle. In the years to come as Helena and her husband gradually built up their own stud farm with all its accompanying vicissitudes, Helena would sometimes think of King. She would remember how before his gelding he would charge at her, teeth bared, rearing above her – how someone would have to hold his head while she mounted and dismounted because he would swing and lunge at her. He would take the slightest opportunity for attack. Yet somehow she felt sorry for him – he touched her. He touched her because his owners never came near him, because he was beautiful and proud and angry. She had been right to geld him, no doubt about it, but inside her there was a sadness that after his castration he had been tamed and broken. That *she* had tamed and broken him.

When Helena was feeling at all logical, which was not often these days, she supposed that Spencer had some right to at least a few of the horses that lived on the property. After all, they had bred them together. But only the day after he'd left, he had come back with a float, to collect his share, he said. And she, well, she had seen red. Seen him off the place, called the police, told them he was intimidating her. 'I'll see you in court,' she said, 'I'll let the judge decide what's fair.' The police had arrived, told him to move on, had backed her up.

That night Spencer had rung her, pleaded with her. 'At least let me get Quintar,' he said. 'He's my horse, Helena, not yours.' Which was true, she didn't even like the horse much, despite the fact that he was their most productive stallion. He wasn't kind to his mares. It was like an organised rape, to her mind, every time they let him loose on a brood mare. He had as much foreplay as a forklift truck as he bore down on his victim, his teeth biting into their necks so hard he always drew blood. So she relented, and the next day Spencer came back with the float, loaded the stallion and left.

Not quite left. Not quite as simple and clean as that. In fact, she followed him around while he collected stuff – a few forgotten shirts, Quintar's tack.

'I only want to know *why*,' she said, not for the first time. 'I mean, being left for another woman is bad enough . . . why can't you tell me? At least give me *something* after all these years.'

And him, turning to her, a look of hate in his eyes. 'Christ, Helena can't you hear yourself . . . have you any idea what it's like to spend your life with someone who believes there is only one way to live a life, and that's her way? Is that the kind of thing you want me to tell you?

I'm not sure you've ever once thought about me, what I might want, what I might be like – who I even *am* . . .'

'But you never *said*.'

'You never listened.'

And that was it, he was off.

The whole episode shook her. The idea that two people who had once loved each other enough to leave their jobs in the city to breed horses, could now hate each other so strongly that they were equally prepared to pull the business apart, felt like an even worse betrayal than the actual infidelity – the unbelievable but undeniable truth that her husband had left her, not for another woman, nothing that simple, but for a man. For, to be precise, the town's gay vet. And she had thought they were, to coin a phrase, just good friends! More than that, she had been pleased for him that suddenly there was a man in town who was not just into football and beer, who seemed to genuinely love horses and the country. It had even – and this, if she was really honest, was what rankled most – occurred to her how attractive Chris was, and when she was with him she had enjoyed being mildly flirtatious.

Worse than anything was this: all the women in

town had fancied him. He was exotic, a Greek Australian, dark and tall. He played opera at full blast. In a small country town he stood out a mile. At first the men mistrusted him, but when they saw how good he was at his job they forgave him his good looks, the fact that all their wives went weak at the knees at the mere mention of his name. They decided he was a good bloke after all. In these dark days Helena can sense no sympathy in the town towards her. Everybody hates her. It is her husband, after all who has destroyed the women's daydreams, her husband who has somehow made a fool of the men. She has not only been left. She has been outcast. She had thought that at least she had organised her life to the point where she would never be an outcast again.

When the whole sordid thing came out in the open, Helena rang her best friend. 'What is it they say?' said Mary. 'Beware of Greeks bearing gifts?' So now, with Tom's note in her hand, it was to Mary that she turned. Saying to her friend, 'I could have had another life . . . I don't know. It must have been my fault, somehow. How on earth can a man leave his wife for a *man*?'

∩ ∩ ∩

When her parents divorced, and Helena and her mother moved into a small one-bedroomed flat, Lawrence was sold. She had pleaded and pleaded but it was no good. Apparently this was going to be her new life, and she would enjoy it once she'd got used to it: living in Oxford, being able to visit friends when she liked. Lawrence was taken to the market, and Helena extracted a promise from her mother that they would know who he would be sold to — that she would able to keep in touch, find out how he was. But somehow it went wrong. Or did it? Her mother always swore that it had been a series of accidents: the farmer that had bought Lawrence while she was having lunch, the lack of paperwork . . . she was sorry, darling, she really was. She mustn't dwell on it, there's a good girl.

Helena, despite her love for her mother, had her doubts. She was very careful from then on to track her loved ones.

∩ ∩ ∩

Helena had meant to get up early, to be back at the stud at first light, but despite, or perhaps because of, her emotional see-saw, Mary had managed to persuade her to spend the night in town, and had then coaxed her to consume such large amounts of alcohol that it was now necessary to employ minimal movement with every part of her body. She required extensive water treatment, externally and internally, followed by tea, followed by food, followed by coffee. So it wasn't until midday that she made the final turn through the white gates, up the driveway.

Oh, she could sense it in the air that something was wrong, the moment she got there, the moment she stepped out of the car. Nothing she could put her finger on. The horses were quiet, the sun was shining, the house looked exactly the same and yet there was a feeling of weight in her chest – a distress she tried to put down to the combination of events. It wasn't until she was making herself a coffee and staring out of the kitchen window while she waited for the kettle to boil, that she realised she knew exactly what was wrong, or more accurately, missing.

It was her broodmare, April, so called because her temperament was every bit as changeable as that month's weather. A real Arab, she could shy violently at a piece of paper, and let a semi-trailer go past without turning a hair. Helena's pride and joy, and she was definitely, quite definitely, not there.

Helena rushed out of the house, her eyes scanning the paddocks, the hangover still throbbing at her temples, the question hanging in the air: Who on earth would want to steal only one horse – her horse? The answer so painfully obvious that she could hardly move with the distress of it, until she heard the phone ringing, and rushed inside, expecting what? Spencer, of course, that it would be Spencer with a reasonable explanation.

But it was Davy, from down the road.

'Helen?' He always called her Helen, couldn't handle Helena. 'Helen? Look, well, I was wondering . . . you know, I couldn't help hearing, seeing . . .'

And Helena almost dying on the spot.

'Dave?'

'Yes . . . well, what I'm trying to say is . . .'

'Look, I've got a bit of an emergency, Dave . . .'

'Yeah, well, I thought you'd like to know. Thought it was strange that's all . . . anyway . . .'

She stopped suddenly in her tracks.

'Thought what was strange, Dave?'

'That's what I'm trying to tell you, see, this van from the knackers going up to your place . . . well, nowhere else it can go up there is there? You're the end of the road. Seen you drive out yesterday, so I knew you wasn't there . . . Thought it was strange.

You would have said if you was putting a horse down, not like you I thought to send a horse to the knackers . . .'

And Helena realising the full import, put down the phone, and picked it up again to call the police, and Dave was still there!

'So that's why I thought I'd better ring you see . . .'

In her mind Helena had always referred to the knack-ery as that *terrible* place out of town, terrible because in Helena's judgment it misadvertised itself. Nowhere did it actually say, 'You send us horses and we turn them into dog food.' Quite the reverse. Instead, the owners had built a false paradise of huge paddocks, dams and trees, and in amongst the verdant surrounds were the horses. Horses of all colours, ages and sizes and kinds. Not just the vicious and the broken down but racehorses who couldn't quite cut it, ponies who had outlived their usefulness, long time pets, dis-carded, injured and forgotten. Helena, every time she drove past, wished she had enough money to save every single one of them. This time, as she turned into the sweeping drive, with the elliptical sign which sug-gested there were horses and dog food for sale with no hint that there was a connection between the two, Helena was filled with anger and fear. What if she was too late? What if April had already been slaughtered, and was lying butchered on the floor?

∩ ∩ ∩

Lying at night in her bed. Always awake. The picture of Lawrence on her wall. Where had he gone? Did he think of her? Her mother, loving and remote. 'Go to sleep poppet, see you in the morning.' Sometimes the loss of her horse, her father and her home felt so great it seemed to her that someone had taken a cleaver and cut her vertically downwards, straight through the middle. The lies her mother told her. That they would be living in Oxford, only for Helena to find that within weeks they had moved to the other side of the world. If her father ever wanted to, how would he find her, here in Australia? Another loved one gone.

∩ ∩ ∩

At first the manager tried to bluster his way through. Shrugged. 'I don't know what you're talking about lady . . .'

'Don't give me that bullshit. You came onto my property this morning and you stole my horse, that's what I'm talking about. And I want her back. Now.'

But the manager had no intention of giving her back. He wasn't a fool, he knew he'd ended up with a prize-winning broodmare on his hands. He'd been well paid to turn her into dog food, but he wouldn't do that, he'd got his principles after all. No, he was going to keep her and truck her off to the country to a friend's place, no questions asked, and sell her in a while for some good money. But the woman in front of him kept up the tirade.

'Before I came I called the police,' she told him, 'and they're on their way. I have an AV order out against my husband and I know that this was his doing – if you just give me back my mare, we'll say no more about it, and I won't press charges. If you don't I'll make sure your life is ruined.'

He looked at her with distaste. He couldn't bear women like her. Women with an education and money and the apparent belief that they were as good as men. He'd like to show her a thing or two, like he'd shown some other sheilas, but even the suspicion that the cops were on their way – although he thought it was unlikely – gave him pause for thought. After all, this wouldn't be the first time.

He sighed, admitted defeat. 'She's over there.'

He led her behind the slaughter house to a row of stables. Helena, seeing April's pretty head over the door, wanted to cry, but she held her ground.

'Get her loaded on my float, you bastard,' she said, 'and if you ever come near me or my property again, I'll shoot you, and I'll say it was in self-defence.'

The manager threw up his hands. 'Steady on!'

As Helena drove away, he muttered under his breath. 'Fucking ballbreaking cunt. No wonder he went fucking homo.'

That night when Helena fell into an uneasy sleep, she dreamt of a golden foal.

The honey and cream palomino — how it shone in the sunlight — was held by a woman, whom she could see was herself. She reached out a hand to touch the foal's velvety nose and saw it was lame, that its near back leg was swollen and sore. She saw its eyes were crusty, and its coat dull. Its eyes were sad, too, as if it had undergone some terrible hardship. As Helena swept her gaze over it, checking its withers, its rump, she spotted the blood dripping from its testicles, iron-red drops on the dust beneath, which as she watched became a steady stream, and then a torrent.

'Is there anything we can do?' she asked her other self.

'No,' the other answered. '*The cutting has happened, there is nothing we can do.*'

In the morning Helena woke clear-headed and certain. Now she knew what she had to do. She must wait until Sunday, when Spencer and Chris would be at the polo match, the matches they all used to go to together.

And she would wait, and she did wait.

When the time came, she gathered up her equipment, her stockman's knife, her twitch, her anaesthetic spray, her sterilising solution, and before she left the house to drive to Chris's property, she took the photograph of Quintar which was still hanging near the front door, the one of him with the ribbons he won for best stallion in his led class and overall champion for the district show, and she took it with her, to leave for Spencer as a reminder to him of what he, Spencer, once was, and of what Quintar once was, and she drove off to do her job.

Elyne Mitchell

Silver Brumby, Silver Dingo

Far up on a high dome of the range, silhouetted against the sky, was a herd of horses – a herd of mixed colours, including piebalds and skewbalds – and, out in front of them standing on a big rock, was a tall roan stallion.

Tiarri and Neera were curious. Although they appeared to be grazing aimlessly, they kept moving steadily closer to the herd. Bomber dived down through the air, flattened out, and landed close to the two young ones. He looked at the distant herd once, then stretched out his wings and began gently urging Tiarri and Neera to turn back and head the way they had come. Tiarri knew that Bomber could see the danger ahead. That stallion was a very big horse. What if he were unfriendly? Might he harm Neera?

Neera did not really want to turn back but Bomber kept pushing him with one wing, so back they went towards the head of the valley that Tiarri had begun to think of as his mother's. Suddenly Tiarri saw a creamy mare on a grassy rise in the far distance, and beside her was a glittering aura of sunlight. The aura seemed to be weaving into the shape and form of a horse. He thought that the mare was his mother and that she was calling him, yet no sound came; and what was that strange glow beside her?

He felt curiously impelled to gallop towards her, obeying that soundless call, but he had not gone very far when he remembered Neera and Neera's short legs, so he stopped and looked back at the pup who was desperately trying to go fast, but was quite unable to catch up. Tiarri hurried back to him. When he reached the little dog Neera gave a funny, exhausted sob and dropped to the ground, his flanks heaving as he gasped for breath. Tiarri rubbed his face on the breathless pup, then filled his mouth with cool water from a nearby soak and gently dribbled it over Neera's face and on to his tongue. He watched anxiously as Neera began to get his breath back.

The sound of drumming hooves came on the air. Tiarri looked quickly in the direction of the sound and was greeted by the sight of a fan-shaped mass of galloping horses being led by the roan stallion. And there, flying low and flying straight for the mob leader, was Bomber.

The roan stallion and his herd kept thundering on, hooves cutting into the grass and clods of earth raining out behind them. Bomber began rushing straight at them, his wings flapping at their faces. He rose upwards again, stalled and turned in the air, then folded his wings and dived at thrilling speed straight back at them, uttering an angry scream as he flew.

Neera, his breath now coming more evenly, struggled to his feet as Tiarri stepped over him and stood four square above him – a half-grown silver horse with a thundering heart standing over his fellow survivor of the killer storm, ready to fight. Neera began to growl. His hackles stood up and he, too, was ready to fight with Tiarri. In the next instant Tiarri and Neera heard another stallion's trumpeting behind them, and there was a different sound of galloping hooves . . . then no sound at all. Sometimes the thudding, sometimes an eerie silence. Tiarri quickly looked around him, but could see nothing except a weird and beautiful corkscrew of light.

The roan's herd was still coming at them despite Bomber's efforts to stop them. Bomber became desperate and started flailing the air with his massive wings. Some of his creamy breast feathers floated down, one of them drifting towards the colt and the pup like a message. The roan faltered, half blinded by the beating eagle wings, and his herd, slipping and slithering, crowded up behind him. Then the stallion, as though possessed, ducked under Bomber's dark wings and charged at Tiarri, charged as if he were mad to destroy. To the stallion, Tiarri and the white dingo pup exuded a supremacy and a mystery that overwhelmed him. Tiarri, blazing with courage, stood firm above the bristling little dog. He threw up his head and gave a defiant neigh.

Suddenly his neigh was echoed from behind, and there was an accompaniment of pounding hooves and the sound of Bomber's beating wings. The pounding of the hooves shook the ground; eagle wings churned the air into a maelstrom. Bomber rose straight upwards, where he hung on the currents of air, watching.

The roan thundered up to Tiarri, but Tiarri could not spring to meet him because Neera was beneath him. All the young colt could do was brace himself, rear up and smash his immature hooves at the stallion's head. He felt his hooves strike the bone of the roan's face before he himself was knocked off balance. Luckily, the roan's large hooves did not connect with Neera. As the big animal sprang again at Tiarri, his teeth bared, the pup leapt and fastened his jaw on the roan's hind leg. The big stallion shook him off like a fly, and Neera went hurtling through the air.

Before any of the struggling animals could clearly see what it was, something that could have been a silver stallion, or a swirling mist, or a tempestuous whirlwind, was suddenly there in its shimmering glory to meet the roan in battle.

Tiarri, his balance restored, leapt to protect Neera, who lay winded. The roan, momentarily frozen, stood staring at he knew not what – a ghost, or a flash of light, or a flesh and blood horse – then he wheeled around and fled for his life. His herd of mares stood as though struck by lightning, with eyes only for the silver wraith who was galloping after their leader.

Bomber rose in circles on a thermal. Tiarri rubbed his nose softly over Neera's body, trying to get the breath back into him. Even with his anxiety for Neera, he kept looking into the distance where the roan stallion was only just managing to keep ahead of his pursuer, who was nipping him on the rump and driving him as fast as he could possibly go.

The abandoned and confused herd slowly followed the path of their fleeing master. A small willy willy carrying snow grass and daisy leaves spiralled and danced up the ridge behind them. Tiarri saw the roan stallion fade into the distance, the mysterious apparition still shining and gleaming in pursuit. He saw the willy willy catch up with them, and then the silver stallion vanished and became part of the twisting wind, dissolving into the brilliant light.

Neera got unsteadily to his feet, and he and Tiarri stared into the distance where a mystery had been but where now, above the willy willy, a white hawk hovered.

Exhausted, Bomber rested on the air currents above his two young charges. Not far away, he saw a real and quite substantial creamy mare take one look towards them before trotting quietly into the trees to become enfolded by the snow gums.

Bomber looked out towards the high-piled rocks of Dicky Cooper's Bogong — his beloved landscape. He had seen the whirlwind of light and half understood the mystery of it. When he had been little more than a fledgling, the legend of the silver brumby had long haunted the mountains of the Ramshead Range, far to the south, and all this country that was now spread below his wings had been woven into the tale. Part of the story told of a great journey northward that the silver brumby had made to meet the daughter of Warrung, the sun, and of the Moon Filly. Together these two had created their own foal, the Son of the Whirlwind.

Legends, legends: legends of the high mountains, of the wild storms, of the wind and the snow, of horses created when God took a handful of the blizzard wind and blew on it.

Bomber felt the currents of air through his feathers. He could still see in his mind the vision of Tiarri standing over Neera, ready to protect the pup with his life against the roan stallion's killing lust. Bomber remembered the time that seemed so long ago when he had dived on the pup, meaning to kill him and carry him away and Tiarri had fought him off. The two visions merged as he watched the two unlikely mates who had been bonded together by the killer storm.

He watched them walking quietly along their snow daisy highway. They were weary also. Bomber knew he would have to protect both Tiarri and Neera until they were fully grown. He, too, was part of that unfailing devotion, the seeds of which had been sown by the storm.

Bomber wondered what terror, what heartbreak, were hidden in the rolling seasons that were to come, or lay hidden beneath the granite rocks and in the blizzard wind. But for now the silver ones were his and he circled quietly down, letting his wings stir the air above them. Another breast feather dropped down to the ground beside them. Neera picked it up in his mouth, then it stuck to his whiskers where it stayed all the way to their camping place.

Bomber went off to catch something for Neera's evening meal. He returned with a small feral pig and put it down beside the pup, who was hunting for rats

in among the horizontal branchlets of a yellow kun-
zea. It was a ritual now for Neera to tear Bomber's
offering apart and put half in front of the old eagle,
sharing his gift of life. The eagle and the pup ate side
by side while the silver colt grazed next to them.

As the sun set, the long fingers of light continued
to weave the mystery that would bind them. As the
last of the sun's rays touched the sky, leaving the
mountains in twilight, a white hawk hovering in the
sky became bathed in the red-gold light of love.
Darkness descended.

As her son slept with his legs around the young
dingo, a pale mare crept up from the valley to gaze
and wonder. From two high peaks there rang out two
wild neighs. They were calling, calling, but of what
they called or to whom their voices bore a message no
one could know. No one that is except, perhaps, a very
old eagle, a lord of the skies who could understand
this communication to the skies and the winds and
the mountain peaks of wild high, deep, all-enduring
love. 'For God took a handful of blizzard snow, blew
on it and created the horse.'

The Book of Job

Hast thou given the horse strength?

Hast thou given the horse strength? hast thou
 clothed his neck with thunder?
Canst thou make him afraid as a grasshopper? the
 glory of his nostrils *is* terrible.
He paweth in the valley, and rejoiceth in *his* strength:
 he goeth on to meet the armed men.
He mocketh at fear, and is not affrighted; neither
 turneth he back from the sword.
The quiver rattleth against him, the glittering spear
 and the shield.
He swalloweth the ground with fierceness and rage:
 neither believeth he that *it is* the sound of the
 trumpet.

He saith among the trumpets, Ha, ha; and he
smelleth the battle afar off, the thunder of the
captains, and the shouting.

Peter Shaffer

Equus

20

[ALAN *moves upstage, and mimes opening the door.*
Soft light on the circle.
Humming from the CHORUS: *the Equus noise.*
The horse actors enter, raise high their masks, and put them
on all together. They stand around the circle – NUGGET *in*
the mouth of the tunnel.]

DYSART: Quietly as possible. Dalton may still be
awake. Sssh . . . Quietly . . . Good. Now go in.

[ALAN *steps secretly out of the square through the central*
opening on to the circle, now glowing with a warm light. He
looks about him. The horses stamp uneasily; their masks turn

towards him.]

You are on the inside now. All the horses are staring at you. Can you see them?

ALAN [*excited*]: Yes!

DYSART: Which one are you going to take?

ALAN: Nugget.

[ALAN *reaches up and mimes leading* NUGGET *carefully
round the circle downstage with a rope, past all the horses on
the right.*]

DYSART: What colour is Nugget?

ALAN: Chestnut.

[*The horse picks his way with care.* ALAN *halts him at the
corner of the square.*]

DYSART: What do you do, first thing?

ALAN: Put on his sandals.

DYSART: Sandals?

[*He kneels, downstage centre.*]

ALAN: Sandals of majesty! . . . Made of sack.

[*He picks up the invisible sandals, and kisses them devoutly.*]

Tie them round his hooves.

[*He taps* NUGGET's *right leg; the horse raises it and the boy
mimes tying the sack round it.*]

DYSART: All four hooves?

ALAN: Yes.

DYSART: Then?

ALAN: Chinkle-chankle.

[*He mimes picking up the bridle and bit.*]

He doesn't like it so late, but he takes it for my sake.

He bends for me. He stretches forth his neck to it.

[NUGGET *bends his head down.* ALAN *first ritually puts the bit into his own mouth, then crosses, and transfers it into* NUGGET's. *He reaches up and buckles on the bridle. Then he leads him by the invisible reins, across the front of the stage and up round the left side of the circle.* NUGGET *follows obediently.*]

ALAN: Buckle and lead out.

DYSART: No saddle?

ALAN: Never.

DYSART: Go on.

ALAN: Walk down the path behind. He's quiet. Always is, this bit. Meek and mild legs. At least till the field. Then there's trouble.

[*The horse jerks back. The mask tosses.*]

DYSART: What kind?

ALAN: Won't go in.

DYSART: Why not?

ALAN: It's his place of Ha Ha.

DYSART: What?

ALAN: Ha Ha.

DYSART: Make him go into it.

ALAN: [*whispering fiercely*]: Come on! . . . Come on! . . .

> [*He drags the horse into the square as* DYSART *steps out of it.*]

21

> [NUGGET *comes to a halt staring diagonally down what is now the field. The Equus noise dies away. The boy looks about him.*]

DYSART [*from the circle*]: Is it a big field?

ALAN: Huge!

DYSART: What's it like?

ALAN: Full of mist. Nettles on your feet.

> [*He mimes taking off his shoes — and the sting.*]
Ah!

DYSART [*going back to his bench*]: You take your shoes off?

ALAN: Everything.

DYSART: All your clothes?

ALAN: Yes.

> [*He mimes undressing completely in front of the horse. When he is finished, and obviously quite naked, he throws out his arms and shows himself fully to his God, bowing his head before* NUGGET.]

DYSART: Where do you leave them?

ALAN: Tree hole near the gate. No one could find them.

[*He walks upstage and crouches by the bench, stuffing the invisible clothes beneath it. DYSART sits again on the left bench, downstage beyond the circle.*]

DYSART: How does it feel now?

ALAN [*holds himself*]: Burns.

DYSART: Burns?

ALAN: The mist!

DYSART: Go on. Now what?

ALAN: The Manbit.

[*He reaches again under the bench and draws out an invisible stick.*]

DYSART: Manbit?

ALAN: The stick for my mouth.

DYSART: Your mouth?

ALAN: To bite on.

DYSART: Why? What for?

ALAN: So's it won't happen too quick.

DYSART: Is it always the same stick?

ALAN: Course. Sacred stick. Keep it in the hole. The Ark of the Manbit.

DYSART: And now what? . . . What do you do now?

[*Pause. He rises and approaches* NUGGET.]

ALAN: Touch him!

DYSART: Where?

ALAN [*in wonder*]: All over. Everywhere. Belly. Ribs. His ribs are of ivory. Of great value! ... His flank is cool. His nostrils open for me. His eyes shine. They can see in the dark ... *Eyes!* —

[*Suddenly he dashes in distress to the farthest corner of the square.*]

DYSART: *Go on!* ... Then?

[*Pause.*]

ALAN: Give sugar.

DYSART: A lump of sugar?

[ALAN *returns to* NUGGET.]

ALAN: His Last Supper.

DYSART: Last before what?

ALAN: Ha Ha.

[*He kneels before the horse, palms upward and joined together.*]

DYSART: Do you say anything when you give it to him?

ALAN [*offering it*]: Take my sins. Eat them for my sake ... He always does.

[NUGGET *bows the mask into* ALAN's *palm, then takes a step back to eat.*]

And then he's ready.

DYSART: You can get up on him now?

ALAN: Yes!

DYSART: Do it, then. Mount him.

[ALAN, *lying before* NUGGET, *stretches out on the square. He grasps the top of the thin metal pole embedded in the wood. He whispers his God's name ceremonially.*]

ALAN: Equus! . . . Equus! . . . Equus!

[*He pulls the pole upright. The actor playing* NUGGET *leans forward and grabs it. At the same instant all the other horses lean forward around the circle, each placing a gloved hand on the rail.* ALAN *rises and walks right back to the upstage corner, left.*]

Take me!

[*He runs and jumps high on to* NUGGET's *back.*]

[*Crying out.*] *Ah!*

DYSART: What is it?

ALAN: Hurts!

DYSART: Hurts?

ALAN: Knives in his skin! Little knives — all inside my legs.

[NUGGET *mimes restiveness.*]

ALAN: Stay, Equus. No one said Go! . . . That's it. He's good. Equus the Godslave, Faithful and True. Into my hands he commends himself — naked in his chinkle-chankle. [*He punches* NUGGET.] Stop it! . . . He wants to go so badly.

DYSART: Go, then. Leave me behind. Ride away now, Alan. Now! . . . Now you are alone with Equus.

[ALAN *stiffens his body.*]

ALAN [*ritually*]: Equus — son of Fleckwus — son of Neckwus — *Walk.*

[*A hum from the* CHORUS.

Very slowly the horses standing on the circle begin to turn the square by gently pushing the wooden rail. ALAN *and his mount start to revolve. The effect, immediately, is of a statue being slowly turned round on a plinth. During the ride however the speed increases, and the light decreases until it is only a fierce spotlight on horse and rider, with the overspill glinting on the other masks leaning in towards them.*]

Here we go. The King rides out on Equus, mightiest of horses. Only I can ride him. He lets me turn him this way and that. His neck comes out of my body. It lifts in the dark. Equus, my Godslave! . . . Now the King commands you. Tonight, we ride against them all.

DYSART: Who's all?

ALAN: My foes and His.

DYSART: Who are your foes?

ALAN: The Hosts of Hoover. The Hosts of Philco.
The Hosts of Pifco. The House of Remington and
all its tribe!

DYSART: Who are His foes?

ALAN: The Hosts of Jodhpur. The Hosts of Bowler
and Gymkhana. All those who show him off for
their vanity. Tie rosettes on his head for their vanity! Come on, Equus. Let's get them! . . . *Trot!*

[*The speed of the turning square increases.*]

Stead-y! Stead-y! Stead-y! Stead-y! Cowboys are watching! Take off their stetsons. They know who we are.
They're admiring us! Bowing low unto us! Come on
now – show them! *Canter!* . . . CANTER!

[*He whips* NUGGET.]

And Equus the Mighty rose against All!

His enemies scatter, his enemies fall!

TURN!

Trample them, trample them,

Trample them, trample them,

TURN!

TURN!!

TURN!!!

[*The Equus noise increases in volume.*]

[*Shouting.*] WEE!... WAA!... WONDERFUL!...

I'm stiff! Stiff in the wind!

My mane, stiff in the wind!

My flanks! *My* hooves!

Mane on my legs, on my flanks, like whips!

Raw!

Raw!

I'm raw! Raw!

Feel me on you! *On* you! *On* you! *On* you!

I want to be *in* you!

I want to BE you forever and ever! -

Equus, I love you!

Now! -

Bear me away!

Make us One Person!

  [*He rides* EQUUS *frantically.*]

One Person! One Person! One Person! One Person!

  [*He rises up on the horse's back, and calls like a trumpet.*]

Ha-HA!... Ha-HA!... Ha-HA!

  [*The trumpet turns to great cries.*]

HA-HA! HA-HA! HA-HA! HA-HA! HA!...

HA!... HAAAAA!

  [*He twists like a flame.*
  Silence.

The turning square comes to a stop in the same position it occupied at the opening of the Act.
Slowly the boy drops off the horse's back on to the ground.
He lowers his head and kisses NUGGET*'s hoof.*
Finally he flings back his head and cries up to him.]
AMEN!
[NUGGET *snorts, once.*]

BLACKOUT

R. Wilkes Hunter

The Breaking

On the ridge-side beneath the shadow of the iron-barks there was a movement, sound: the sharp 'Clop' of an unshod hoof striking upon the beaten track, and the occasional clatter of a dislodged stone.

Presently a horse emerged from the timber and stood upon the edge of a spur, where it shelved down precipitately to the river's edge, gazing back in the direction from whence he had come.

He was not a pretty horse. His head, for instance, was hammerlike and vicious, his neck, too thin for a domestic stallion, was almost scrawny.

In colour he was a greyish roan, an unattractive

colour, like sunburnt granite. His long mane and tail were thickly matted with lagourra burrs and studded with many a thorn of the lawyer vine and wait-a-while.

He appeared to have travelled hard, for he was lean and gaunt, and foam dried white upon his flanks and behind the rippling muscles of his shoulders. His whole appearance was both cruel and repellent – yet withal he was strangely beautiful standing thus. Or perhaps this fleeting beauty was merely an illusion, lent by the gleam of his dark eyes, as he gazed back at ridge and scrub that he did not see – for he looked farther than these. Back through the days of hard travel, of pursuit and escape and haunting fear; back in the lonely ranges, high up where the Timbarra River winds along through granite ridges, behind the Solferino and Canghi goldfields, to the range which to him was home. There where a solitary mountain peak seemed to watch benignly over the bushland below.

It was there, three days ago, that he had lost the last of his mob; had lost the long-legged colt whose blooded dam he had seduced away from some lone cattle station. He had stayed with them till the last; sometimes impatiently leading them through fern-clad gullies where the light of day seldom penetrated;

sometimes driving them before him up slopes before which they hesitated, appalled and weary. Then their flagging strength had brought them within reach of the strange and terrible death, the unseen death, which the man-creatures inflicted from a distance. So they had died; and Tiarra had stood over them, and even nudged them gently, lying there so still, until the blood-smell and the knowledge of death had swept him through the gamut of the emotions, from red rage to an overwhelming panic of fear, and he had fled, blindly, the burn of a rifle bullet along his ribs spurring him on to a greater effort.

Now, in spite of the certain knowledge of death, he could not believe they would not be there, grazing quietly in some hidden gully, awaiting his return. So, later, when his fear had abated somewhat, he had sought to return. Yet for the last twenty-four hours, double and twist as he might, he had found that impossible — for between them always was the most implacable foe in all creation . . . man!

It seemed that he had always hated man, had feared him, too, terribly, ever since the day, four years ago, when his brumby mother had brought him down from the deeper recesses of the scrub, seeking sustenance.

That had been during the severe 'dry-time,' and it was then that the scattered remnant of the Timbarra tribe had given him the name – Tiarra, son of the wind. Not one of the old men of the tribe could recall a drought as severe as that one. Living had been at best a precarious business, even for humans; and Tiarra's mother, weakened by her privations and the hungry life of her long-legged colt, had fallen an easy victim to their spears. But Tiarra, by his fleetness of foot, had eluded them, for he was as agile as a deer, and could leap sure-footedly over obstacles that would have taxed the powers of a mountain goat. So, frightened and wondering, he had fled, with her dying screams and the warm blood-smell to act as goad.

Then had come the rain.

But in the lean, fleet-footed colt fear had been born – and hatred.

Later, passion had come to him...lust...the strong urge that had made him outlaw – a brumby stallion...

Many lonely prospectors had wakened in the night to the thunder of his hoofs, and, finding themselves stranded and on foot, had hurled curses after him – and hot lead.

More than one boundary rider, too, at the lonely outstations, had sought vainly for the mare which he had left picketed the night before, and had cursed at the sight of his tracks.

Now he was alone.

Tiarra raised his head higher and sent his shrill call rocketing back up the spur. The trees and ridges caught the sound, tossing it backwards and forwards and from side to side, far up the river, until it seemed that a phantom army of horses was there, watching him.

As the echoes died he was still, listening, waiting for the response that never came. He whinnied again, lowly, with a whimpering sound like a frightened child, and presently he picked his way wearily down to the river.

It would be pleasant to stay here in this quiet valley, to camp in the cool shade of the brush; but he was still uneasy, continually turning his head and seeking for the scent which he hated, and of which this strange dread was born, which drove him onward.

At the river he drank thirstily, wading in belly-deep and abandoning himself to its cool caress. Diamond drops gleamed upon his soft muzzle, and he flirted them off impatiently.

Again he stood at gaze, head high flung, testing the wind. All was peaceful, still; only the familiar scent of the Bush, of gum and eucalypts, greeted him with aromatic friendliness.

He crossed the river slowly, his sensitive nostrils blowing suspiciously at its surface before each step, for the sandy river bottom was strange to him, and bred distrust.

Beyond the river a patch of sweet Bush grasses lured him aside. He tarried awhile, his strong white teeth tearing the top from a clump of grass here, another there. Presently he worked his way out on to a ridge-top. To the north, range on range of scrub-clad ridges rose in tiers to the distant bulk of the McPherson Ranges and the clear-cut silhouette of Mount Lindsay. A country of deep gullies and impenetrable scrub – and freedom.

He faced about.

Southward the immediate ridges rose higher than the one on which he stood, shutting him in closely.

Tiarra stood very still, his eyes remotely dreaming. Suddenly a wave of burning nostalgia swept over him, enveloping his senses, blinding him to reason – and to fear. Abruptly he moved off down the ridge, breaking

into a loping trot, that changed presently to a swinging gallop . . . heading south.

Ridge and gully and fragrant bushland passed
beneath the steady beat of hoofs. Now, eastward, the
ground sloped away to lush grasslands where red and
white cattle grazed, enclosed by mile on mile of
barbed-wire fence. Presently he stopped. Here the
fence approached closer to the river, leaving only a
scant half-mile of bushland between. He could see
the cattle more plainly now; could hear the low moan-
ing bellow of the big red bull, grim and menacing like
distant thunder, as, scenting the brumby, he offered
battle. He could see the lowered head and the slow
scrape of the forefoot that cast spurts of red dust
high behind the broad shoulders. Presently the bull
knelt, and fell to horning the ground in sudden rage.

But it was not this which brought the light of stark
fear to Tiarra's eyes; cattle he disdained. It was the
man-scent, coming downwind and growing momentarily stronger!

Even as he stood in indecision a rider appeared
high on the crest of the ridge before him, and his
view-hulloa rose high and clear as he urged his horse
forward down the slope.

Tiarra flattened his ears and thrust his head forward, until from his withers to his snapping teeth was one cruel straight line, and took a few tentative steps forward. He saw the rider fling up his arms, heard his ringing shout, and from the shelter of the scrub farther to the left came a faint, whip-like report, and sand and grit spouted up in a dusty fountain beside him. Tiarra's ears pricked and he snorted in sudden terror, bounding sideways from the stinging particles. Again came the faint report, this time from a still different position, and an unseen something hummed past overhead.

Panic gripped Tiarra, an all-powerful animal panic caused him to swerve and run, blindly, anywhere, to be away from these terrifying creatures and the terrible, unseen death.

The fence loomed up before him, and he reared, pivoting to the right and stretched low in a dead run along the cleared patch of ground beside it.

The man-scent was stronger now; it was all about him. To the rear the shouting lessened and faded, and then before him a stockwhip cracked in a ripple of vicious sound.

Tiarra slid to a standstill, wild-eyed and heaving.

Sight of the sleek gelding the man bestrode maddened him, set him rearing and screaming his hate. But fear of man was stronger even than the primitive lusts. On his left a break appeared in the monotony of the fence. A grassy lane that stretched away into profound distance, narrowing, lessening, vanishing into the quivering heat-haze.

Behind him the scrub erupted riders, converging upon him in a scattered line. Before him the solitary rider advanced slowly, swinging his whip.

Fear blinded caution, and Tiarra swerved into the lane as the men swept down upon him.

The nearest rider yelled exultantly, and the ranges re-echoed to the song of his whip.

Tiarra fled, fear-ridden, in a mad burst of speed that sent the fence-posts flying past in a blurring, solid wall as the chase thundered in behind him...

Foam flecked from his outflung muzzle, back upon his shoulders and sides; he turned his head from side to side continually, watching his pursuers dropping farther behind.

A five-barred gate seemed to jump at him from a hollow in the plain ahead; man-made, it terrified him anew; but his headlong pace carried him up and over to a landing that jarred every bone in his gaunt body.

His excited pursuers set up a fresh shout at sight of that leap, spurring him on to greater effort, for it brought back a memory from his lonely colthood, of the clamour of starving wild dogs hunting him through the mountain fastnesses.

The cattle beside the lane had given place to sheep — foolish creatures that rippled away from his passing like dirty grey water. He has never seen sheep before, and loathed them instinctively. The stench of them was heavy in his flaring nostrils, overpowering the man-scent. It was unclean, sickening; it nauseated him.

The men behind were gaining now, for their horses were upon familiar ground, heading for home, but he...he was in a world that was new and fearful, where every stride brought fresh terrors.

The hollow reverberation of a bridge beneath his hoofs set his heart pounding wildly, made his legs feel strangely weak.

Queer, squat structures of slab and iron appeared on his right, enclosed by countless lines of interwoven fence — sheep pens. And then, as he topped a small rise, crowning horror, a rambling iron-roofed home-stead, low stone outbuildings, more yards.

He stopped tremblingly, snorting his distrust, and whirled to face his pursuers.

They were silent now; grim, dark-visaged riders, already crossing the bridge.

Fear of them drove him on recklessly to the very end of the lane, and through the fence beside the gate, with the twang, and sting of parting wires to spur him on.

Before him, the station buildings surmounted a low hill, surrounded by a straggling garden containing a few stunted fruit trees, the whole enclosed by a picket fence that had once been white.

On his left, between the hill and the boundary fence, two post-and-rail wings led into a massive stockyard.

To the right, the road wound up to some concealed entrance behind the homestead. In the centre of the road a small man-child played in the dust.

The small creature did not appear formidable; like all young things, it was friendly and curious.

Tiarra faltered in his stride; and then he was flying down the wing fence towards the stockyard, with the riders spreading out in a half-circle hard on his heels.

He shot through the big gate with one tremendous

bound, as though clearing some unseen obstacle, and plunged to a halt, the red dust of the stockyard spurting from beneath his hoofs.

Behind him, the foremost rider crowded his horse against the gate, and it clanged shut with sound of terrible finality that started the brumby racing around and around the yard, dazed and terror-stricken, with their exultant shouts stirring him to a culminating frenzy of fear, that presently left him weak and trembling, huddled in the farthermost corner of the yard.

All the wildness of him, all the surging vitality, seemed submerged in a numbing dejection. For a time he was cowed and trembling, like a child faced with some overwhelming catastrophe, which has descended upon it from out of the blue.

There was something childlike, too, in the transient impulses, that, as a ruffling wind ripples the surface of some placid gilgai, were reflected in his still eyes. They came and went, these disturbing impulses — now stark, cowering fear; now rage, as yet unborn — with each abrupt gesture, and with each rise in inflection of the voices of men, now staring through the rails at him, and excitedly discussing the chase.

The approach of two men from the direction of

the homestead stilled their excited comment.

One was the largest man-creature that Tiarra had ever encountered – a perfect colossus.

The other was his direct antithesis.

From the small feet enclosed in tight-fitting riding boots to the crown of his wide-brimmed felt hat, he was so small as to seem almost insignificant. Yet his quick, nervous movements, and the quality of his bird-like black eyes, never still, hinted at a dynamic energy.

'Luck! Sheer luck!' he was saying to his Herculean companion. 'Couldn't yard him like that again in a lifetime!'

His companion grunted phlegmatically.

'Unbreakable!' he said slowly. 'As well have shot him out in the ranges!'

Tiarra watched them furtively as they leaned their arms upon the gate and stood staring at him.

'I'll lengthen the odds!' the big man said suddenly. 'Ten to one you can't break him!'

The little man bent his keen gaze on Tiarra anew, his eyes darkening, dilating with the strange human lust to conquer, to subdue, and to enslave. He appeared oblivious to his companion's remark, but as

Tiarra moved uneasily beneath that arrogant stare, he followed the brumby's restless pacing with quick, bird-like movements of his head.

Tiarra shivered with a sudden dread; his whole unreasoning fear of humans seemed concentrated in these two men.

The small man handled a pliable manilla rope, flexing it through his fingers and shaking out the loop; then abruptly he slipped through the gate into the yard.

Tiarra tensed, a little shiver running through him at the man's daring, and watched him with slowly reddening eyes.

As the man advanced, Tiarra leaped in deadly action, his mouth wide open, showing the strong white teeth; but quicker even than his tigerish rush, the rope shot out, the loop expanding in the air and tightening around his neck.

He stopped in mid-stride at its touch, rearing and striking the air with his forefeet in a soundless rage as the rope tightened, strangling him.

He plunged towards his tormentor, feeling the rope slacken as he advanced, but the man leaped lightly aside as willing hands dragged in the slack. Tiarra whirled in pursuit, and as he reached the end of the rope it gripped at his throat like a steel band, jerking his head around, throwing him.

He yielded then to an excess of rage, and again and again his fear-maddened plunges brought him down in the dust of the stockyard. There followed chaos, and the firm grasp of human hands. Tiarra came to his feet slowly. There was something tight around his massive chest, some terrifying thing that pressed along his neck, gripping him firmly by the head and jaws, moulding his every action to the will of man.

Hours later they left him, the bridle still in place, secured by curbing reins to the tight surcingle.

He huddled in a far corner, exhaustion and fear of the curb keeping him still, and stared with bloodshot eyes out over the bare paddocks to where the vanished sun incarnadined the stark outline of his beloved mountains with rosy colour that presently softened, mellowing to dark smoky blues, and purple shadow pools, and the softening mantle of night.

He stood very still, the pain and rage and fear fading from his eyes, leaving them still, placid pools, remotely dreaming.

The night, and the night sky, was so familiar; the

flickering sheen of sheet lightning upon the tumbled banks of cumulus storm-cloud in the south; the rising moon, clear and pale like a drowned human face; the dark shadows of distant timber; the plaintive cry of a curlew – these were still the same; but he . . .

He champed tentatively at the bit, and presently he moved a few paces experimentally, and whickered softly. The sound set a score of dogs barking, and he moved restlessly, pacing slowly around the fence, his hoofs heavy in the dust.

Then from somewhere behind the homestead, shrill and high, came an answering call and the ring of iron-shod hoofs.

Presently they came to the gate, two sleek, pampered station mares, and tried to touch noses with him through the bars, whirling in skittish play as he responded awkwardly to their advances, and kicking up their heels at him in foolish coquetry.

Once his eyes blazed with a strong lust, and he bit back at one of them, his ears flattening at her squealed response. But the implacable curb of the bit as he moved forward brought fear again, and the lust faded.

Presently Tiarra ignored them completely, staring out over their heads to the dark bulk of the mountains, where storm-clouds gathered, driven by blinding spears of lightning.

He listened to the slow rumbling of distant thunder, and seemed to hear the rain pattering upon the leaves and swelling the river. Burning thirst consumed him at the thought, but stronger, more intense even than this, was the terrible nostalgia that succeeded it, that set him vainly circling the stout fence.

So passed the night.

The shadows were lengthening again ere the riders returned, the small man half-hidden beneath a heavy stock-saddle.

Tiarra whirled and faced them, snorting his defiance.

He watched his enemy swing the saddle upon the rail and enter the gate, whip in hand, whilst deadly hatred that had strengthened during the still noonday hours bred hot, unreasoning lust within him. A lust to rend, to tear; to trample this insignificant man-thing back into the dust whence he came and to which he belonged.

Tiarra rushed his enemy without warning with the swift, deadly charge of the wild stallion. The man stepped back a pace quickly and the whip whirled and sang, the lash cutting deep into Tiarra's soft muzzle, stunning him with a numbing wave of pain, stopping him in mid-stride. He backed helplessly, blinded with agony, and again he knew the drag of the rope and the crack of the whips forcing him up to the fence.

He pulled back and fought frantically as his head was jerked tightly against the rough ironbark. Then came a hideous, terrifying blackness as the folds of a sack covered his eyes, shutting out light.

A deadening fear that left him weak and trembling possessed him, for the unnatural darkness, to him, was ultimate horror, and for a time he stood still, oblivious to the strange things that were happening to him — unheeding the bony knee pressed into his soft belly, or the drag of girths or surcingle, and the indignity of the crupper.

Then the bag was whisked away, and for a moment he stood, dazzled by the brilliant flood of sunlight, seeing men scurry from about him to the shelter of the fence. But only for a moment . . . and then an all-enveloping rage, savage as the northern typhoon, swept over him . . . for the terrible little man-creature was seated, jauntily erect, upon his back.

For an instant Tiarra cringed beneath the unaccustomed weight, and then his back arched like a rainbow, his first wild leap taking him to the centre of the yard, the rip of the rider's spurs driving the last vestige of sanity from his brain. He screamed on an eldritch note that paled the face of the little man and caused him to drive the spurs home viciously; then Tiarra's flying hoofs sent the red dust spurting, and his head, almost tearing the reins from the man's grasp, curled in between his forelegs.

He bucked high in a frenzy of whirling action, spinning like a child's top, and each time his hoofs jarred down in the dust he screamed and screamed again, bucking in a mad frenzy, terrible to behold, that awed the men upon the fence, silencing their shouted encouragement.

But through it all the rider clung burr-like to the saddle, though his head jarred forward upon his breast with each plunge, and on his lips now was the frothy blood of an internal haemorrhage.

Red dust rose in a choking cloud, enveloping horse and rider, so that sometimes they were quite invisible to the men on the fence.

Tiarra felt himself slowly weakening. He ceased the bucking spin as abruptly as he had commenced it, and leaped sideways, throwing his weight draggingly along the fence, seeking to crush the rider against the rough timbers.

The man swung his leg up with little to spare, his face ashen, and left a long strip of cloth flapping from a splinter of rail.

Tiarra bucked straight ahead then, around the fence, and time and time again he tore and bruised his own gaunt body against the rough logs in vain effort to unseat his rider.

Nothing human could have stood that terrible pounding much longer. The rider could feel the girths slipping, but the reckless abandon of racial pride kept him in the saddle. To subdue, to break this maddened creature — or to die.

Tiarra wheeled away abruptly into the centre of the stockyard again, and his long neck came up, his hammer-like head, dust-begrimed and bloody, the eyes white and staring, his strong teeth bared suddenly as he stopped screaming and reached back to savage at his rider's legs. The man drew his foot back quickly and struck forward with his spurred heel. Tiarra took the blow upon his writhing upper lip, and screamed again, rearing and striking at the air in impotent fury. The rider leaned forward and struck Tiarra's high-flung head with clenched fist, smiling grimly through the haemal froth upon his lips the while – for this was an old, old trick.

But some clamouring instinct drove Tiarra up again. He reared higher with an excess of effort, toppled for an instant beneath the man's frantic blows, and crashed over backwards.

The fall winded Tiarra, but he scrambled up, his sides sweat-caked and heaving . . . for the rider was no longer on his back!

And now a fresh fear seized him, fear of the twitching thing hanging from one stirrup. He leaped away from it, snorting his terror, and the thing leaped after him, raising the dust and dragging the saddle sideways, as shouting men swarmed into the yard and tried to seize him.

He avoided them easily; they seemed slow of movement, stricken, and the weight swung heavily against his back legs. He kicked at the sodden body furiously, trampling it beneath his hoofs.

A flying rein caught in the fence and snapped off with a sound like a whip-crack. The weight beneath dragged the saddle backwards over his rump, the crupper pulled out, and he was free.

A gate opened suddenly before him; a whip flicked a long wale along his ribs, and he leaped through into a larger yard and fled snorting to the farthest corner.

Behind him the rider lay very still, face downward in the dust. The dust smeared his fair hair redly; it was the colour of the blood upon his lips.

The small man had lost a bet!

Anna Sewell

Black Beauty

One day, whilst our cab and many others were waiting outside one of the parks where a band was playing, a shabby old cab drove up beside ours. The horse was an old worn-out chestnut with an ill-kept coat, and with bones that showed plainly through it. The knees knuckled over, and the forelegs were very unsteady.

I had been eating some hay, and the wind rolling a little lock of it that way, the poor creature put out her long, thin neck and picked it up, and then turned round and looked about for more. There was a hopeless look in the dull eye that I could not help noticing; and then, as I was thinking where I had seen that horse before, she looked full at me and said, 'Black Beauty, is that you?'

It was Ginger! but how changed! The beautifully arched and glossy neck was now straight, lank, and fallen in; the clean, straight legs and delicate fetlocks were swollen; the joints were grown out of shape with hard work; the face that was once so full of spirit and life was now full of suffering; and I could tell by the heaving of her sides and by her frequent cough how bad her breath was.

Our drivers were standing together a little way off, so I sidled up to her a step or two that we might have a little quiet talk. It was a sad tale that she had to tell.

After a twelve-month's run off at Earlshall, she was considered to be fit for work again, and was sold to a gentleman. For a little while she got on very well, but after a longer gallop than usual, the old strain returned, and, after being rested and doctored, she was again sold. In this way she changed hands several times, but alway getting lower down.

'And so at last,' said she, 'I was bought by a man who keeps a number of cabs and horses, and lets them out. You look well off, and I am glad of it; but I cannot tell you what my life has been. When they found out my weakness, they said I was not worth what they gave for me, and that I must go into one of the low cabs and just be used up; that is what they are doing — whipping and working me, with never one thought of what I suffer. They paid for me, and must get the money out of me, they say. The man who hires me now pays a deal of money to the owner every day, and so he has to get it out of me first; and so it goes on all the weeks round, with never a Sunday rest.'

I said, 'You used to stand up for yourself if you were ill-used.'

'Ah!' she said, 'I did once, but it's no use; men are stronger, and if they are cruel and have no feeling, there is nothing that we can do but just bear it — bear it on and on to the end. I wish the end was come; I wish I was dead. I have seen dead horses, and I am sure they do not suffer pain; I hope I may drop down dead at my works, and not be sent off to the knacker's.'

I was very much troubled, and I put my nose up to hers, but I could say nothing to comfort her. I think she was pleased to see me, for she said, 'You are the only friend I ever had.'

Just then her driver came up, and with a tug at her

mouth backed her out of the line and drove off, leaving me very sad indeed.

A short time after this a cart with a dead horse in it passed our cab-stand. The head hung out of the cart tail, the lifeless tongue was slowly dropping blood; and the sunken eyes! — but I can't speak of them, the sight was too dreadful. It was a chestnut horse with a long thin neck. I saw a white streak down the forehead. I believe it was Ginger; I hoped it was, for then her troubles would be over. Oh! if men were more merciful, they would shoot us before we came to such misery.

Lewis Carroll

The White Knight

Whenever the horse stopped (which it did very often), he fell off the front; and whenever it went on again (which it generally did rather suddenly), he fell off behind. Otherwise he kept on pretty well, except that he had a habit of now and then falling off sideways; and as he generally did this on the side on which Alice was walking, she soon found that it was the best plan not to walk *quite* close to the horse.

'I'm afraid you've not had much practice in riding,' she ventured to say as she was helping him up from his fifth tumble.

The Knight looked very much surprised, and a little

offended at the remark. 'What makes you say that?' he asked, as he scrambled back into the saddle, keeping hold of Alice's hair with one hand, to save himself from falling over on the other side.

'Because people don't fall off quite so often, when they've had much practice.'

'I've had plenty of practice,' the Knight said very gravely: 'plenty of practice!'

Alice could think of nothing better to say than 'Indeed?', but she said it as heartily as she could. They went on a little way in silence after this, the Knight with his eyes shut, muttering to himself, and Alice watching anxiously for the next tumble.

'The great art of riding,' the Knight suddenly began in a loud voice, waving his right arm as he spoke, 'is to keep . . .' Here the sentence ended as suddenly as it had begun, as the Knight fell heavily on top of his head exactly in the path where Alice was walking. She was quite frightened this time, and said in an anxious tone, as she picked him up, 'I hope no bones are broken?'

'None to speak of,' the Knight said, as if he didn't mind breaking two or three of them. 'The great art of riding, as I was saying, is – to keep your balance properly. Like this, you know . . .'

He let go the bridle, and stretched out both his arms to show Alice what he meant, and this time he fell flat on his back, right under the horse's feet.

'Plenty of practice!' he went on repeating, all the time that Alice was getting him on his feet again. 'Plenty of practice!'

'It's too ridiculous!' cried Alice, losing all her patience this time. 'You ought to have a wooden horse on wheels, that you ought!'

'Does that kind go smoothly?' the Knight asked in a tone of great interest, clasping his arms round the horse's neck as he spoke, just in time to save himself from tumbling off again.

'Much more smoothly than a live horse,' Alice said, with a little scream of laughter, in spite of all she could do to prevent it.

'I'll get one,' the Knight said thoughtfully to himself. 'One or two — several.'

Jean Giono

The Horseman on the Roof

Dawn found Angelo mute and yawning but awake. The brow of the hill had protected him from the slight dew that falls in these regions in summer. He rubbed his horse down with a handful of heather and rolled his saddlebag.

The birds were stirring in the valley into which he descended. It was not cool, even in the hollows still covered by the darkness of the night. The whole sky was lit by shafts of grey. At last the red sun, smothered in a thicket of dark clouds, emerged from the forests.

Despite the already stifling heat, Angelo longed for

something hot to drink. As he descended into the middle valley separating the hills on which he had spent
the night from another, higher and wilder range, two
or three leagues ahead of him, where the first rays of
the sun were burnishing the bronze of the tall oak
woods, he saw a small farm building by the roadside
and, in the field, a woman in a red skirt, picking up the
washing that she had spread out in the evening dew.

He drew near. Her shoulders and arms were bare
above a coarse linen bodice, which also displayed
enormous, deeply sunburned breasts.

'Excuse me, madame,' he said, 'but will you let me
have a little coffee? I'll pay for it.'

She did not answer at once, and he realized that he
had adopted too polite a manner. 'That "I'll pay for
it" is clumsy,' he thought.

'I can give you some coffee,' she said; 'come in.' She
was tall, but so nimble that she swung around slowly
in one place, like a ship. 'The door's over there,' she
said, pointing to the end of the hedge.

In the kitchen there were only an old man and a
great many flies. But on the low stove with its roaring
fire, alongside a cauldron of bran for the pigs, the
coffeepot emitted such a good smell that Angelo

found the soot-blackened room altogether charming. Even the pig-bran spoke a language of magnificence to his stomach, poorly satisfied by a supper of dry bread.

He drank a bowl of coffee. The woman planted herself in front of him, giving him a good view of her brawny shoulders, full of dimples, and even of the huge pink blossom of her breasts. She asked him if he was an official gentlemen. 'Careful!' thought Angelo. 'She's regretting her coffee.'

'Oh no,' he said (taking care not to say 'madame'), 'I'm in business at Marseille; I'm going to see clients in the Drôme and I thought I'd get some fresh air on the way.'

The woman's face grew more kindly; especially when he asked the way to Banon. 'You'd like an egg,' she said. She had already pushed the cauldron of bran to one side and put the frying-pan on the fire.

He ate an egg and a piece of bacon with four slices of coarse, extremely white bread, which seemed to him as light as feathers. The woman was now bustling maternally around him. To his surprise he didn't mind the smell of her sweat at all, nor even the thick tufts of red hair in her armpits when she raised her arms to adjust her bun. She refused payment and even began to laugh when he insisted, roughly pushing his purse away. Angelo felt painfully awkward and ridiculous in her presence; he would have liked to be able to pay and depart with that dry, detached air which was his timidity's usual defence. He rapidly murmured his thanks and pocketed his purse.

The woman showed him his road rising on the other side of the valley into the oak woods. Angelo walked his horse for a while in silence along the little plain, through bright green fields. He was under a spell from the food, which had left a most pleasant taste in his mouth. At length he sighed and set his horse to trot.

The sun was high; it was very hot but there was no violence in the light. It was white and so diffused that it seemed to butter the earth with dense air. Angelo had been climbing for a long time through the oak forest. He was following a narrow road covered with a thick layer of dust, and each step of his horse raised a smoke that did not settle again. Through the ragged and withered undergrowth he could see, at each turning, how the signs of his passing remained upon all the windings of the road below him. The trees brought no coolness. Instead, the small hard oak leaves reflected the heat and light. The shade of the forest dazzled and stifled.

On these banks, burned to the bone, a few white thistles cracked as his horse went by, as though the metal earth all around were vibrating under the iron-shod hoofs. There was nothing but this little thorny noise, crackling with extreme clarity above the sound of the hoofs, dulled by the dust and a silence so total that the presence of the great mute trees became almost unreal. The saddle was scorching. The movement of the girths raised a lather of sweat. The animal sucked its bit and from time to time cleared its throat by shaking its head. The steady rising of the heat hummed like a boiler mercilessly stoked with coal. The trunks of the oaks cracked. Through the under-growth, dry and bare like a church floor, flooded by the white light that had no sparkle, but a blinding powderiness, the horse's gait set long black rays slowly turning. The road, hoisting itself in stiffer coils up over ancient rocks covered with white lichens, some-times headed straight into the sun: then, in the chalk sky, there opened a sort of abyss of unbelievable phosphorescence, and out of it came a breath of fur-nace and fever, sticky, the slime and fat of it visibly quivering. The huge trees dissolved within this dazzle; great stretches of forest engulfed in the light showed only as a vague foliage of cinders, shapeless forms, almost transparent and suddenly coated by the heat with a slow sway of shimmering viscosity. Then the road would turn westward, instantly shrunken to the dimensions of the mule track that it had become; it would be hemmed in by living, violent tree trunks supported by pillars of gold, with branches twisted by crackling twigs of gold, and still leaves all gilded like little mirrors set in thin gold threads that closely framed their every outline.

C. S. Lewis

The Horse and His Boy

You must not imagine that Shasta felt at all as you and I would feel if we had just overheard our parents talking about selling us for slaves. For one thing, his life was already little better than slavery; for all he knew, the lordly stranger of the great horse might be kinder to him than Arsheesh. For another, the story about his own discovery in the boat had filled him with excitement and with a sense of relief. He had often been uneasy because, try as he might, he had never been able to love the fisherman, and he knew that a boy ought to love his father. And now, apparently, he was no relation to Arsheesh at all. That took a great weight off his mind. 'Why, I might be anyone!' he thought. 'I might be the son of a Tarkaan myself – or the son of the Tisroc (may he live for ever) – or of a god!'

He was standing out in the grassy place before the cottage while he thought these things. Twilight was coming on apace and a star or two was already out, but the remains of the sunset could still be seen in the west. Not far away the stranger's horse, loosely tied to an iron ring in the wall of the donkey's stable, was grazing. Shasta strolled over to it and patted its neck. It went on tearing up the grass and took no notice of him.

Then another thought came into Shasta's mind. 'I wonder what sort of man that Tarkaan is,' he said out loud. 'It would be splendid if he was kind. Some of the slaves in a great lord's house have next to nothing to do. They wear lovely clothes and eat meat every day. Perhaps he'd take me to the wars and I'd save his life in a battle and then he'd set me free and adopt me as his son and give me a palace and a chariot and a suit of armour. But then he might be a horrid cruel man. He might send me to work on the fields in chains. I wish I knew. How can I know? I bet this horse knows, if only he could tell me.'

The Horse had lifted its head. Shasta stroked its smooth-as-satin nose and said, 'I wish *you* could talk, old fellow.'

And then for a second he thought he was dreaming, for quite distinctly, though in a low voice, the Horse said, 'But I can.'

Shasta stared into its great eyes and his own grew almost as big, with astonishment.

'How ever did *you* learn to talk?' he asked.

'Hush! Not so loud,' replied the Horse. 'Where I come from, nearly all the animals talk.'

'Wherever is that?' asked Shasta.

'Narnia,' answered the Horse. 'The happy land of Narnia — Narnia of the heathery mountains and the thymy downs, Narnia of the many rivers, the plashing glens, the mossy caverns and the deep forests ringing with the hammers of the Dwarfs. Oh the sweet air of Narnia! An hour's life there is better than a thousand years in Calormen.' It ended with a whinny that sounded very like a sigh.

'How did you get here?' said Shasta.

'Kidnapped,' said the Horse. 'Or stolen, or captured — whichever you like to call it. I was only a foal at the time. My mother warned me not to range the

Southern slopes, into Archenland and beyond, but I wouldn't heed her. And by the Lion's Mane I have paid for my folly. All these years I have been a slave to humans, hiding my true nature and pretending to be dumb and witless like *their* horses.'

'Why didn't you tell them who you were?'

'Not such a fool, that's why. If they'd once found out I could talk they would have made a show of me at fairs and guarded me more carefully than ever. My last chance of escape would have been gone.'

'And why –' began Shasta, but the Horse interrupted him.

'Now look,' it said, 'we mustn't waste time on idle questions. You want to know about my master the Tarkaan Anradin. Well, he's bad. Not too bad to me, for a war horse costs too much to be treated very badly. But you'd better be lying dead tonight than go to be a human slave in his house tomorrow.'

'Then I'd better run away,' said Shasta, turning very pale.

'Yes, you had,' said the Horse. 'But why not run away with me?'

'Are you going to run away too?' said Shasta.

'Yes, if you'll come with me,' answered the Horse.

'This is the chance for both of us. You see if I run away without a rider, everyone who sees me will say "Stray horse" and be after me as quick as he can. With a rider I've a chance to get through. That's where you can help me. On the other hand, you can't get very far on those two silly legs of yours (what absurd legs humans have!) without being overtaken. But on me you can outdistance any other horse in this country. That's where I can help you. By the way, I suppose you know how to ride?'

'Oh yes, of course,' said Shasta. 'At least, I've ridden the donkey.'

'Ridden the *what?*' retorted the Horse with extreme contempt. (At least, that is what he meant. Actually it came out in a sort of neigh – 'Ridden the wha-ha-ha-ha-ha.' Talking horses always become more horsy in accent when they are angry.)

'In other words,' it continued, 'you *can't* ride. That's a drawback. I'll have to teach you as we go along. If you can't ride, can you fall?'

'I suppose anyone can fall,' said Shasta.

'I mean can you fall and get up again without crying and mount again and fall again and yet not be afraid of falling?'

'I – I'll try,' said Shasta. 'Poor little beast,' said the Horse in a gentler tone. 'I forget you're only a foal. We'll make a fine rider of you in time. And now – we mustn't start until those two in the hut are asleep. Meantime we can make our plans. My Tarkaan is on his way North to the great city, to Tashbaan itself and the court of the Tisroc –'

'I say,' put in Shasta in rather a shocked voice, 'oughtn't you to say "May he live for ever"?'

'Why?' asked the Horse. 'I'm a free Narnian. And why should I talk slaves' and fools' talk? I don't want him to live for ever, and I know that he's not going to live for ever whether I want him to or not. And I can see you're from the free North too. No more of this Southern jargon between you and me! And now, back to our plans. As I said, my human was on his way North to Tashbaan.'

'Does that mean we'd better go to the South?'

'I think not,' said the Horse. 'You see, he thinks I'm dumb and witless like his other horses. Now if I really were, the moment I got loose I'd go back home to my stable and paddock; back to his palace which is two days' journey South. That's where he'll look for me. He'd never dream of my going on North on my own.

And anyway he will probably think that someone in the last village who saw him ride through has followed us to here and stolen me.'

'Oh hurrah!' said Shasta. 'Then we'll go North. I've been longing to go to the North all my life.'

'Of course you have,' said the Horse. 'That's because of the blood that's in you. I'm sure you're true Northern stock. But not too loud. I should think they'd be asleep soon now.'

'I'd better creep back and see,' suggested Shasta.

'That's a good idea,' said the Horse. 'But take care you're not caught.'

It was a good deal darker now and very silent except for the sound of the waves on the beach, which Shasta hardly noticed because he had been hearing it day and night as long as he could remember. The cottage, as he approached it, showed no light. When he listened at the front there was no noise. When he went round to the only window, he could hear, after a second or two, the familiar noise of the old fisherman's squeaky snore. It was funny to think that if all went well he would never hear it again. Holding his breath and feeling a little bit sorry, but much less sorry than he was glad, Shasta glided away over the grass and went to the donkey's stable, groped along to a place he knew where the key was hidden, opened the door and found the Horse's saddle and bridle which had been locked up there for the night. He bent forward and kissed the donkey's nose. 'I'm sorry we can't take *you*,' he said.

'There you are at last,' said the Horse when he got back to it. 'I was beginning to wonder what had become of you.'

'I was getting your things out of the stable,' replied Shasta. 'And now, can you tell me how to put them on?'

For the next few minutes Shasta was at work, very cautiously to avoid jingling, while the Horse said things like, 'Get that girth a bit tighter,' or 'You'll find a buckle lower down,' or 'You'll need to shorten those stirrups a good bit.' When all was finished it said:

'Now; we've got to have reins for the look of the thing, but you won't be using them. Tie them to the saddle-bow: very slack so that I can do what I like with my head. And, remember – you are not to touch them.'

'What are they for, then?' asked Shasta.

'Ordinarily they are for directing me,' replied the Horse. 'But as I intend to do all the directing on this journey, you'll please keep your hands to yourself. And there's another thing. I'm not going to have you grabbing my mane.'

'But I say,' pleaded Shasta. 'If I'm not to hold on by the reins or by your mane, what *am* I to hold on by?'

'You hold on with your knees,' said the Horse. 'That's the secret of good riding. Grip my body between your knees as hard as you like; sit straight up, straight as a poker; keep your elbows in. And by the way, what did you do with the spurs?'

'Put them on my heels, of course,' said Shasta. 'I do know that much.'

'Then you can take them off and put them in the saddlebag. We may be able to sell them when we get to Tashbaan. Ready? And now I think you can get up.'

'Ooh! You're a dreadful height,' gasped Shasta after his first, and unsuccessful, attempt.

'I'm a horse, that's all,' was the reply. 'Anyone would think I was a haystack from the way you're trying to climb up me! There, that's better. Now sit *up* and remember what I told you about your knees. Funny to think of me who has led cavalry charges and won races having a potato-sack like you in the saddle! However, off we go.' It chuckled, not unkindly.

And it certainly began their night journey with great caution. First of all it went just south of the fisherman's cottage to the little river which there ran into the sea, and took care to leave in the mud some very plain hoof-marks pointing South. But as soon as they were in the middle of the ford it turned upstream and waded till they were about a hundred yards farther inland than the cottage. Then it selected a nice gravelly bit of bank which would take no footprints and came out on the Northern side. Then, still at a walking pace, it went Northward till the cottage, the one tree, the donkey's stable, and the creek – everything, in fact, that Shasta had ever known – had sunk out of sight in the grey summer-night darkness. They had been going up-hill and now were at the top of the ridge – that ridge which had always been the boundary of Shasta's known world. He could not see what was ahead except that it was all open and grassy. It looked endless: wild and lonely and free.

'I say!' observed the Horse. 'What a place for a gallop, eh!'

'Oh don't let's,' said Shasta. 'Not yet. I don't know how to – please, Horse. I don't know your name.'

'Breehy-hinny-brinny-hoohy-hah,' said the Horse.

'I'll never be able to say that,' said Shasta. 'Can I call you Bree?'

'Well, if it's the best you can do, I suppose you must,' said the Horse. 'And what shall I call you?'

'I'm called Shasta.'

'H'm,' said Bree. 'Well, now, there's a name that's *really* hard to pronounce. But now about this gallop. It's a good deal easier than trotting if you only knew, because you don't have to rise and fall. Grip with your knees and keep your eyes straight ahead between my ears. Don't look at the ground. If you think you're going to fall just grip harder and sit up straighter. Ready? Now: for Narnia and the North.'

Katharine S. Prichard

The Grey Horse

He was young, a draught stallion, grey, and Old Gourlay worked him on the roads.

Old Gourlay kept the road in order on the back of Black Swan and lived with his housekeeper in a barefaced wooden box of a house beside the road, where it loped over the mountain to Perth, by way of the river and half a dozen townships scattered across the plains. Gourlay was a dry stick of a man, and deaf; but Grey Ganger – the beauty of him took the breath like a blast of cold wind. There was nothing more beautiful in the ranges, not the wild flowers, yellow and blue, on the ledges of the road, nor the tall white gums gleaming through the dark of the bush from among thronging rough-barked red gums and jarrah.

A superb creature, broad and short of back, deep-barrelled, with mighty quarters, the grey stallion carried Old Gourlay, on the floor of the tip-dray, uphill in the morning, curveting with kittenish grace, as though the tip-dray were a chariot; prancing and tossing his head so that silver threads glinted in the spume of his mane. He brought loads of gravel down-hill, gaily, prancing still, with an air of curbing his pace to humour the queer, fussy insect of an old man who clung to the rope reins stretched out beside and behind him.

Wood-carters who worked on the Black Swan road envied the old man his horse. They wanted to buy him; but Gourlay would not sell the Ganger. Their great, rough-haired horses laboured along the bush tracks and came slowly down the steep winding road, sitting back in the breeching; the roughly split jarrah for firewood stacked on the carts jabbing their haunches.

O'Reilly had offered good money, cash down, for Grey Ganger; he had told Gourlay to name his own figure. But Old Gourlay shook his head. Nothing but cussedness, it was, O'Reilly declared. Gourlay had not enough work for the Ganger: a less powerful horse would suit him better, cost less, and be easier to manage. O'Reilly would have liked to mate the Ganger with his Lizzie when he found he could not buy the horse. Lizzie was a staunch enough working mare, shaggy and evil-smelling, with a roach back, and splay feet, but she had been 'a good 'un in her day', he said.

Gourlay would have none of that either.

'Aw—aw,' he stuttered; 'she's rough stuff. He's only a baby. There'd be no holding him if —'

Old Gourlay had pride in his horse, enjoyed crying his measurements, the size of his collar. The Ganger was always in good condition, close-knit and hard, his hide smooth and sheeny as the silk of a woman's dress. Not that Gourlay seemed to have any affection for him: rather was there hostility, a vague resentment in his bearing. He nagged at Grey Ganger as though he feared and had some secret grudge against him.

But no one envied Old Gourlay his horse more than Bill Moriarty, who, against the advice of every fruit-grower in the district, had taken up the block of land adjoining Gourlay's, and had planted vines and fruit-trees to make an orchard there, a few years before

Gourlay, Mrs. Drouett and the grey stallion had come to live on the Black Swan road. As he cleared and grubbed, burnt off, and cultivated his land, Young Moriarty had watched Gourlay and Grey Ganger.

On the wildest, wettest nights he had seen the flickering, loose golden star of Gourlay's lantern as he went to feed the Ganger and shut him into his stable for the night. He had been up when the old man pulled the board from across the stable door in the morning, and the Ganger, released, dashed round the small, muddy square of the yard, flinging up his heels, snorting and gambolling joyously, with such a clumsy, kittenish grace that Moriarty himself would laugh, and sing out to old Gourlay: 'He's in great heart, this morning, all right.'

Gourlay would mutter resentfully, and swear at the Ganger, clacking the gate of the stable-yard to, as he went up to breakfast. Nothing annoyed him more than to see Grey Ganger disporting himself.

When first he and his housekeeper had come to live at Black Swan, Old Gourlay had made those trips to feed and shut the Ganger in his stable for the night with zest, swinging his lantern religiously and whistling. And he had gone afterwards into the shed beside the stable, where a bed was made up, put the light out there and slammed the door. But Young Moriarty had seen him stumble uphill in the starlight, or when he thought all Black Swan was sleeping, open the back door quietly, and go into his house.

Black Swan people did not appear to mind where Old Gourlay slept, really. They were too busy in their orchards or clearing and cultivating land for vines to bother much about what their neighbours were doing. Besides, Gourlay's and Mrs. Drouett's story had gone before them. Nobody expected Old Gourlay to sleep in the shed beside the stable. Even the children going along the road to school, as they passed Gourlay's, said mysteriously to each other: 'He's got one mother up-country . . . and living here with another.'

The neighbours were kind and friendly enough when they met either Gourlay or Mrs. Drouett. Their story had created a slightly romantic sympathy. It was said Old Gourlay had been a well-to-do farmer with a wife and family when Laura Drouett had come his way. He sold his farm and left his family to go away with her. They had wandered about for years and grown old together.

Mrs. Drouett had been a comely woman and still

kept her figure tight at the waist. Her hips were thrust out from it, plump and heavy; she had a bosom and a fringe of brown curly hair, which she wore above the withered apple of her face when she was dressed for the afternoon, or going driving with Mr. Gourlay. She was older than he, perhaps, but better preserved; deaf also, and nervy, under the strain of living with Mr. Gourlay, 'seeing how I am placed', as she explained to Young Moriarty when he hopped on over the fence to talk to her, and cheer her up, sometimes.

Old Gourlay did not like Bill Moriarty hopping over the fence to talk to Mrs. Drouett.

'He's as mad as a wet hen if he finds me having a yarn with the old girl,' Bill explained to O'Reilly. 'She's a decent sort . . . a bit lonely . . . and I've been trying to get round her to make the old man lend me his horse, now and then.'

O'Reilly laughed. He thought he guessed what was at the back of Old Gourlay's mind. Bill was a good-looker, thick-set and swarthy, with crisp dark hair and blue eyes set in whites as hard as china, and so short-lashed that they stared at you unshaded from the bronze of his face. Though he was still more or less coltish, Young Moriarty, O'Reilly knew, was working too hard, and too much in love with a girl who lived down on the flats, to be bold with any woman or give Tom Gourlay cause for doubting the fidelity of his Laura. But O'Reilly could not resist rubbing it in when, a few days later, the old man stopped him on the road, not far from where Bill was pruning his vines.

'Good cut of a fellow, that,' he shouted, waving an arm towards Moriarty. 'Isn't a better made man in the ranges. Ever seen him stripped? By God, he's got good limbs on him.'

In the evening, mean-spirited and vindictive, Gourlay gave Mrs. Drouett the benefit of that praise of Bill and the gall he had stewed in all day. The old woman cried; but she was coy and self-conscious with Young Moriarty next time she saw him. She put on her brown hair in the morning and pulled the strings of her corsets tighter. Old Gourlay guessed what she had done, and was madder than a wet hen, though Bill, for all Laura's youthful figure and hair, saw only her poor grandmother's face. He was soaked with the sight and shape of Rose Sharwood, her warm bloom; thirsty with desire for the sound and the smell of her. He was all a madness for Rose. So when he could not get a horse to do his spring ploughing, he went again to Old Gourlay. He had asked before for the loan of his horse, and the old man had refused him, churlishly enough, but with excuses. And Bill had not pressed him. But this was different. It meant a great deal to him, getting that ploughing done.

Black cockatoos had whirled about the clearing, shedding their wild cries high in the air that morning. A long spell of dry weather was breaking and Bill Moriarty needed a horse to cultivate between his vines after the rain.

'How's it for a loan of the Ganger to plough my orchard?' he asked Old Gourlay, leaning over the weatherworn saplings of the stallion's yard.

'Nothing doing,' Old Gourlay growled.

Moriarty explained the difficulty he was in. He was hard up. He could not buy a horse: he could pay for the hire of one by the day. But every man in the district with working horses was waiting for the rain and required his horses to plough, and make the most of the ground while it was soft. Young Moriarty could not get the promise of a horse from anyone. And it meant everything to him, to have the earth turned and sweetened about his vines, this year; all the difference between a good, or a poor, yield of the grapes. Bill let Old Gourlay know, with all the sentiment he could muster, that he was praying for a good harvest because he wanted to get married. He soft-pedalled about Rose, and the skinflint of an aunt who threatened to take her away to the Eastern States at the end of the autumn if Bill had not built a house and married the girl before then.

Old Gourlay pretended not to hear half of what he was saying.

'T-too busy to do any ploughing,' he said. 'Rain'll w-wash away half the road up by The Beak . . . Couldn' spare the Ganger . . . plenty of work for him to do on the road . . . Too much for one man and one horse.'

He stuttered away from the subject, irritably. Moriarty let him go, watching the stallion as he frisked and plunged about the yard where the grey sapling posts and rails, silvered by the early light, shook as he bumped against them.

'Ever mate him, Mr. Gourlay?' Young Moriarty yelled.

'No!' The old man's eyes leapt, sharp and startled in the weathered fallow of his face. 'There'd be no holding him if ever I did.'

So that was it, Bill thought. He and the Ganger were in the same boat. Old Gourlay would thwart them both if he could; defeat their instincts. Vaguely Bill understood that what Gourlay resented in the Ganger, and in himself, was their youth and virility, when the sap had dried in his old man's bones.

It was beginning to rain as Bill went back to his work.

'Mean old blighter,' he muttered. 'Had two women himself, and won't give a handsome animal like that his dues. Him breaking his neck . . . and me too.'

Young Moriarty went out to the road to meet O'Reilly as the wood-carts came downhill that evening, looking top-heavy, the wood piled high on them red and umber with rain, the shaggy, brown-furred horses stepping warily for fear they might come down on the slippery road beside which the feather-white torrents of rain-wash were flying.

Moriarty asked the wood-carter for the loan of his mare, Lizzie, some Sunday soon, when he was not using her. He told O'Reilly how Old Gourlay had refused to let him have the Ganger although the stallion spent most of his time on Sundays galloping up and down and cavorting about his yard beside the stable; and how he had explained to Gourlay what it meant to him to get his ploughing and harrowing done just then.

O'Reilly knew about Rose Sharwood and that Bill wanted to marry her.

The rain beat around them as they talked, Bill hat-less, hugging himself in the coat of his working clothes buttoned up to the throat; O'Reilly, his tarred overalls shining, his ruddy, unshaven face with dropped lip and lit eyes laughing from under his sod-den hat. The raindrops quivering on its brim ran and fell as he laughed, getting the gist of Young Moriarty's grievance, and the way he proposed to pay for the hire of old Lizzie.

Squalls swept up over the purple and green of the plains all week, flung themselves against the ranges, scattering hailstones, and passed on inland. A film of fine chill rain veiled the timbered hills about Black Swan for days. Then the sunshine of late spring leapt, shimmering on the water lying down on the flats, and drying the land in the hills quickly.

O'Reilly did not appear with Lizzie that Sunday. Moriarty was desperate. Rains had lashed the blossom from the almond-trees along the boundary of his fences. The tooth of green was everywhere; the flame of young leaves. Down near Grey Ganger's stable and yard, where Moriarty had put a row of nectarines below the vines, pink flowers were spraying wide-spread, varnished branches. It would soon be too late to conserve moisture for the vines. And the thought that Rose would go away with her aunt if he did not do well out of his grapes that year, overhung Young Moriarty like a doom.

But the next Sunday morning, while the Ganger was galloping about his yard, just from his stable, as fresh and beside himself as Bill had ever seen him, O'Reilly brought old Lizzie to cultivate the orchard.

O'Reilly and Bill stood watching the Ganger's gam-bollings for a moment, laughing and exclaiming their admiration. Then they got to work. O'Reilly drove the mare as they ploughed, across the crest of the hillside, while Bill, stooping along before Lizzie, cleared stones and pruned branches out of the way. O'Reilly ploughed well down the slope before he swung Lizzie from an upper to a lower furrow, uphill and along, downhill and along.

The Ganger came to the end of his yard as he sighted them. He watched Lizzie curiously, snorted as she passed, and galloped up and down, throwing himself about to attract her attention. When they had finished ploughing that side of the hill, Moriarty and O'Reilly spelled Lizzie while they went up to the lean-to Bill lived in, for a meal.

They left her down near the fence where the young nectarines were in blossom. The grey stallion was trembling against his yard as they did so; taut, the breath blowing in gusty blasts from his nostrils. Lizzie swung her bland, white-splashed face towards him and blinked at him from behind her wide black winkers. Her tail moved gently. A hot, herby aroma reached the men. Young Moriarty went to lead her away, as if to avoid trouble and propitiate Old Gourlay. But it was too late. Grey Ganger rushed and broke his fences. He whirled round Lizzie, charging Moriarty. Bill got away from his plunging fury and flung heels. He picked up the dead branch of a fruit-tree as though to defend himself, or beat off the Ganger. O'Reilly ran away over the broken earth of the hillside.

The noise of the breaking fence and the stallion's whinnied blast brought Old Gourlay running from the house. Mrs. Drouett jiggled marionette-wise on the back veranda for a moment; then when she saw what was happening at the bottom of the paddock, near Young Moriarty's flowering fruit-trees, she put her hands over her face and scuttered into the house again.

Old Gourlay writhed beside the fence, brandishing his whip and shrieking in a frenzy of rage. Moriarty tried to explain, but Gourlay would have no explanations. He was deaf to what Moriarty was saying, though he heard O'Reilly laughing up under the almond-trees. He knew well enough there was only one explanation, Old Gourlay, and Moriarty was not likely to give that.

'It's a put-up job,' he spluttered; 'a buddy put-up job. I'll have the law of ye for it. Taking the bread out of a man's mouth. There'll be no holding him now.'

And there was not. Gourlay was right about that. At the sidings there was no keeping the Ganger from passing mares; and he was as flighty as a brumby, on the roads. He dragged Gourlay, powerless at the end of his reins, behind the tip-dray as they came down-hill, the old man looking more than ever like some dry, twiggy insect as he jogged there, shrilling fiercely. He was at his wits' end, and went in danger of his life, trying to manage the stallion. He could talk of nothing but the life the horse was leading him; and worry about each new incident in his career, as if an only son had kicked over the traces and was disgracing him in the district.

Mrs. Drouett got nerves with it all. She went about with her head in a shawl and said she was ill. She and Old Gourlay quarrelled incessantly. Their voices could be heard cracking and rattling at each other in the evening. Nothing seemed left of their old passion except its animosities. But when Mrs. Drouett took to her bed, Old Gourlay became alarmed. He thought she might die, and he threw up his contract for mending the road to stay at home and nurse her.

Without telling anyone in Black Swan what he was going to do, or where the horse was going, he sold Grey Ganger then. O'Reilly called him by every name he could think of. But Gourlay would not have forgone his vengeance for a fiver. As it was, he had taken less for the horse than O'Reilly, and many another man round Black Swan, would have given. He sold his house and land too; and he and Mrs. Drouett went to live nearer to town, where, if people were not as kind and friendly, at least they were less free with their neighbours' property.

Moriarty married Rose Sharwood soon after old Lizzie had foaled in O'Reilly's paddock beyond The Beak. At the end of the winter it was. His vines did well in that fifth year: he had expected so much from them. He dried currants, raisins, sultanas, and sold them at top prices on the London market. Even Rose's aunt was satisfied with the cheque he showed her from his agents.

It was not until the following season that 'the bottom fell out of the market for dried fruit', as fruit-growers around Black Swan said. And about the same time Rose gave birth to a son.

Bill was not sorry when the baby died, a few months afterwards during the summer. He believed it was better for a weakly child, as for a sick chicken or calf, to die. But the birth, brief screaming existence and death of the small puckered red creature were a shock to him. He had not reckoned on a child from him being a weakling; and Death, like a hand out of the dark, had gripped, shaken, and squeezed life out of the youngster. There was something brutal and unfair about the whole business. If the thing was to die, why had it ever been born? Young Moriarty was dazed, numb and angry under the shock.

As he worked out of doors, milked the cows he had

bought to make up for the falling price of dried fruit, fed pigs and fowls, ploughed and harrowed the orchard, or cleared land for fodder crops, he still glanced often down to the Ganger's yard. Through his numbness and anger about the child, the cleaning of sties and cowyards, breaking of earth, slopping of milk into pig-troughs, thoughts of the stallion were fugitive.

Life with Rose was not what he imagined it would be. It was mostly a fitting-in of domestic jobs, talking about the cost of things, eating frugally, and sleeping without touching her. He had taken her as he wished, sometimes; and now she pushed him away, saying he was 'low . . . a lustful brute'.

Moriarty was depressed about it. He had not expected Rose to be like that; his joy in her to fade so soon. As he toiled, ploughing, harrowing and pruning, he was conscious of belonging to the fecund earth and life, and yet of being apart from them.

Rose did not want any more children; she dreaded having another baby. It seemed simple and natural enough for a man and woman to have children. But not for Rose, or for him . . . He snipped the shoots from a budding fruit-tree . . . Perhaps they were burnt cats who feared the fire, he and Rose.

He noticed that grass had grown in the Ganger's yard and under his stable door.

Rose herself had no strong feelings, he was sure, except for the things that did not matter: dust in out-of-the-way corners, pennies spent unnecessarily. But she was keen on the scent of any hankering Bill might have for another woman, and so shrewish about it that for the sake of peace, at least, he had come to heel. He no longer sought other women.

But Lord, what was there to live for? His days tasted all the same to him, from dawn till dark, flat and dull. He worked hard but without the old zest. Couch had made its appearance in his orchard, his tilth was not what it had been. He invariably struck a bad day if he had cows to sell; and he missed the best price for eggs.

He was a fool, Moriarty told himself, as Rose had often said. He had been wrong about Rose; he had made a mistake about the orchard. There was no money in fruit, fresh or dried. He worked as hard as any of O'Reilly's draught horses for food and a room over his head: and that was all there was to it. He was sick to death of pottering about pigsties, cowyards, fowl-houses, fruit-trees; and he supposed he would go on pottering among them, and being sick to death of them.

It was the rut of life he had made and must stay in.

As he sprawled before the fire that evening, morose and weary, this was swarming over him, the thoughts crawling in and out of his brain and breeding, as did fruit-fly on rotting nectarines in his orchard.

O'Reilly swung into the kitchen.

'That draught stallion of Old Gourlay's,' he said, 'he's been bought by Purdies. Standing the season at The Beak farm and will travel the district. Be up at my place this day next week ... Thought you'd like to know.'

Moriarty went to see the horse when he was at O'Reilly's stables. As the groom led him out, the stallion came, arching his neck and tossing his head.

Grey Ganger was more beautiful than he had ever been; no longer skittish, but imperious, his quarters moulded to perfection, the grey satin of his skin sheening under its dapples as he moved. Bill walked across and stood beside him, rubbing a hand over his shoulders, the anguish of his dissatisfaction with life breaking.

'I wish it was me, old man,' he groaned. 'I wish it was me. It's all I'm fit for really.'

Rodney Hall

The Island in the Mind

1661

The village was well off, as villages went, and tidily kept. Cottages clustered quaintly along the river bank, rowboats were set in ice where they had drifted at the end of their moorings, and the watermill stuck at a fixed angle. Diminutive figures in black hats and wraps skated on the new wide sparkling estuary of ice. Remote children's cries, carrying on the still air, reached me shrilly, joyfully. And, sure enough, some town merchants approaching the far bank did urge their slithering horses towards the ice. Loaded wagons swayed down the bumpy slope, the beasts baulking at a risk which perhaps they judged more accurately than their masters. A skein of wheel tracks across the river marked the same route taken by previous expeditions, ending on my side in slushy ruts zigzagging up into the village and then out along the road snaking away to the south-west.

I was so interested I stayed a while to watch. Strolling now and again, I still watched, not even conscious of where I trod. The leading wagon, now safely on level ice, skidded a little. The horse puffed out worried exclamations of steam, his hooves slipping and rising too sharply off the surface. Other spectators from the village on my side of the river stood to watch also – village women carrying babies. A second wagon creaked steadily to the edge in its turn, this one was drawn by two horses. Laden with a huge heap of firewood, it jolted down on to the ice and set out to cross. The driver slid from his bench to take the bridle. He led the way, treading gingerly. I thought what a fool he was to risk it if he felt so apprehensive. Arriving after both wagons, a horseman reined in on the far bank and waited – no doubt wise enough to see them safely over before adding any extra weight to the ice.

Both wagons, the one loaded with some sort of live-stock wagging their heads and the one piled high with firewood, crept our way. Perhaps those dobbins pulling them could hear the ice yield, as we could not. They wavered along hesitantly. A couple of our villagers deduced something humorous from this; and a young woman with several brats clutching her skirt let out shrieks of laughter. The rooks flocked up out of their new roost among the elms and dipped away towards the town, uttering desolate cries. On the second wagon, with its teetering heap of firewood, a huddled person flapped one hand at the driver who held the bridle. He noticed. He spared a moment to look up and say something. Then he turned again to the task of listening to his boots and creeping forward. A sudden breeze sprang out from nowhere, agitating scarves and chilling our skin. Then it was gone.

The first wagon, more than halfway across, began to hurry, the horse now plainly frightened and losing rhythm, kicking up chips of ice in little flurries. 'You'll soon be safe,' the laughing woman called, 'and a pennyworth of trouble the better off!' By the tone of her mockery I gathered he was famously close-fisted. But he dared not shout back or his nag might bolt altogether. They plugged on mutely. The main sound was wheels grinding and whistling. You could hear the beast's laboured breath too. Also the beasts behind, grunting. And you could hear the strain of loads borne by aching timbers. One after the other they came on with a dull rumble, as if rolling across a drum-skin. (I forgot my own concerns, forgot the message still inside my shirt.) Dangling chains clanked, leather straps stretched and squeaked on the traces. Harnesses jingled.

A child in a woollen hat, holding her mother's hand, jumped up and down on the spot. The first horse lifted its head in alarm and gazed up at us, nostrils wide and pale. Suddenly it made a dash for the bank. The wagon slewed, wheels chafing, its freight of caged pigs – for that's what they were – catching the panic, let out a chorus of screams. The driver furiously tugged the reins. The whole thing threatened to topple over as it reached land, hit a hard ridge of frozen clay and bounced up the bank. Jolted crates thudded at the impact and pig trotters drummed with a frenzied pattering. The sideboards bent. The overworked vehicle yawed, timbers joggling loose at the joints. The horse stamped, kicked and reared, then dug its hooves in. Lashed by the whip, haunches quivering with strain, the terrified creature drove itself, wide-eyed, up the bank to the road where it crabbed for a few yards until the owner could calm its panic. The pigs, having scented death as only pigs do, kept up their chorus of screams, seething and milling in the cages. Fat hard naked bodies rasped against one another. The outfit rolled past us smelling of desperation. I saw their darting eyes. And their upraised snouts, as expressionless as the soles of feet.

The gentleman on the far bank edged his pretty horse on to the ice.

The way being clear, the wood wagon groaned closer, its load uncertain, the half-standing passenger still teetering. There was something odd about the way she stood. Something irresolute – not fully straightened up, and being thrown about by the least jerk. Now that the noisy pigs had passed well down the road on their way to the slaughterhouse, her voice came to us, clear in the frosty air. She was talking continuously, patiently. We could also hear the woodcutter answer in a similar monotone an octave lower. On they came, advancing, so steady for a moment that they seemed not to move at all. We stood watching, our toes grown numb. Each breath we let out hung in the air as a tiny apprehensive cloud.

A bent old man joined us, snow creaking under his felt boots. Another brief coil of wind leapt up from the cold ground, spiralled among us and sank back again. I shivered.

Abruptly, without warning, the wagon tilted sharply: one wheel appeared to have collapsed. The horses stamped and strained, feeling the load tug them back. When the bridle twitched in his hand the man swung round to look up at them, as if their eyes might tell him more than his lurching vehicle. He reached out with a soothing hand to pat the nearside animal. The load leaned the other way. And then leaned further. The standing woman lost her balance. She pitched right off, tumbling on to the ice, flat and still. She lay there in a huddle of winter clothes. She had fallen with scarcely a sound, there was just the bitter cold pinching our ears. The woodcutter jerked at the bridle — setting studded traces and little brasses on the swingletree jittering — and began to shout commands to his horses. He knew now what was wrong. He watched the load heel to one side. Yet he made no move to help the injured woman. Only then did I guess the truth that, from where he walked, with those large beasts of burden between them, he had not seen her fall. So how could he know that, right then, the swaying load of wood hung above her? How could he know that if it rolled over, which might happen at any moment, she would be crushed?

The ice cracked with a noise as loud as a gun.

Women near me shrieked in distress and began running along the bank, but dared not go closer; most, as I say, had babies in their arms or small children grabbing their skirts. Nothing could be done in any case. Yet I did notice, to my surprise, the gentleman on horseback urging his mount to a trot, already halfway over.

The ice gave under the other wheel on that same side of the stricken vehicle. The pile of branches swayed dangerously, straining the ropes lashed tight around it. The horses were nearly thrown by shafts bending with strain. They braced their weight the other way. They whinnied in terror. They kicked each other, hooves skittering wildly as they bunched and struggled to drag the cart up out of that widening hole of sinister black water. They were so close to the bank. Yet there was no saving the load. With a long protesting creak of bowed timbers it sagged. One by one, the ropes snapped. 'Ma!' yelled the man — just that one frantic guttural cry of heartbreak. He sloshed among separating plates of ice as he let go the bridle. The jagged black map underfoot broke open. The effort was doomed. He could not keep his balance to reach her or rescue her. Firewood, piled high as a haystack, groaned and sank down on her — squashed her and forced her body under, deep into the freezing current flowing under the ice — the hole like a jagged island of nothing in a white sea. The woodcutter plunged in.

Too late, the gentleman rode over, his own mount fracturing the crust and lurching, floundering belly-deep, struggling to get a foothold, then heaving itself up on the margin, awash and lucky to be out of danger. Without hesitation he slid down from the saddle. Releasing his terrified beast to gallop away along the palace road, he tugged a dagger from its sheath, braved the swirling waters and waded toward the wagon. Once there he hacked at the traces while the drowning horses fought for life, stretching their long necks — lips pulled back, yellow teeth slashing at him, their manes swishing like wet whips. They humped and rose a moment only to sink down to the eyes again and then fight their way back. He freed one. The animal flipped, threshed and churned away to safety, suffering so tremendously, coughing such violent great coughs I thought it must die in any case.

The woodcutter's streaming head emerged from beneath his overturned wagon as it rolled completely upside down and sank. Amazingly he had survived. Sleek as an otter, he goggled and squinted around him, lost. Then he struggled free and breasted a passage through the jostling fractured ice. Women reached out to help him up. Setting their infants down in the snow they stretched their arms toward him. I never saw so mournful a sight, even at war. And the gentleman too, deathly pale, shivering in his sodden clothes, dragged himself to safety. The remaining horse, still entangled in tackle, drowned a frightful convulsive drowning. Perhaps the two men wept, the woodcutter and the gentleman. There was no way to tell. They were holding on to one another when I reached them to offer my aid. I noticed then that the chunks of broken ice contained frozen perch and even a hawk with its wings askew. 'Ma was blind,' the fellow explained as if apologizing. His voice broke in blubbering sobs, while the other stared at me very particularly, even though he hunched double from spasms of cold. Surprisingly this gentleman turned out to be an oldish person. What's more I recognized him. Primo Tranquilli.

'But I was looking for you!' I complained idiotically.

I wrapped him in my cloak. The women hitched wailing babies on their hips and led us to a nearby cottage, a train of wide-eyed children following them. Here they stripped soggy garments from the survivors and bundled them in rough blankets. Tranquilli, blue already, lost consciousness. So I found him after all, when I had given up looking for him. But there was no longer any urge to disencumber myself of Scarron's message. Once he revived, if he did not die of the chill, I would find an occasion to pass on the composer's advice that, in order to present the Beast as both misleader and guardian of mysteries, he might need to put away his drawings and discover the means by dreaming it. I set off for the palace at a run, mind filled with horrors. Only now did I see the tragedy for what it was. And the expression I had caught in those heavy-lidded eyes was the look of someone who recognizes a monster.

Damon Runyon

Old Em's Kentucky Home

The grounds and the house itself all look as if they can stand a little attention and there is not a soul in sight and it is rather a dismal scene in every respect. The gate is closed, so I get down off the truck and open it and Itchky drives the truck in and right up to the front door of the house under a sort of porch with white pillars.

Now the truck makes a terrible racket and this racket seems to stir up a number of coloured parties who appear from around in back of the house, along with a large white guy. This large guy is wearing corduroy pants and laced boots and a black moustache and he is also carrying a double-barrelled shotgun and he speaks to Itchky in a fierce tone of voice as follows:

'Pigface,' he says, 'get out of here. Get out of here before you are hurt. What do you mean by driving in here with a load of dog meat such as this, anyway?'

He points a finger at old Em who has her head up and is snuffling the air and gazing about her with great interest, and right away Itchky climbs down off the seat of the truck and removes his derby and places it on the ground and takes off his coat and starts rolling up his sleeves.

'It is the last straw,' Itchky Ironhat says. 'I will first make this big ash can eat that cannon he is lugging and then I will beat his skull in. Nobody can refer to Emaleen as dog meat and live.'

Now the front door of the house opens and out comes a thin character in a soiled white linen suit and at first he seems to be quite an old character as he has long white hair but when he gets closer I can see that he is not so very old at that, but he is very seedy-looking and his eyes have a loose expression. I can also see from the way the large guy and the coloured parties step back this is a character who packs some weight around here. His voice is low and hard as he speaks to Itchky Ironhat and says:

'What is this?' he says. 'What name do I just hear you pronounce?'

'Emaleen,' Itchky says. 'It is the name of my race mare which you see before you. She is the greatest race mare in the world. The turf records say she is bred right here at this place and I bring her down here to see her old home, and everybody insults her. So this is Southern hospitality?' Itchky says.

The new character steps up to the truck and looks at old Em for quite a spell and all the time he is shaking his head and his lips are moving as if he is talking to himself, and finally he says to the large guy:

'Unload her,' he says. 'Unload her and take good care of her, Dobkins. I suppose you will have to send to one of the neighbours for some feed. Come in, gentlemen,' he says to Itchky and me and he holds the front door of the house open. 'My name is Salsbury,' he says. 'I am the owner of Tucky Farms and I apologise for my foreman's behaviour but he is only following orders.'

As we go into the house I can see that it is a very large house and I can also see that it must once be a very grand house because of the way it is furnished, but everything seems to be as run-down inside as it does outside and I can see that what this house needs is a good cleaning and straightening out.

In the meantime, Mr Salsbury keeps asking Itchky Ironhat questions about old Em and when he hears how long Itchky has her and what he thinks of her and all this and that, he starts wiping his eyes with a handkerchief as if the story makes him very sad, especially the part about why Itchky brings her to the Bluegrass.

Finally Mr Salsbury leads us into a large room that seems to be a library and at one end of this room there is a painting taller than I am of a very beautiful Judy in a white dress and this is the only thing in the house that seems to be kept dusted up a little and Mr Salsbury points at the painting and says:

'My wife, Emaleen, gentlemen. I name the horse you bring here after her long ago, because it is the first foal of her favourite mare and the first foal of a stallion I import from France.'

'By Christofer, out of Love Always,' Itchky Ironhat says.

'Yes,' Mr Salsbury says. 'In those days, Tucky Farms

is one of the great breeding and racing establishments of the Bluegrass. In those days, too, my wife is known far and wide for her fondness for horses and her kindness to them. She is the head of the humane society in Kentucky and the Emaleen Salsbury annual award of a thousand dollars for the kindest deed brought to the attention of the society each year is famous.

'One night,' Mr Salsbury continues, 'there is a fire in the barns and my wife gets out of bed and before anyone can stop her she rushes into the flames trying to save her beautiful mare, Love Always. They both perish, and,' he says, 'with them perishes the greatest happiness ever given a mortal on this earth.'

By this time, Itchky Ironhat and I are feeling very sad indeed, and in fact all the creases in Itchky's face are full of tears as Mr Salsbury goes on to state that the only horses on the place that are saved are a few yearlings running in the pastures. He sends them all with a shipment a neighbour is taking to Saratoga to be disposed of there for whatever they will bring.

'Your mare Emaleen is one of those,' he says. 'I forget all about her at the time. Indeed,' he says, 'I forget everything but my unhappiness. I feel I never wish to see or hear of a horse again as long as I live and I withdraw myself completely from the world and all my former activities. But,' he says, 'your bringing the mare here awakens old fond memories and your story of how you cherish her makes me realize that this is exactly what my wife Emaleen will wish me to do. I see where I sadly neglect my duty to her memory. Why,' he says, 'I never even keep up the Emaleen Salsbury award.'

Now he insists that we must remain there a while as his guests and Itchky Ironhat agrees, although I point out that it will be more sensible for us to move on to Louisville and get into action as quickly as possible because we are now practically out of funds. But Itchky takes a look at old Em and he says she is enjoying herself so much running around her old home and devouring grass that it will be a sin and a shame to take her away before it is absolutely necessary.

After a couple of days, I tell Itchky that I think absolutely necessary arrives, but Itchky says Mr Salsbury now wishes to give a dinner in honour of old Em and he will not think of denying her this pleasure. And for the next week the house is overrun with coloured parties, male and female, cleaning up the house and painting and cooking and dusting and I do not know what all else, and furthermore I hear there is a great to-do all through the Bluegrass country when the invitations to the dinner start going around, because this is the first time in over a dozen years that Mr Salsbury has any truck whatever with his neighbours.

On the night of the dinner, one of the male coloured parties tells me that he never before sees such a gathering of the high-toned citizens of the Bluegrass as are assembled in the big dining hall at a horseshoe-shaped table with an orchestra going and with flowers and flags and racing colours all around and about. In fact, the coloured party says it is just like the old days at Tucky Farms when Mr Salsbury's wife is alive, although he says he does not remember ever seeing such a character sitting alongside Mr Salsbury at the table as Itchky Ironhat.

To tell the truth, Itchky Ironhat seems to puzzle all the guests no little and it is plain to be seen that they are wondering who he is and why he is present, though Itchky is sharpened up with a fresh shave and has on a clean shirt and of course he is not wearing his derby hat. Personally, I am rather proud of Itchky's appearance, but I can see that he seems to be overplaying his knife a little, especially against the mashed potatoes.

Mr Salsbury is dressed in a white dinner jacket and his eyes are quiet and his hair is trimmed and his manner is most genteel in every way and when the guests are seated he gets to his feet and attracts their attention by tapping on a wineglass with a spoon. Then he speaks to them as follows:

'Friends and neighbours,' he says. 'I know you are all surprised at being invited here, but you may be more surprised when you learn the reason. As most of you are aware, I am as one dead for years. Now I live again. I am going to restore Tucky Farms to all its old turf glory in breeding and racing, and,' he says, 'I am going to re-establish the Emaleen Salsbury award, with which you are familiar, and carry on again in every way as I am now certain my late beloved wife will wish.'

Then he tells them the story of old Em and how Itchky Ironhat cares for her and loves her all these years and how he brings her to the Bluegrass just to see her old home, but of course he does not tell them that Itchky also plans to later drop her in a race at Churchill Downs, as it seems Itchky never mentions the matter to him.

Anyway, Mr Salsbury says that the return of old Em awakens him as if from a bad dream and he can suddenly see how he is not doing right with respect to his wife's memory and while he is talking a tall old guy who is sitting next to me, and who turns out to be nobody but the guy who directs Tucky Farms, says to me like this:

'It is a miracle,' he says. 'I am his personal physician and I give him up long ago as a hopeless victim of melancholia. In fact, I am always expecting to hear of him dismissing himself from this world entirely. Well,' the old guy says, 'I always say medical science is not everything.'

'My first step toward restoring Tucky Farms,' Mr Salsbury goes on, 'is to purchase the old mare Emaleen from Mr Itchky Ironhat here for the sum of three thousand dollars, which we agree upon this evening as a fair price. I will retire her of course for the rest of her days, which I hope will be many.'

With this he whips out a cheque and hands it to Itchky and naturally I am somewhat surprised at the sum mentioned because I figure if old Em is worth three G's War Admiral must be worth a million. However, I am also greatly pleased because I can see where Itchky and I will have a nice taw for the races at Churchill Downs without having to bother about old Em winning one.

'Now,' Mr Salsbury says, 'for our guest of honour.'

Then two big doors at one end of the banquet hall open wide and there seems to be a little confusion outside and a snorting and a stamping as if a herd of wild horses is coming in and all of a sudden who appears in the doorway with her mane and tail braided with ribbons and her coat all slicked up but old Em and who is leading her in but the large guy who insults her and also Itchky on our arrival at Tucky Farms.

The guests begin applauding and the orchestra plays My Old Kentucky Home and it is a pleasant scene to be sure, but old Em seems quite unhappy about something as the large guy pulls her into the hollow of the horseshoe-shaped table, and the next thing anybody knows, Itchky Ironhat climbs over the table, knocking glasses and dishes every which way and flattens the large guy with a neat left hook, in the presence of the best people of the Bluegrass country.

Naturally, this incident causes some comment and many of the guests are slightly shocked and there is considerable criticism of Itchky Ironhat for his lack of table manners. But then it is agreed by one and all present that Itchky is undoubtedly entitled to the Emaleen Salsbury kindness to horses award when I explain that what irks him is the fact that the large guy leads old Em in with a twitch on her lip.

Well, this is about all there is to the story, except the Itchky and I go over to Louisville the next day and remain there awaiting the Kentucky Derby and we have a wonderful time, to be sure, except that we do not seem to be able to win any bets on horse races at Churchill Downs.

M. E. Patchett

Tam the Untamed

Because of a serious injury, the horse-breaker who worked every year at Gunyan could not come, and another man turned up and applied for the job. My father gladly took him on, for he had a great reputation as a horseman. His name was Tom Hessler, and it did not need Ajax's warning growl to tell me I would not like him very much. But nevertheless I respected his reputation as a horseman and also as a judge of horses. So when he said to me:

'They reckon you've got a champion here – a grey horse – what's his name?'

'Tam,' I said. 'It's short for Tamburlaine. He belongs to me.'

'I'd like to have a look at him sometime,' he went on, and I, silly little mutt, always loving to show Tam to anyone, especially a good judge, said:

'Would you like to come along now?'

So we started off for the stables. Hessler was a small, slender man with a graceful walk, and the strong hands and wrists that belong to horsemen. He had sandy hair and a narrow, cunning face; he wore an old felt hat, and it struck me that he looked very like a fox with a hat on. He had rather a bragging manner, and I liked him less than ever when he gave a whistle and pointed at Ajax, saying:

'Where'd you get *that* mong from? He's as big as a lion!'

'Ajax isn't a mongrel, he's half dingo and half kangaroo dog – we think –'

'Ajax, eh? Well, he's the biggest dog I've ever seen.'

Ajax, hearing his name spoken, growled away in his throat. It was easy to see what *he* thought of the new man, horseman or not.

Tam, when I was in my twelfth year, had just reached his full beauty. He was a proud, silver horse, and I doubt if even Hessler had ever seen one to equal him. Tam was standing in his orchard, his head thrown up, listening. For a moment I almost liked Hessler when I saw the expression of absolute amazement that spread over his face:

'W-e-l-l – that's a *horse!*' was all that he said.

We moved nearer, and Tam dilated his nostrils and moved nervously away.

'You stay here until he gets used to you,' I said, and went over and fondled Tam.

While I held him he let Hessler examine him. There was no doubt that the man knew horses. He moved his sure hands over Tam, and Tam relaxed.

'I'd like to ride this fellow,' Hessler said off-handedly.

I answered that no one ever rode Tam but me, and I told him about Willis. He laughed.

'I used to know that bloke, not a bad horseman,' he said in a tone that implied that he himself was better.

'He must have been pretty good,' I admitted, 'but Tam threw him when he wanted to. You know Tam's the son of Bobs?'

'Well, buck-jumpers don't come any better than Bobs – can this fellow buck?'

'Ask Willis,' I said grimly.

He laughed again. 'Don't tell me he's as good as

Bobs, because I won't believe you. Bobs is the greatest buck-jumper Australia has ever seen.'

'And Tam's just as good,' I said defensively. 'I've seen Bobs plenty of times, and Tam bucks just like him — only Tam's more nervous than Bobs.'

'You ought to sell him, he'd make a fortune in a buck-jumping tent – why, if he's as good as you say I could get you hundreds for him.'

'I've been offered hundreds; Tam isn't for sale.'

All the time we were talking Hessler was rubbing Tam down, across his back, down his legs, with strong, swift movements of his big hands. Tam liked it. For the first time in his life he turned and looked at a stranger with friendly eyes. Hessler stayed around for about half an hour, then it was time for me to feed Tam, and he walked along to the stable with me. It was plain that he was fascinated by the horse. I wished he would go away, but he turned to and helped me to get the feed, found my cache of carrots and gave Tam one, and was altogether what I thought to be very officious. Still I could not find it in my heart to be nasty to anyone, however much I disliked them, who felt such an admiration for my horse.

Through the next days I often saw Hessler ride the

horses he was breaking-in; he was undoubtedly a fine horseman. In his off hours he often walked over to Tam's stable, and Tam got quite used to his rubbing him down, and even feeding him. I disliked it, and I did not like that man; but as he never did anything to offend me there seemed to be nothing I could do about it.

I noticed that the stockmen were not as cordial to Hessler as they had been at first, so I supposed that they found he did not improve on closer acquaintance. Once my father had to speak to him about using excessive cruelty to one difficult horse he was breaking, and that did not make me like him any better either. When he came along to the stable, Algy and Ben greeted him quite happily; but Ajax never unbent, and if Hessler moved near him, Ajax growled deep in his throat and moved away.

Word came that the Bill Brady Buck-jumping Show was to play two nights in Texas. It was the rival show to the one that Bobs was in, but not nearly as good. Brady simply could not get a buck-jumper of anywhere near Bobs' quality; there was not one – or, if there were, then he was not for sale.

Still, we all loved buck-jumping shows, and on that

first night we set off and had quite an exciting evening. It was my governess Miss Brown's first view of this sort of entertainment, and she was thrilled. Brady had one jumper that was not bad, but on the whole the horses were poor. As Miss Brown did not know the difference between pig-rooting and buck-jumping she was quite happy, and clapped loudly for every event. The show was to be on for one more night, but my father decided that it was not really good enough to see again. Rumour said that Brady was very worried that his show was not pulling in better audiences, and he was a good enough showman to know that it never would unless he could improve the quality of the buck-jumping.

Next day I went round to my father's office to give him a message, and I found him paying Hessler off.

'Where're you making for now?' my father asked.

'Oh, I'll stay in Texas a day or two; then I'm off down Goondiwindi way.'

'It's the last night of Brady's show; you'd better look it over. You're the sort of horseman who wouldn't find it difficult to pick up a few pounds riding any of Brady's horses.'

Hessler smiled, a nasty smile.

'Oh, I'll take a look at it,' he said and turned away. 'I'll drop along and say good-bye to the horse later on, Miss,' he added to me, and I was glad to think it would be the last time he would touch Tam.

Hessler came along and lingered round the stable, petting Tam, rubbing him down and generally taking his time. As last he left with a casual good-bye to me, and accompanied by a velvety growl from Ajax. I stood in the doorway and watched him go through the orchard gate, very thankful indeed that I had seen the last of him. Then I went back into the stable and gave Tam another rub-down to remove the touch of those horrid hands, said good night to him and went to have my supper.

The moon was a little past full and it rose late, but even so it was as bright as daylight outside. I went to bed early and lay looking at the white, magical world around me. Ajax was restless, and kept moving about and growling a little. Algy and Ben were snoring loudly after a long day's rabbiting – and not one catch! My parents had guests to dinner, and they were play-ing bridge afterwards. Ajax got more and more restless; he kept turning his head towards the old orchard, which was on the other side of the house, and I got to wondering if it was something to do with Tam that worried him. It was about half-past eight, and I had not seen my horse since I bedded him down before seven.

I put on my dressing-gown and slippers and followed Ajax quietly out of the house. I could hear my family and the visitors having coffee in the sitting-room. My mother had been out to say good night, and I knew that they would not move from the card-table for hours.

As we went into the orchard, Ajax's hackles were high and he made soft, thunderous noises deep in his chest, which made me hurry. I broke into a run, pulled up short at the stable door and looked in – Tam was not there. Perhaps he was in the orchard, and, intent on reaching the stable, I had not noticed him. I looked around the orchard – no Tam. My heart was pounding with fear, and a dreadful suspicion grew in my mind. I went back to the stable – my saddle and bridle were there – then I retraced my steps, looking closely at the moonlit ground of the little path the dogs and I had worn from the gate to the stable. Here and there Tam's fresh hoof-prints showed up clearly. I followed them to the outer garden gate – then it was no longer a suspicion: I knew.

A fury of rage and despair gripped me; that was why Hessler had made friends with Tam. I tried to make myself think calmly, to reason what he would do with him. If he kept the horse to sell, Tam was so well known that the thief would be caught. No, Hessler was not fool enough to do *that* — the last man who had tried it was still in gaol. Then there was only one answer — the buck-jumping show! Suddenly I remembered the scene in the office, Hessler's nasty smile and his casual words about the show: 'I'll take a look at it.'

As clearly as though I was watching him do it, I knew that Hessler was going to take Tam to Brady's buck-jumping tent. The audience would recognize Tam as my horse, but everyone knew Hessler had been working on Gunyan. It seemed impossible for anyone to realize the depth of my love for Tam; to them it would seem credible that I would let a horseman of Hessler's class try out the son of Bobs.

I had never spoken to Brady, nor had he seen my horse; he would be only too willing to believe anything that Hessler chose to tell him, particularly when he had seen Tam buck and knew what a draw he would be; Hessler knew his stuff well enough to make Tam buck full out in the ring. The very boldness of his plan would make it succeed. By to-morrow he would be well away, and Brady would be the one to have the trouble.

Instead of the sadness and misery I felt the time before when Tam had been kidnapped, this time I was full of rage and fury and a longing for action. That Tam should have been betrayed by those cunning hands smoothing his hide was a Judas-act too bitter to dwell on. I made up my mind; I would not ask for help, I would get Tam myself.

I put on my riding-clothes, my fingers clumsy with haste, and put the latch on the wire door of my veranda, so that Algy and Ben could not get out. They woke as I moved about, but I made them stay where they were, and put my dressing-gown on the foot of the bed so that they climbed up on it, which is what I always did to show them that they must stay there, and that I would be back.

Then I slipped out and crossed to the big stables where Belle was in the yard with the horses that were to be used in the morning; the stockhorse; the horse the milkman rode to round up his milkers; the general-purpose mare that anyone took to go short distances – this animal was always known as the 'square mare', which strange title came from the fact that it was allowed to graze in the square paddock around the house.

Belle was plainly annoyed at being saddled at that time of night, and surprised that I was so brusque with her. She was even more surprised when I rode her relentlessly as fast as she could gallop along the six miles of unmade, often rough road that led to Texas. I passed no one as I galloped along, with Ajax just ahead of me, silvered by the moonlight, running effortlessly and beautifully.

It was not much after nine when I saw the big white tent pegged out on a bare stretch of river flat. In the distant background there was a jumble of wooden houses. Vehicles were left around the tent, wherever their owners had unharnessed the horses and tied them, along with a number of saddle-horses, to the trees that grew round.

Not much light seeped out of the tent; over the entrance was a big banner tied at each end, on which was printed:

BILL BRADY'S GIGANTIC
BUCK-JUMPING SHOW

in letters so big that they were easy to read even by moonlight. Inside the tent I could hear the voices of the crowd; a sudden cheer broke out, then a great clapping of hands and the general buzz of human voices.

Poor Belle was winded. I jumped off her and pulled the reins over her head, not waiting to tether her among the other horses, and then I ran towards the entrance. Most of the audience was standing, and I slipped through the door unchallenged, as the show was half over. I could not see into the ring over the tall heads of the bushmen massed in front of me. I pushed my way round the inside of the tent until I came to where the crush, through which the horses were led into the ring, was beside me, and then I turned and wriggled and fought to the front.

My heart almost stopped with horror. Ajax had wormed his way forward with me, and I put my hand down and touched him for help to bear this awful sight. Tam was in the ring, a Tam I scarcely knew, one I never would have known except for that episode with the snake. His eyes were wild with terror and his splendid body streaked and darkened with sweat — and across it were two great weals.

I moved my eyes away from Tam, and saw Hessler,

a furious expression on his face and one side of his clothes torn and dirty. It was obvious he had been thrown, so he must have ridden Tam for a time. In his hands he held a stock-whip, and I shuddered, for I knew what had made those cruel marks on the satin hide which those hands had so lately fondled.

Tam was plunging and rearing, and as he backed against the rough, stout railings that fenced him in with his tormentor, the wood cracked and the crowd moved back. Then that terrible whip snaked out at him and caught him across the shoulder, and my horse screamed – a terrible, high sound, full of pain and madness.

That, I think, must have driven me to a kind of madness, too. I took my hands off my dog and said:

'Get him, Ajax!'

The great golden body shot into the ring, and in an instant Hessler was on his back and Ajax, his eyes blazing with red light, lips drawn back from his wolf's teeth, stood astride the man's body, his savage mouth almost touching Hessler's throat. The madness in me wanted to let my dog tear out that throat, but some touch of sanity told me I must not do this thing, for if I did, then Ajax would have destroyed himself, too.

Tam was lashing himself about the ring, twisting his body, swinging his head, rearing and pawing and backing away from the thing on the ground that he had thought his friend. The crowd fell into a stupefied silence, and I saw a man I knew to be Brady trying to push his way towards me. I called:

'Hold him, Ajax.'

Then I called to Brady and the crowd, and my face was hot and wet, so that I knew that the wetness must be the overflow of the scalding tears that burnt my eyes.

'Stay there, Brady – and you – all of you. If you move one step Ajax will tear that beast's throat out – and then I'll set him on *you*, Brady! Stand still – all of you!'

I could hardly see through my tears to pull open the gate of the crush. The sudden hush and my voice made Tam cease his agonized struggling for an instant. I held the gate and called:

'Tam! Tam! I want you – here, boy.'

But the ceaseless turning, plunging and twisting began again. Suddenly Tam reared, and his whole weight thrust for a moment on the railings behind him. There was a splintering crash, the crowd scrambled hastily to the sides, pushing and crushing each other. Tam wheeled, saw a way of escape through splintered wood, and crashed through and out of the open flap before him.

Glancing at Ajax, I saw that his body vibrated with the intensity of his growls, his lips still writhed back in a snarl and saliva dripped on to Hessler's throat where he lay, his hateful face yellow with terror, his body rigid between my dog's legs. I slipped through the railings and ran across the ring shouting:

'If any of you move, Ajax will get you! Don't try to follow, or I'll have Ajax pull your horse down – and he can do it – don't try to follow.'

I scrambled through the opposite side, and when I reached the tent-flap I turned and shouted:

'Hessler! If you ever set foot on Gunyan again I'll have Ajax tear your throat out! Ajax – come on, boy!'

I waited an instant until I saw my golden panther of a dog leap through the railings towards me, then I turned and sprinted for Belle.

Poor Belle! it must have been an awful night for her. I slowed up so as not to frighten her, caught the reins and flung them on to her neck, and jumped into the saddle and tore towards where I could see a silver form rapidly disappearing in the distance. Tam was going towards home, led, I suppose, by some instinct deep within his tortured brain. I leaned forward on Belle's neck and urged her on. She was a fast mare, but she could not catch Tam; still, we were not far behind. I turned my head and saw gaps in the tent where light streamed out and excited people were jostling each other, and then we dipped down into a gully, and the patch of flat ground, the tent and the people passed from sight.

Belle, her head turned towards home, did not need as much urging as she had on the way out, but she had already done a fast six miles that night, so her pace in general was slower. We passed the first gate more than a mile from the township, and I could see how Tam had cleared it like a bird, and was still following the road. Three miles farther on Belle toiled up the hillside to a gate on the top. The mare was tiring fast and slugged her head against the bit, but much as I loved her I had to urge her on.

My heart was full of Tam . . . Tam the betrayed. Again Tam had cleared the next gate; just through it he turned off to the right down the slope of the hill. I pulled Belle up and followed Ajax, who in turn followed Tam's tracks. When we could see down the hillside, Tam was there, his silver brightness darkened by sweat. He was standing still, but as we looked he began to back and rear and toss his head in an aimless way, and a new terror smote me – supposing he never recovered?

I forced this thought away, jumped off Belle and threw the reins over her head, gave her a little pat on the rump, so that she moved off towards the fence and began grazing. Then I walked down the hill a little way and called Ajax. Together we went towards where Tam was doing aimless movements over and over again. Then I sat down on the grass and said:

'Ajax – go to Tam. Softly now – softly.'

Ajax went towards my horse, but Tam never stopped his horrible, idiotic movements. Ajax stood near him and lifted his head to Tam to nuzzle him the way he always did. The big dog might not have been there for all the notice Tam took of him. And then I saw the quality of the movements change; they became more frenzied, more jerky, full of a crazy fear.

I rose and walked towards Tam, calling softly. The movement stopped, the horse stood quite still except for a terrible shuddering that gripped and shook his powerful body. Ajax, with his sensitive animal instincts, recognized the change in the horse, and backed towards me, growling a little in a puzzled way.

I called again — and snaking his neck and giving a whistling scream, the horse charged me. I was terrified; this mad thing was not Tam, it was some dreadful unbalanced force I could not control. Only my immense pity for my horse made me stand there. I wanted to run blindly away, but even if I had been able to move my legs, which I could not, it was futile to run from this great muscular engine if it was bent on my destruction; it bore down on me with the speed and power of a great wind.

Not a yard from me Tam stopped his rush and reared high above me. My mesmerized eyes saw his thrashing legs as his huge silver chest and belly towered uncertainly over my head, blotting out the night sky. Then his front hooves dropped to the earth, missing me by inches, his neck curved inwards and he seized me in his teeth; fortunately as I ducked he caught my riding-shirt at the back of my neck. It was tough material, and it held as Tam swung me high in the air and shook me, his head tossing from side to side. I was not conscious of much except an awful shaking, and of the moment when, high in the air, Tam let me go and flung me curving through the air to fall to the ground yards away. All I thought of then was relaxing my body in the way I had been taught to fall. That and the resilience of my young bones saved me from multiple breakages. I hit the earth; it shook, bruised and knocked the wind out of me, but I was unbroken, and I struggled to sit up.

It was then that Ajax showed me once and for always that in spite of his love and companionship for Tam, his love for me was greater. I sat up, groggily conscious that Tam was gathering himself for another rush at me, and this time I knew that those flailing hooves would not miss; but in that instant Ajax sprang across my body, protecting me, facing Tam's powerful rush. I heard my horse's mad scream, the thud of hooves as he backed away and then came rushing towards me. When the horse was almost on top of us, Ajax's great body rose above me and drove at Tam.

He must have hurled his whole considerable weight where the horse's neck joined the shoulder. As Tam began to rear, Ajax struck him and threw the horse off-balance. He came down on his four hooves, and Ajax crouched for another spring. Silent and still, the horse and dog faced each other, and I lay, not daring to move, scarcely daring to breathe.

In that moment I knew that the madness had gone out of Tam. I called him softly, and Ajax turned and sat down beside me, pressing his strong, comforting body close to my side. Tam stood as if listening to something far away. I called again, just his name, 'Tam, Tam, Tam . . .' over and over again, and presently he came hesitantly towards me.

I sat where I was; he put his head down and I put my hand on his nose; the madness had passed. It was a tamed, an infinitely sad Pegasus that came back to me. I slipped the saddle and bridle off Belle where she stood farther up the hill, placidly grazing, then I patted her and left her to graze. Poor Belle! she had done her part. Then I put the bridle and saddle on Tam, and for a while I led him, his head on my shoulder. I stroked and fondled him, talking incessantly, and every now and again Ajax joined me, and he and Tam nuzzled at each other.

Jim Crace

Continent

How had they reacted, these people, when the young teacher came to the valley, earnest and eager? Old Loti brought him down to the village on horseback on his second day and took him round to shake grave hands at the mayor's house and informal ones at the village store. People smiled at him smiling and waited until they got to know his particular ways before they showed any warmth to the newcomer, the 'volunteer' from Canada. His pupils due back at school within a week, kept away but watched. The men who had met foreigners before, while working in the mines or in the markets and warehouses of the city, stayed close but silent. Those that shook his hand saw that his horse did not like him and that he sat awkwardly on it and pulled too closely on the reins. The horse was reserving judgment, looking for something to trust, and so would they. Horses knew a lot. Did not the white horse escape the flood which drowned the shepherdess?

They did not see him on a horse again, though all the young men of the mountains rode horses, for on the fourth day, at dusk, Eddy Rivette took his shorts and running shoes from their bag and set off at a soft pace across the compound of the school. He tested the ground and the stones and the thorns until he was sure of them, and then, lengthening his step, turned to the steep ridge which separated his half-valley from that of the village and the store. Alone on the tracks worn by animals and borrowed by men, he encountered everything which he had expected: sunset, warm earth, a sense of liberation amongst a landscape and a people equally dispossessed. He picked his way, running all the time but choosing, heading for landmarks, and favouring distance to the hard work of gradients. By the time he was in sight of the store and was surprising those who sat outside, Eddy Rivette had followed for the first time the track which he was to run every day for the fifteen months he stayed in the hills.

'What's that teacher doing, running half-dressed across the hard ground of the hills?'

Old Loti could not give the answer. Men walked or rode in the village but perhaps in Canada they ran in white shorts. He did not know.

'Perhaps in Canada they don't have horses,' he said, and the men nodded that this was so because they remembered how the teacher had sat on his horse two days before.

'Children run,' said the storekeeper. 'They run just for the pleasure of it.'

'Yes, but not alone,' said Loti. 'And anyway, watch him. He doesn't run like a child. He runs as if he has some purpose ... but without any urgency. That's Canada for you.'

But they got used to it and after a while began to look forward to it, like anything reliable and harmless. Within an hour of the children from the school slowly picking their way down the hillside towards the village at the end of their day, the slim, tense figure of their teacher would appear briefly at the summit of the ridge above the village, disappear into the slip of

an erosion gully and then come in view again lower
down the hill where the track was quite flat. There, the
teacher came forward on his toes, head down and fists
clenched, and ran the last two hundred metres in a
sprint, not slowing and stopping until he had passed
the smiles and grins of the men who sat at the store.
Then he turned, cool and with breath to spare, and
smiled himself and said Hello to all who had been
watching.

He got to be quite famous. But fame is something
different from popularity. It is less demanding for a
start and has more to do with talent than virtue. But
not even much to do with talent. The fame which
Eddy Rivette enjoyed was just that of someone behaving strangely but purposefully in a place where there
were enough old men with the leisure to watch. When
they smiled and clapped at his daily approach at the
store it was not with affection or welcome but at what
he was providing for their day. If they had genuinely
known and liked him, the running would have embarrassed them. It was strange. It was quirky. It separated
them from him. Not to be wished of a friend.

'Isra-kone, however, *was* a friend of the village. He
was a young man, uneducated in school ways but

knowing and intelligent and, best of all, a fine talker
and a great horseman. These two things mattered to
the men of the village who were too old to be judged
by the recent talents which were taught at the school.
'Isra was one of the last initiates of the valley, having
spent twelve days, two of them drugged unconscious,
at the circumcision lodge in the mountains. He knew
the secret songs in the old Siddilic, drummed end-
lessly at him and his fellows at the lodge. They had
repeated the words, their stomachs pressed to the
walls to ease the pains of hunger. After 'Isra's lodge
the old mayor had died and the new mayor, old Loti's
brother, discontinued circumcision of the young villagers and the lodges and the secret alliances which
sprang from them, not because he was modern but
because he feared the new directives of the govern-
ment officers in the city more than he feared the
criticism of the old gossips in the village.

And so 'Isra and the young poor men of his age
were the last 'brotherhood' and the old gossips whom
the mayor didn't fear put their hopes on them. It was
foolish, for the younger, uncircumcised brothers and
sons of the 'brotherhood' were better for the village.
They read and wrote and spoke English with the

runner at the school as if it were their own language.
But still the old men preferred 'Isra and his friends.
And secretly they mistrusted the ponderous troupe of
pupils who left with their pens and books for the
school at eight each day.

Of the brotherhood 'Isra was their favourite, more
popular than their own mayor's son who had gone
away to colleges in England and Italy and got new
wild ideas. They didn't need much excuse to like 'Isra.
He was so easy. But when they retold how he had ridden his white mare that night of the rains across the
hills to bring help for the mayor's chest, where his
heart was beating and flapping like a trapped bird,
they found all the excuse to like him thoroughly. The
helicopter had come from the town on to the flat edge
of the village and taken the mayor away to hospital.
Four foreign doctors had slaved to quiet his heart and
keep the mayorship with this old fearful man and
away from the wild ideas of his wild college son. And
'Isra had returned to tell of his ride and that the chief
would be well. Even the smallest children will say it.
'Isra-kone is the finest horseman in the valley.

'Isra was a quiet man, though a great talker when he
chose, who had few certainties. He did not trust the

weather or his cattle or the life of his horse whom he loved. When the weather was fine and his stock was healthy and he woke in the morning to find the horse bright-eyed and vigorous, then he let himself enjoy that day. But he did not expect it to hold for the next day. He expected only what he could see approaching with his own eye, and (since the night darkness blocked his vision) his anticipations ended each day at sunset.

He had known, since the first swollen stomach of his boyhood, what it was to sit watchful at night beneath the stars. That was the extent of his mysticism. For the rest, he was happy while he had maize and fulfilled while he was popular in the village. In the two years since his ride across the mountains to bring the helicopter, he *had* allowed a small certainty into his life, that his comings and goings were commented on. That as he rode down from the lands the old men at the store nodded and smiled with affection and said, 'There's young 'Isra with his horse. What's he up to?' and called, 'Go well, 'Isra. Where are you riding?' Or, 'From where are you come?'

When the old men stopped calling and nodding and commenting they did not like him any less. It was just that their interests were elsewhere, fixed a little to the right of the wide erosion gulley on the ridge above the village where the teacher appeared each evening for an instant before disappearing and appearing again, jogging doggedly towards them and their gossip at the store.

'Isra watched his rival with the old men for a season until his own fame had eroded away and not even the men of his brotherhood turned to admire him and his white mare or whisper his name. Their eyes were not for one of their own whom they loved and trusted and understood but for the foreigner for whom they cared nothing, but who came faster and faster each day from the ridge below the sunset and who seemed to tell them something about man and their mountains which they had never guessed – that men were like hares who could bounce across the black-studded basalt earth around which they had stumbled for centuries until the horse had come.

'Isra missed his fame for a season until he saw how he and his horse could regain it, bringing the attention of the villagers once again back to his entries and exits and his fine horsemanship and story-telling. Not planning ahead further than that day 'Isra timed the meeting with his rival for the evening.

He told old Loti. 'Me and the teacher are going to race tonight from the school to the store. Will you be there? Don't let anybody miss the race.'

Neither he nor old Loti nor the other gossips at the store doubted for an instant that 'Isra and his mare would beat the teacher. The horse was born to the mountains. But they looked forward to the contest. It would be interesting to see what the foreigner and his bony legs could do against the mountain and the horse.

The word soon spread through the village that 'Isra would race the teacher. But the last man to hear was the teacher himself. It was Sunday and the school was closed. He sat at the door of his house and ran his fingers across the ripple soles of his shoes. Still good. Good perhaps for another month or so ... and then it wouldn't matter. His 'term' would be over and he would be back in Canada and running on track again. He'd need harder soles there. These ripples were good for the dry sloping hills which surrounded the school, for turning sharply on the thorny goat-ways and the rubble of the yearly erosion – but not for 'track'. Another month or so ... and he'd have needed new running shoes, the thatch on the staff house would have to be replaced, new boys would be coming to the school. And he'd be in Montreal with his colour slides and a life-long commitment to this seventh and shabby continent, to the village in the next valley. Melvyn John Murphy was coming. His replacement. From Detroit, Michigan – motor city. He'd already written to the American and told him about the place, the school, the trick the sunlight had of flecking the aloes long after the light in the valley had gone. He hoped that Melvyn John Murphy would respect the place like he had, would give what he had (though not quite as much) and take what was offered. They had their own ways, these people. Brashness would not be welcome.

He thought all this and decided that he would miss his running across the hills into the village. He decided, too, that he would preserve his sense of loss, even when his memory was faint and when his body and pace had got used once again to the flat white-lined cinder tracks and the soft spring-time training runs across the campus of Joliette college and along the lip of the river where girls sat with their bicycles on the grass. Somehow it was more noble and more worldly amongst the slipping soils and half-chewed thorns to pad pad pad along, nearly always dry, nearly always warm, always alone and with no competition, no other runners but yourself to run against.

He would preserve the loss of that.

The wind was dropping now as it did the hour before dusk. He pulled the ripples on and tied them tight and double so they would not loosen or snag on the low dry bushes. He turned his socks close down over his shoes so that his shins were exposed and could be cut on the sharp twigs and coarse grass of the track. It was good to scratch and draw blood in that safe place.

When he stood he saw 'Isra-kone standing next to his tough white mare at the edge of the school compound. Eddy Rivette walked over and greeted his visitor.

'Did you come to see me?'

'Isra nodded.

'What is it? To do with the school?'

'No, running. I want to race with you to the store.'

Eddy Rivette was half-pleased. It was good that one of the villagers should want to run with him, but this man was not dressed for running nor built for it. It was strange, that—for the man's decision to come to

him at the school seemed firm and old but his appearance was that of a man who wanted to run on
impulse, whatever he wore and despite his build.

'I go fast,' said Eddy discouragingly.

'My horse goes faster!'

'Your horse? You want to race me on your horse?
Not running?'

'No, riding on my horse!'

The both laughed at the thought of 'Isra running.
This was to be more of a contest because 'Isra was a
fine rider and his horse was strong and used to the
hills and the ways across them.

'Why do you want to run against me? Must the
loser give something?'

'No,' said 'Isra. 'It is for the race only'.

'Okay. When?' asked Eddy.

'Now,' said 'Isra.

∩ ∩ ∩

And that was how the Great Race between the schoolteacher and the horseman began — a simple challenge
brought to the school compound by a small uneasy
man with a horse to another small man, a runner from
Canada. Not a brother. Not a man from the villages

amongst the hills, but a stranger with a stranger's ways. 'When?' asked the one. 'Now,' answered the other. And so the race waited a few moments to begin, for the two men to understand the race, that it was two different strengths that were being matched.

'When you kick your horse I will start running,' said Eddy Rivette. 'Isra nodded. 'It's the first to the store, is that it?' 'Isra nodded again. 'We can go any way we want, just get there first?'

'That's right,' said 'Isra.

'Let's go then!'

'Isra kicked his horse and turned the rein towards the foot of the steep ridge which stood between him and the crowd of villagers, his villagers, who waited at the ground by the store. The horse speeded from a trot to a canter and cut firmly and confidently into the slow gradient away from the school. Eddy Rivette set off in pursuit, surprised at the speed with which the horse was gaining ground. He saw 'Isra choose the same cattle track which he himself had used nightly for visits to the store. 'Isra had been watching him, he realised. Any advantage that Eddy had from knowing the most economical route across the ridge was lost now that 'Isra had chosen it for himself. It would be impossible to pass, too, on that track. It was too narrow and its borders too treacherous for the delicate ankles of a man. Used to adapting his tactics to the dictates of the pack in the point-to-points and marathons that he had run in Canada, Eddy Rivette saw that the race was lost by his usual route. The horse had the advantage of speed on the flat and the advantage of being first and unpassable on the steep track. He would not be able to pass 'Isra until they reached the gentle gradient at the tree before the store and, by then, the horse's speed would make her the winner. He had to beat them on the hill or lose the race.

He made his mind up quickly, full-heartedly. When he reached the spot where the flatness of the school's half-valley turned abruptly upwards away from the loose stones and thorns into the erosions and cattle paths of the ridge, instead of following the horse and 'Isra, now sixty metres ahead and twenty metres above, Eddy Rivette turned at right angles. He paced out along the wide dry track, which rounded the foot of the ridge with scarcely a change of height before it reached the next valley, the valley of the village and the store. There it joined the broad sandy stream bed, the dead river of the valley, and climbed imperceptibly towards the single tree, the store and the waiting villagers. It was the long way round, perhaps twice the distance of the ridge route, but there wasn't an obstacle nor even a difficult stretch in the whole track. The obstacle was just one of distance. Eddy opened out his pace. It developed easily and his wind was with him. This was easy, plain sailing, after the difficulties that he had tamed daily on the cattle tracks of the ridge, the constant watching and skipping and allowing for hazards and the jarring of hard heels into an aching stomach, the creeping heartbeats waiting to pain him to a standstill. No, this was easy. He could forget those problems and just let his speed stretch with his step, his mind free to calculate the distance and tell himself again and again that it could not be done.

'Isra did not turn to look behind, to see the schoolteacher running along the flat floor of the valley. It was bad luck to look behind. He fixed his eye on the summit of the ridge and rode happily, knowing that he was leading and that the schoolteacher, wherever he was, was behind. But he was careful not to tire his horse. She must be fresh enough to finish strongly, like a victor. 'Let the horse be slow enough to step firmly,' he told himself, 'but fast enough to arrive in time, like when I rode across the mountains to bring the helicopter to the mayor.' 'Isra reached the flat ledge of soily stone a few yards below the summit of the ridge where he had to turn the horse through a tight passage of rock to take the track to the top. The horse paused for a footing and 'Isra let himself glance at the track below. No sign of the teacher. Perhaps he was running in one of the deep gulleys and would appear in a moment. He listened . . . No, not a sound. He would have heard the slapping soles of the foreigner's shoes if he had been moving on that hillside, but not a sound and not a sign.

'Isra looked along the ridge to either side, fearing that the teacher had taken a new, quicker route. Still no movement. 'Isra laughed. 'He is resting,' he said aloud, to the horse and the hills. 'He is tired and he is resting. We have won this race.' He spurred the horse up the last few metres of track and let himself enjoy both the pleasure of reaching the top and of having won midway through the race.

'He is resting,' he thought. 'Or perhaps he has fallen and is lying in the stones with his ankles twisted. We will send a horse to bring him down. *I* myself will ride to bring him down on the back of *my* horse.'

And when 'Isra, the rider of the village, reached the summit of the ridge he was laughing to himself.

At the village store old Loti and the villagers were waiting, their eyes crannied against the evening light silhouetting the hills before them. Loti and the old men knew which spot on the ridge to watch, the spot where the teacher had crossed each evening. They knew where the leader of the race would appear briefly before disappearing into the slip of an erosion gully and then come in view again, lower down the hill where the track flattened. And though the villagers were watching the ridge too, it was their ears which were nervous, waiting for the old men to cry out 'Here he comes. It is . . .' and then the name of the man who led. They formed the two possible shapes on the still ridge, the runner or the horse, its tail frisky with victory.

And then Loti called, just one word, 'Isra, and they saw him there, the man of their village, winning on the ridge. A cry went up from the villagers, carrying across the evening to 'Isra. They saw him spur his horse and start to descend the track into the deep gulley, ferociously. 'He should stay calm,' the old men thought. 'He is in the lead.' But they did not know what 'Isra had seen jogging along the dry valley floor firmly and resolutely towards the village and the store. The schoolteacher had taken the long valley route and was running strongly on the obstacle-free road while he, 'Isra-kone, had still to take care amongst the treacherous descents, though he and his horse were nearer, much nearer, to the store.

'Isra's descent brought him to the valley track twenty metres ahead of the schoolteacher. He lost a metre only turning the horse on to it and urging her to the new course. But the last scrambled descent from the ridge after 'Isra had spotted the schoolteacher had unnerved her and she settled badly. Eddy Rivette, however, had not changed his pace. He had kept his steady step from the moment that he had decided not to challenge 'Isra on the ridge route but follow the contours of the valley. His steadiness kept him behind the horse and he knew from experience that the race depended on the sprint. But when and how? A fast one now to take the lead and keep it with stamina? Or leave it till the end and take it at the post? Or split it in two? Two half sprints – the first to worry the horse and the rider, the second to pass them. Yes, by far the best tactic and the safest one, not taking things too early or leaving them too late. Eddy Rivette·

went forward on his toes and opened his pace. He closed the gap between him and the horse but it had tired him and he was glad to tuck in behind 'Isra and let the animal do the work for the fifty metres before the final bend at the single tree towards the store. He had meant it as half his sprint but he realised that he had no more race in him, that that sprint was all that was left and that now, at best, he could hang on behind the horse, drawn in to her flanks, and come in level at least with the horse's tail though a saddle's length behind 'Isra.

Eddy Rivette knew the race for him was lost, but 'Isra did not know it was won. The sight of the schoolteacher easing across the flat valley had worried him but he had thought he was safe when he reached the track, ahead. But the schoolteacher had closed *that* gap in moments and with the speed of a young dog and was pressing him close, running at the horse's speed and drawing tighter and tighter into the movement of the mare. They must go faster, faster, before the teacher ran like that again and ate up the metres and 'Isra's fame in the village. His knees were sharp in the horse's side and his toes were fierce. Go horse, he said, go go. And he was fierce with the white mare, nagging her across those last few metres. The school-teacher, with hardly a breath finding space in his lungs, hung on in the wake of warm air between the animal and its dust.

And then Eddy Rivette heard something new: a rasp in the horse's lungs that told him 'Isra was driving her too harshly and that, maybe, if only he could stay the pace of that gallop, the horse would have to slow sometime.

Both men heard both lungs racking, the runner and the horse both wanting the race over so that they could halt the pounding and gasp in air and air and normalise their hearts and lungs and shocked legs. No distance now. Just the turn and the few metres to the villagers at the store.

Eddy Rivette's lungs gave. He slowed and stooped a little, his hand on his chest below his heart, the pain building up, the horse moving ahead. He would finish. He was professional enough to finish and he was strong enough to recover quickly. But he would finish last, second to 'Isra and his horse, and that good race would be run.

Horse and 'Isra were at the last bend, taking it with panic and joy, not sure but sure enough that in a moment there would be cheers and the cheers would be theirs. 'Isra glimpsed the flagging schoolteacher a metre and a half behind, half caught up in the hoof dust. He leant with his horse into the bend at the tree and urged her into it, leaning far out like a yachtsman as pivot to the bend. The white mare was upright and tired, taking the turn as best she could. She felt her rider's weight shift towards the tree and went with it, too tired to resist. Her body came down. Her feet went away. She hit the dust of the track with her shoulder, the rest of her body bunched behind, hoofing the air, and sliding for a moment, doing the real damage to her tired white shoulder and to the man's thin leg on which she had fallen.

Not a whinny from her, too tired and breathless. Not a cry from 'Isra, too shamed already. One small gasp from the teacher, a cry of victory suppressed through experience until the line was crossed. A great whoop from the villagers, from the cackle of Loti to the yelp of the schoolchildren, as the winner of the race crossed the line of shadow marked at the side of the store by a low and sinking sun.

Notes on the authors

LOUIS DE BERNIÈRES was selected in 1993 as one of the twenty Best of Young British novelists. His novels, *The War of Don Emmanuel's Nether Parts*, *Senor Vivo and the Coco Lord*, *The Troublesome Offspring of Cardinal Guzman*, and, most recently, *Captain Corelli's Mandolin*, have all won major prizes. He lives in London.

LEWIS CARROLL was the pseudonym of Charles Lutwidge Dodgson (1832–98). He was a children's writer and mathematician, and was born in Lancashire. His most famous work is *Alice's Adventures in Wonderland*, which was first published in 1865 and has remained popular with children ever since. The sequel was *Through the Looking-Glass and What Alice Found There*, published in 1871.

JIM CRACE was born in 1946 in London. He began writing fiction in 1974 and his first story was published by *New Review*. In 1983 he was the initiator and director of the first Birmingham Festival of Readers and Writers. He is married with one son and a daughter.

ROBERT DREWE was born in Melbourne, Victoria, in 1943. He is the author of the novels *The Savage Crows*, *A Cry in the Jungle Bar*, *Fortune*, *Our Sunshine* and *The Drowner* and two volumes of short stories, as well as plays, screenplays, journalism and film criticism. His work has been widely translated, won national and international prizes, and been adapted for film, television, radio and the theatre.

NICHOLAS EVANS worked for ten years as a writer and producer of films. *The Horse Whisperer*, his first novel, has now been made into a major film, directed by and starring Robert Redford. His second novel, *The Loop*, will be published in 1998. Nicholas Evans lives in London with his wife and their two children.

TESS GALLAGHER is a poet, essayist and short-story writer. She has written four books of poetry, a book of essays and the short story collection *The Lover of Horses*.

JEAN GIONO was born in Manosque, Provence. He has written more than thirty novels and numerous essays and stories. In 1953 he was awarded the Prix Monégasque for his collective work.

RODNEY HALL left school and went out to earn his living in Brisbane at the age of sixteen. He was poetry editor of the *Australian* from 1967 to 1978 and from 1991 to 1994 he was chairman of the Australia Council. He has twice won the Miles Franklin Award. His numerous books are available in many translations as well as English editions in the UK and the US.

ERNEST HEMINGWAY (1988–1961), American novelist and short story writer, was born in Illinois. His career started as a cub reporter in 1918, which he gave up after a few months to volunteer for ambulance duties in World War I. He married three times, and received the Nobel Prize for Literature in 1954. Amongst his most famous works are *The Sun Also Rises* (1926), *For Whom the Bell Tolls* (1940) and *The Old Man and the Sea* (1952).

ALICE HOFFMAN is the author of twelve successful novels, including *At Risk*, *Turtle Moon*, *Second Nature* and *Practical Magic*.

R. WILKES HUNTER wrote over a thousand short stories, which have been published (under his own name and various pseudonyms) in every English-speaking country.

D. H. LAWRENCE (1855–1930), novelist, short story writer, poet, dramatist and critic, was born near Notthingham. His first published story won a prize, and he gave up work to write full-time once his first book was published (*The White Peacock*, 1911). There followed novels and nonfiction, including *Sons and Lovers* (1913), *The Rainbow* (1915) which was prosecuted for obscenity, *Kangaroo* (1923), and *Lady Chatterley's Lover* (1928) which was not freely available until 1960, after a case was also brought against it for obscenity in London.

HENRY LAWSON (1867–1922) was born at Grenfell, New South Wales. His first published work was in 1887 in the *Bulletin*, an influential weekly with which he was associated for the rest of his life. His reputation as a short story writer was established with the publication of *While the Billy Boils* in 1896. A national figure, a bush poet strongly identified with Australian values, he died in poverty in Sydney, where he was given a State funeral.

ALAN LE MAY was born in Indianapolis and began writing in 1927. For a long time his main occupation was as a rancher and he continued to write part-time. In the 1950s he was forced to take up writing full-time to support his failed ranch, and the result was some of the finest novels of western life, such as *The Unforgiven* and *The Searchers*.

C. S. LEWIS (1898–1963) was born in Belfast. He was a critic, popular theologian, novelist and children's writer. His 'Narnia' sequence of seven novels beginning with *The Lion, the Witch and the Wardrobe* (1950) and ending with *The Last Battle* (1956) are probably his most favoured works.

ALISTAIR MACLEOD was born in Cape Breton, Canada. His

stories have appeared in a number of magazines and have been reprinted in *Best American Short Stories* and *Best Canadian Short Stories*. Although one of Canada's most acclaimed writers, his entire life work consists of little more than a dozen published short stories, which were collected together in *The Lost Salt Gift of Blood*.

LARRY MCMURTRY is the author of twenty-one novels, two collections of essays, and more than thirty screenplays. His reputation as a writer about the American West is unequalled. His books include *The Last Picture Show*, *Terms of Endearment* and the Pulitzer Prize-winning masterpiece *Lonesome Dove*, the first in the four volume cycle of novels of which *Comanche Moon* is the last. Larry McMurtry also runs two bookshops, one in Washington D.C. and one in Archer City, Texas.

ALEX MILLER was born in England. He came to Australia on his own at the age of sixteen and has lived here ever since. His novels include *Watching the Climbers on the Mountain* and *The Ancestor Game*.

ELYNE MITCHELL's interest in horses began when she was a young girl. Her father commanded mounted troops in the First World War. On his return to Australia, her father taught her to ride. When she married, she moved to her husband's cattle station in the Snowy Mountains. Her first books, written for adults, were about the Snowy

Mountains and the work of the cattle station. Elyne wrote *The Silver Brumby* for her eldest child, so beginning the famous series.

MARY O'HARA (1885–1980) was an author and composer. Her novel *My Friend Flicka* became a classic when it was published in 1941. She was to write two more books about the range country, *Thunderhead* and *The Green Grass of Wyoming*.

MARY ELWYN PATCHETT (1897–1989) was born in Sydney. She spent her childhood on a cattle station in northern New South Wales, an experience which worked its way into many of her books, although she lived in England from the 1940s. She wrote over fifty novels, including children's books, adult fiction and science fiction.

KATHARINE S. PRICHARD (1883–1969) was born in Fiji but lived most of her life in Australia, where she worked as a novelist and journalist. Her novels include *Haxby's Circus* (1930) and her trilogy *The Roaring Nineties* (1946), *Golden Miles* (1948) and *Winged Seeds* (1950), which traces the life of Sally Gough. She also published two volumes of poetry and several collections of short stories.

MONTY ROBERTS was thirteen years old when he went off on his own to the deserts of Nevada to watch mustangs in the wild. What he learned about their methods of communication changed his life forever, and were written about in his book *The Man Who Listens to Horses*.

DAMON RUNYON was born in Kansas in 1884. In 1898 he enlisted in the Spanish–American War, after which he returned to the States and worked on various newspapers, becoming a sportswriter for the *American* in 1911. His first collection of short stories was *Guys and Dolls* (1932), which was made into the hit musical of the same name. He died in 1946.

ANNA SEWELL was born in Norfolk in 1820. Due to an injury in her teens, Anna never walked properly and was crippled for the rest of her life. She thus grew to rely heavily on horses as her main mode of transport. In 1871, she was given a short time to live and determined to write a book 'to induce kindness, sympathy and an understanding treatment of horses'. Five years later, she was still working on *Black Beauty*, which was to be her only book. It was completed and published in 1877, and Anna died a few months after its publication.

PETER SHAFFER's first big success was in 1958 with *Five Finger Exercise*. This play ran for two years in London and won the *Evening Standard* Drama Award. Other successes were *Private Ear: The Public Eye, The Royal Hunt of the Sun, Black Comedy, The Battle of Shrivings* and *Amadeus*, which won the Tony Award for Best Play of the Year (as did *Equus* in

1975), as well as the *Evening Standard* Drama Award, the Plays and Players Award, and the London Theatre Critics' Award.

JOHN STEINBECK (1922–1968) was born in Salinas, California. In 1935, he became a full-time writer and was a special writer for the United States Army Air Force during World War II. Among his most renowned works are *Of Mice and Men, Cannery Row, East of Eden* and *The Grapes of Wrath*, which won the Pulitzer Prize in 1940. In 1962, Steinbeck was awarded the Nobel Prize for Literature as a mark of his outstanding contribution to literature.

Acknowledgments

I would like to thank many people for their help with this anthology. My publishers at Penguin: Bob Sessions for his initial and continuing enthusiasm for the idea; Julie Gibbs for her percipient comments and astute judgment; Lisa Mills for her excellent editing. The many writers from around the world who offered advice, pieces and contacts: my thanks to Larry McMurtry, Bernard MacLaverty, Louis de Bernières, Marianne Wiggins, and Rodney Hall. My thanks too, to my two researchers Kathy Woolley and Christine Westwood; to Jane Albert for helping me round up the missing books; to William Fraser for lending me his horse books for more years than I care to think about; to George Baker, my father, who passed on to his daughter his lifelong love of horses, and finally to my husband, Robert Drewe, for his editorial advice and support.

Candida Baker *In the Cut* by Candida Baker © Candida Baker 1998.

Jim Crace extract from *Continent* by Jim Crace © Jim Crace 1986. Reprinted by permission of the author and David Godwin Associates.

Louis de Bernières extract from *The War of Don Emmanuel's Nether Parts* by Louis de Bernières © Louis de Bernières 1990. Reprinted by permission of the author.

Extract from *Our Sunshine* by Robert Drewe reprinted by permission of Pan Macmillan Australia Pty Ltd and Granta Books UK. Copyright © Robert Drewe 1991.

From *The Horse Whisperer* by Nicholas Evans. Copyright © 1995 Nicholas Evans. Used by permission of Dell Books, a division of Bantam Doubleday Dell Publishing Group Inc and A. P. Watt Ltd.

Jean Giono: Lines from *The Horseman on the Roof*, first published in France in 1951 by Gallimard, in Great Britain in 1953. Copyright © 1951 Librairie Gallimard. Translation copyright © 1953 Alfred A. Knopf. Reproduced by permission of The Harvill Press Ltd.

Tess Gallagher extract from *The Lover of Horses* by Tess

Acknowledgments

© C. S. Lewis Pty Ltd 1954. Reprinted by permission of HarperCollins Publishers.

Larry McMurtry extract from *Commanche Moon* reprinted with the permission of the Orion Publishing Group Ltd and Simon & Schuster Inc. New York. Copyright © Larry McMurtry 1997.

Alistair Macleod 'In the Fall' from *The Lost Salt Gift of Blood* by Alistair Macleod © Ontario Review Press 1998. Reprinted by permission of Ontario Review Press and Jonathon Cape Ltd.

Alex Miller extract from *The Tivington Nott* by Alex Miller © Alex Miller 1989. Reprinted by permission of the author.

Elyne Mitchell extract from *Silver Brumby, Silver Dingo* by Elyne Mitchell © Elyne Mitchell 1993. Reprinted by permission of HarperCollins Publishers (Australia) Pty Ltd.

Mary O'Hara extract from *My Friend Flicka* by Mary O'Hara © Mary O'Hara 1943. Reprinted by permission of Random House UK and Egmont Books.

Mary Elwyn Patchett extract from *Tam the Untamed* by Mary Elwyn Patchett. Reprinted by permission of James Clarke & Co., Ltd and the Lutterworth Press.

Katharine Susannah Prichard 'The Grey Horse' from *Kiss On The Lips and Other Stories* by Katharine Susannah Prichard. ©